My Name is Molly

To Alamo,
Hope you enjoy

Barbara Sattler

My Name is Molly

BARBARA C. SATTLER

ISBN-13: 9781539591290
ISBN-10: 1539591298
Library of Congress Control Number: 2016918272
CreateSpace Independent Publishing Platform
North Charleston, South Carolina

To Kenney, my biggest supporter without whom this book would never have been finished
To Toby and Teddy for always bringing me joy

One

I maneuver my silver Mazda Miata MX-5 to the middle of the tiny parking space numbered 109. The Miata's new, dent-free. I love it. I can't believe I have to park, no squeeze, between an old Camry and a truck that looks like it belongs to a meth-addicted landscaper. Not long ago the Miata rested happily and safely between a hunter green Jag and a midnight black BMW. All the cars in this lot are cheap, low-end except for a black Cadillac Escalade. Probably belongs to a drug dealer.

My name is Molly. I had top grades. I was admitted to every college I applied to. Early admit to law school. Hired by a top firm before graduation. I'm good at interviews. I've been called charming. Yet here I am. My first day as a public defender.

I slip on cheap taupe pumps that match the nondescript outfit I bought for my new job. I don't know what to expect, but I know enough to leave my expensive designer clothes home. I flatten my body to avoid the Camry which looks as if it hasn't seen a carwash since Hurricane Sandy. I can do this. I have to do this. It's only till something worthwhile comes along.

I never intended to use my legal talent to represent druggies, rapists and murderers. From the moment Dad put law school into my head, I planned to land a high paying job. I didn't study my ass off to help losers. People work at the public defender's office because they can't get a real job. Bad grades, bad interview skills, bad breath.

I received a job offer, *before graduation,* from Bellwood, Adams, Roth and Klein, a premiere Phoenix firm. My unemployed classmates were jealous. My lesser-employed classmates were jealous. My future plans were to make everyone jealous. Yet here I am in this uncovered parking lot dotted with potholes.

My parents hosted a big party to celebrate my success. Everyone came except Rose, my older sister. We couldn't find her. She's in Africa somewhere feeding starving children or fighting malaria. I blame Mom. What kind of name is Rose? Like a 60's movie, her first real job was the Peace Corps. Next, a college degree in third world countries, finally on to Africa to do good. She could be thousands of miles away and I still hear her nag.

"Molly, you're wasting your education. The rich don't need help getting richer. Use your brains to help people. Being rich won't make you happy."

OMG

I met Derrick my first year of law, his last of business school. After his graduation he got a job at a small insurance company. We moved in together. We both had big dreams which meant good bye Tucson. Three months before law school graduation, Derrick was offered a job at Winthrop Financial in Phoenix. He was ecstatic. Derrick bought a condo in the newly renovated portion of downtown Phoenix close to shopping, clubs and sports arenas. He proposed the night of my graduation. I loved my ring.

Life was great. By the time I passed the bar my new law firm, affectionately nicknamed BARF, was home. I spent twenty hours a day there. Ate most meals there. Slept on the couch in my office. Weeks passed before I realized the initials of the firm spelled BARK not BARF. Months passed before I found out after working twenty-four straight, several inebriated associates joked "this place makes me want to barf." Barf became an 'in' joke and BARK became BARF.

My first assignment was in the real estate division. I was at the beck and call of two senior partners and one workaholic lawyer who'd been there four years. I was exhausted trying to achieve the mandatory billable hours, and keep up our social calendar, but this was the life I was meant to have. Fancy clothes, expensive jewelry, visits to the spa (when I had time). All I had to do was keep up the pace until I made partner.

Then came the recession.

At first everyone thought we'd get through untouched. Even when Winthrop Financial went bankrupt and Derrick was out of a job, I didn't think my life would change. BARF wasn't Winthrop. BARF had tons of assets and had been around forever. It took only a month till the rumors started. I ignored them. Kept my billables high, my conversation upbeat, and my toes pedicured.

But denial didn't work. It doesn't keep the wolf from your door. "We're going to have to let you go. Nothing personal. Many firms are in the same position. We can offer you three months severance pay and a good reference. Sorry."

Sorry?

Before I could speak, I was out the door and out of a job. My savvy colleagues had started the hunt for new jobs, but I didn't have the energy to find out who was hiring, send out resumes, or make calls.

"Molly, get dressed. Let's celebrate. Seattle made me an offer," Derrick announced several days or weeks after I lost my job.

"You're going to Seattle?"

"Yes, I told you the interview went great, and I'd take it if they made me an offer."

"Take what? I can't practice in Washington until I pass their bar. That will take months, maybe a year."

"I told you. Administrator for the city parks."

"What do you know about parks?"

"Nothing. That's not the point. We talked about it."

"I don't remember."

"That's because everything's always about you. All you do is sit here day after day and complain. You're not even looking for a job."

"I'm paying my share."

"It's not about money you don't pay any attention to me."

"So when are you leaving?"

"I start in a month, but I need to go earlier to look for a place."

"You're just going to pack up and leave me jobless and homeless." I tried hard to stop my tears. I hate weak women.

"I'm not leaving you homeless. You can stay in the condo."

"But I need you."

"Need me? We haven't had sex since I can't remember."

"Sex is the only thing you think about. . ."

That was the most civil conversation we had until he left. No matter what either of us said, the other one argued. The weekend he moved out I stayed with Emily. He left me his address on an otherwise blank piece of paper. After he left either of us could have called the other, but neither of us did. He didn't seem interested in a relationship now that I wasn't a hotshot lawyer. My pride wouldn't let me call him, but not calling was easier than I expected.

Without Derrick around, I didn't even get dressed. I slept on the couch, ordered food in, and drank up Derrick's expensive wine stash. I didn't call anyone or answer my cell. I was watching reruns of the Biggest Loser when Derrick's land line rang. I wasn't going to answer until I recognized the name on the display.

"Molly O'Rourke?" a voice asked when I picked up.

"Yes."

"This is Jack Windsor, AGF Management. Derrick has arranged for new tenants to move in the first of the month. You need to be out by the twentieth so we have time to clean the unit and get it ready for the new renters." He paused for a moment and added, "Sorry."

"Sorry?"

He patiently repeated himself.

Derrick didn't even have the nerve to tell me himself. I threw my wine glass at the TV. The TV wasn't damaged, the glass didn't crack, and there was barely enough wine to make a spot on the carpet. Bastard.

Two

"Do you have any job leads?" Dad asks.

"Don't worry. I've got feelers out and someone will call." I lie.

BARF had fired me. Nicely with a severance package and good references. Ha. Derrick had dumped me. Not nicely. Didn't take me to a fancy dinner and drop the bomb. Didn't call me. Didn't email me. Fucker didn't even text me. That piece of dog turd had his condo management company evict me.

I swallow my pride and call my parents. I'm still not looking for a job.

"Oh, honey I'm sorry. Why didn't you get in touch before?" Mom asks as she slides into fixer mode. "Get some clothes together. We can get the rest of your stuff later. I'll get your room ready. It'll be so great to have you here. We can have that chicken casserole you like for dinner. Dudley will be so happy to see you."

Life is almost like my teenage years. I get up after my parents go to work, toast a bagel and watch TV with Dudley. I stop drinking during the day. My parents will know I'm hitting their booze, and I don't have enough energy to go out and buy my own. Not only will I have to leave the house, I'll have to hide the used bottles. My mom notices everything. Instead, I munch on the cookies, cake, and pies that Mom bakes for Dad. I've inherited his metabolism, unlike Mom and my sister Rose.

By the time they get home, I make sure I'm dressed, TV off, looking productive.

"So how's the job search?" Dad asks every evening as he comes home from work.

"Doing the best I can."

At dinner Mom and Dad talk about their work and people I don't know. I shut them out unless I hear my name.

At night I can hear them talk about me through an air conditioning vent Rose and I discovered shortly after we moved into the house.

"I'm worried about her; she doesn't seem happy," Mom says. "Breaking up with Derrick must have hit her hard."

"Derrick's a jerk. Wasn't good enough for her. I'm worried she's not looking for a job."

"Maybe she's depressed. She's never had anything like this happen to her before. You think she needs therapy?"

"Why would you ask me that? You're a counselor for godsakes."

"Shh, I don't want her to hear us."

I don't want to hear them. I put on my ear phones and drift off listening to Cindy Lauper.

Two weeks after I return home, I open my computer. I browse through emails mostly hitting delete until I see one from Elizabeth Elan. *Call ASAP.* Elizabeth became a friend after she's assigned to me as part of the law school women's mentoring program which hooks up students with attorneys. I thought the whole business was stupid, but I try it and luck out. Elizabeth is attractive, smart, and knows the right people. We hit it off and met for drinks every month or so until she moved to LA for a job. I wonder what she wants. The area code is Arizona. I procrastinate for a day or so, then I call.

"Pima County Public Defender. Elizabeth Elan's office."

I almost couldn't talk. What was she doing there?

"May I speak to Elizabeth? Molly O'Rourke returning her call."

She asks me a few questions to make sure I'm a friend, not some felon trying to talk to the boss.

"Molly, great to hear from you."

"Great to hear from you, but what are you doing at the PD?"

"Quick version—I got married, my husband was offered a job he wanted in Tucson, so we moved back. I was offered head of the office. I took it."

"You like it?"

"It's a great place to work. The lawyers are smart. I don't have much in common with them, but I like being in charge. Why didn't you get in touch sooner? What happened anyway?"

What happened? She must know what happened. She wants me to say it. "Big layoffs at the firm because of the economy. I guess I've been in denial. I'm living with my parents."

"We have a trial position open here. You'd be perfect. I'll send you an email with information on how to apply. You've got to get your resume in by tomorrow."

Me, a PD? No way. "I'd never fit in there. They'd figure it out in a minute."

"Don't worry. I've stacked the hiring committee with my buds. All you need to do is apply."

Not my kind of job, but the bright side I'll be a star among all those losers.

Three

My new office is a joke. Institutional beige. A metal desk that looks like it belonged to generations of unruly middle school students and takes up most of the space. An old-fashioned two-drawer file cabinet jammed in a corner. Nails, holes and tape on the walls left from the last employee.

"Sorry we couldn't get you a window, Molly, but offices are assigned by seniority." Another sorry.

"The good news is you're free to paint any color and hang whatever you like on the walls as long as it doesn't violate Elan's good taste directive." Paint the walls? I'm a lawyer, not a janitor. I'm not going to be here long enough to decorate.

"There's a kitchen at the end of the hall, refrigerator, microwave and some people have coffee pots. There's a snack stand on the first floor. We try to support the place, it's managed by an ex-client but. . . ."

She looks at me like she expects an answer but I can't remember her name, or why she's in-charge of the grand tour, or think of anything appropriate to say. I stay quiet.

"Denise Covington's your secretary. You share her with Steve and Lisa. She's busy—a last minute motion. Almost everyone has court in a few minutes. Feel free to wander over and watch. I've left a couple files on your desk. Barry Singer's your team leader. He'll explain more later."

"Okay."

"And Double, I mean Elizabeth, said to tell you she's sorry she can't be here to welcome you, she's at a conference."

Share my secretary. Team leader. At BARF we each had our own secretary and at least one paralegal. We had partners, junior partners and associates like a normal law firm. Team leader sounds like we're here to shoot hoops or . . . people.

Once I'm alone, I open the first of three files, "State v. Charles Walter Osborne." Less paper than a BARF file. Maybe criminal law's easier. Only good thing so far.

DOCUMENT #1

Dear Mr. Osborne,

My name is Steve Tillis. I'm an attorney with the Public Defender's Office. Your case has been assigned to me.

I need to meet with you as soon as possible. Please call my secretary, Denise Covington 520-444-4819, to schedule an appointment before your November 15 court date. If we don't talk before then, you must appear in Pima County Superior Court on that date or a warrant will be issued for your arrest.

Don't talk to anyone about your case including your family and friends. If you are contacted by the police tell them you have a lawyer and you do NOT want to speak to them. Make sure you follow your bail conditions.

I look forward to meeting you.

DOCUMENT #2

Dear Mr. Osborne,

My name is Gloria Rhodes. The purpose of this letter is to advise you that Mr. Tillis has left the office. I am your new lawyer. Please contact my secretary, Denise Covington at 520-444-4819, to make an appointment before your next court date of December 1. I look forward to meeting you.

It is important not to speak to anyone about your case.

DOCUMENT #3

Dear Mr. Osborne,

I am your new lawyer, Paul Terrazas. Your next court date is a Pretrial Conference, Jan. 11. You must appear at court or a warrant will issue for your arrest.

Since your court date is so soon, I will meet you there. If you need to contact me before your court date, contact my secretary, Nancy, at 444-4819.

Remember, don't talk to anyone about your case but me. That means not your family, friends, or girlfriends.

DOCUMENT #4

Dear Walter,

I am your new lawyer, Anne Levy. Mr. Terrazas is no longer with the office. I am sorry to tell you that he passed away. I know it must be frustrating to have so many different lawyers. I hope we can talk soon, as there are new developments in your case.

I have filed a motion contesting the search in your case. It has not yet been set for hearing. I have also received a new plea offer in your case. The deadline for accepting the offer is two weeks from today. Please call Denise, 444-4819, and set up an appointment.

Remember not to speak with anyone about your case.

DOCUMENT #5

Dear Walter,

I wanted to let you know I am leaving the office at the end of the month for personal reasons. I've tried to call you, but the number you gave me is out of service.

I don't know who your new lawyer will be, but if I find out before I leave I will let you know. Again, I'm very sorry that you have had so many lawyers, but whoever your lawyer is we are all trying our best to help you.

I have written the County Attorney requesting the plea be reduced to a Class 5 felony as we discussed.

Your case is set for trial on March 15. It will be continued due to the change of lawyers. You must appear in court that date even though the trial is going to be continued.

Remember not to talk to anyone about your case, to check in with Pretrial Services and drug test if your number is called. Best of luck. I've enjoyed working with you.

The other side of the file has legal documents and more handwritten notes. The first document is labeled: Indictment.

INDICTMENT

On or about the first day of April 2014, in the County of Pima, State of Arizona CHARLES WALTER OSBORNE intentionally or knowingly entered the property on 4141 E. 5th with the intent to commit a felony to wit: burglary.

On or about the first day of April 2014, in the County of Pima, the State of Arizona CHARLES WALTER OSBORNE intentionally or knowingly possessed a dangerous drug to wit: methamphetamine

On or about the first day of April 2014, in the County of Pima, the State of Arizona CHARLES WALTER OSBORNE intentionally or knowingly possessed burglary tools to wit: a screwdriver.

On or about the first day of April 2014 in the County of Pima, the State of Arizona CHARLES WALTER OSBORNE intentionally or knowingly possessed drug paraphernalia: to wit: a baggie

My first client. A meth head— breaks into people's homes with a screwdriver. They expect me to talk to this drug addicted jerk who probably hasn't showered in weeks. They expect me to argue he's innocent.

I haven't met him and I think he should be locked up—for a long time.

I imagine my letter.

Dear Mr. Osborne,

Ms. O'Rourke is no longer working here. She has received an offer at a prestigious law firm and is delighted she never met you. Go ahead and tell anyone who gives a shit the details of your crime of the century.

Molly O'Rourke
Former Public Defender

Four

Saturday night, alone. Mom, Dad and Dudley are gone. On their way back to Phoenix. They had a dinner engagement or might never have left. It's a major coup to get them to bring Dudley. He doesn't shed much, he's a poodle, but Dad's fanatic about his Lincoln looking pristine. Maybe that's where I got the same concern about the Miata. Mom agrees after days of nagging they can use her car. She drives an older Infiniti SUV left over from the days she hauled me to friend's houses and Rose, a candy striper, to hospitals. I looked forward to their visit, but shortly after they arrive I want them to leave except for Dudley. Now I miss 'em.

Probably a bad idea to let Dad buy me this place, but without him I couldn't afford a brand-new, three bedroom condo with a sunken living-room, top-of-the line kitchen appliances, modern landscaping and a fireplace. Like most of Tucson who could afford one I wanted a fireplace even though it rarely got below 40 degrees. A couple of pools and spas. A state of the art gym. Someday I might use it. We got it for a steal when the previous owner, a widow, died. Her only child lived out of state, hated Tucson, and wanted to sell quickly.

Mom's contributions are furnishings. I have a few things I'd bought over the years, but none of it's classy enough. Mom has impeccable taste and doesn't look at price tags.

I know gifts, even gifts from parents, no, especially from parents, come with strings. But if it's a choice between a low-class apartment with used furniture, noise and the possibility I can run into a client, I'll take the strings and hope they don't tighten anytime soon.

I'd like to get together with someone, but I haven't made friends. The lawyers at the PD are surprisingly nice. They answer my myriad of questions without acting like I'm a moron. I have so many. All I did at BARF was research and write documents and contracts. I learned nothing practical like the protocol of covering a hearing. The sense of competition that swirled around BARF seems absent. Colleagues stop by my office to chat and invite me to lunch but the camaraderie stops when I leave the office.

Everyone avoids the mystery surrounding the death of Paul Terrazzas. I asked a couple colleagues what happened and each said something like, "A terrible accident. He drank too much and drowned in his Jacuzzi". There is something off in their tone. I hope Elizabeth will fill me in.

Elizabeth pisses me off. She pulled strings to hire me, but seems to have no interest in speaking to me. She checks in every couple days, but hasn't invited me to lunch or dinner. Not even a drink. I haven't met her husband. I don't get it.

Maybe its best. Nobody trashes Elizabeth to my face, but the atmosphere changes when she enters the room. I hear, "Double E questioned her case count," "Double E is at it again," "Double E thinks she's. . ." I know they mean Elizabeth. I don't know why they call her that, but it's not a compliment. I don't want to choose between her and my colleagues.

My biggest problem's the lack of a man. Since I learned how to get one, I've never been without. When I was a teenager, I thought no guy would like me. High school was a nightmare. I was taller than most of my classmates, male and female, not to mention clumsy and awkward. The kids called me "Molly Green Giant." The popular girls were petite and curvy. I was all angles. The clothes that flattered the popular girls did nothing for me, but I thought if I dressed like them it'd help me fit in.

Besides towering over everyone, I was nearsighted and had to wear thick coke-bottle glasses. They didn't make stylish ones then. My mother insisted I wear contacts when the ophthalmologist said I was old enough. I hated them. They made my eyes red, itchy and teary. They hurt. I lost dozens. "Molly, can't you be careful? You're costing us a fortune." Half the time I went without. The kids thought I was a snob because I ignored them, but I ignored them because I couldn't see who was talking.

Summer after senior year, my parents went to Europe for six weeks. I stayed with my mom's sister, Margaret, in Tucson. Rose insisted she had to be in Phoenix to work at the hospital. She stayed with our grandma. My best summer. Aunt Margaret was divorced, childless and cool. She acted more like an older sister than a mom.

"Molly, you have a figure like a model. You could wear almost anything and look hot, except you pick little girl clothes. What's with that?"

I didn't know what to say. Too embarrassed to admit I copied the popular girls. "Not sure what to buy," I mumbled.

"Let's go shopping." Like my mom she had exquisite taste. Unlike Mom, she wanted me to look sexy.

"Stand up straight and use height to your advantage."

"Okay," I said, not sure about that.

"And you're eyes are always red and teary. Do you need a new prescription?"

"No, it's my contacts. I hate them."

"Let's get some glasses. Once your eyes stop tearing, I'll show you how to put on make-up."

I felt like a new person. Aunt Margaret said I was beautiful. I didn't believe her, but for the first time I liked what I saw.

I started seeing Kent, the son of one of Aunt Margaret's friends. Twenty-one years old, he was the first real man I dated. The first anyone I dated. Instead of telling me he was too old and trying to stop it, like Mom would, Aunt Margaret made sure I looked great. Gave me advice. "Never let a man think you care more than he does; Don't put all your eggs in one basket; If you like him, don't nag."

By the time my parents returned, he was history so was my virginity. When he left to go back east to finish college I was devastated. He wasn't interested in a long-distance romance. I tried to keep my hurt from Mom, but she guessed. "He was too old for you. You'll find someone more your age." I learned to not to throw myself at men and not to tell my mom about my love life.

College wasn't high school. The first freshmen mixer I met a guy. Then another. Kent became a memory. Since that summer I'd always had a boyfriend, sometimes more than one. My mantra became "Love the one you're with."

When Derrick ended it, I was stunned. No one had dumped me since Kent. I decide when it's over. If I hadn't been messed up because of BARF, I'd have ended it first. Trashed his condo or his reputation. Goodbye Derrick and good riddance.

I'm ready to get back in the game. Jack Clarke's interested. He doesn't seem like my type. Not much ambition. Thinks being a PD is top of the charts. His favorite t-shirt says, *"My mom doesn't know I'm a Public Defender. She thinks I'm a piano player in a whore house."* He thinks that's funny. His taste in clothes is abysmal. Out-of-style suits that hang wrong. Shirts with frayed collars and sleeves. Gaudy ties. On the positive side. Tall. Sexy. Self-confident. I find the card with the lawyers' private numbers and dial Jack.

The phone rings and rings. Loser doesn't have voice mail. I'd barely hung up when my phone rings.

"Jack?"

"Not Jack." For a moment only silence.

"Who is it?" I ask. The voice's familiar, but . . .

"You've forgotten me already? Moved on to Jack?"

"Derrick? No, I haven't moved onto Jack, like it's your business." I begin to pace.

"I didn't call to fight. I'm sorry about kicking you out of the condo."

Sorry again. You're wrong Elton, sorry isn't the hardest word. "It's a little late for that."

"I know. I was going through a bad time. I was in debt, drinking. The Seattle job didn't seem to be working out."

"Don't worry about me. Everything's fine. I love my new job. Tucson's great."

"I'm surprised you're happy at the PD."

"How do you know where I work?"

"One of our friends. Emma maybe." Again silence.

"What do you want?"

"I'm in Tucson. Thought we could get together."

"What'd you have in mind? Dinner, drinks, sex?"

"Sounds great."

"How 'bout drinks and sex, forget dinner?"

"Better."

"How 'bout just sex?"

"Should I come to your place?"

I'm quiet for a moment. Why is it so hard to come up with the right words to tell someone they're a complete fucking asshole, dickhead jerk? I finally give up on originality.

"Go fuck yourself."

Five

"You look fetching," Jack Clarke says as he walks into my office. Unlike BARF, lawyers keep their office doors open when they aren't with a client or on a deadline. They stop to chat. At BARF there's no time to chat, unless you can figure out how to bill it. Jack's office is close to mine in location, but since he's worked here forever, he has a large corner space and a window that overlooks a parking lot. He stops by often.

"Its good to have someone notice," I say. Denise chooses that moment to stop in. She knocks on the open door.

"Hi Molly, Jack. I'm sorry to interrupt, but here's a file you need to look at."

"No problem." I sigh, roll my eyes as Denise hands me the file and leaves.

"I know how Denise comes off if you don't know her, but you're lucky she's assigned to you. She's had a lot of trauma in the past and is in a tough situation now. Her husband has PTSD and one of her kids is disabled. Money's tight. But she's a great secretary."

"Thanks for telling me," I lie. I don't want to hear about her personal life.

"I've got 8:30 court. I've got to get going."

"So do I."

From that day Jack shows up in my office every morning before court. He compliments my clothes, makes me laugh, and saves my career. I try to learn as much as I can, but I'm at a deficit. In law school I'd avoided criminal law and any litigation clinics where I might have learned how court worked. The only practical skill I learned at BARF was how to bill fourteen hours of work in an eight hour day. It's of no use here. We don't bill clients.

I browse the file Denise handed me. There's a sticky on top, Probation Revocation Hearing - Feb. 14 - Div. 8, 9:30 am.

Fuck, a probation revocation hearing. What the hell? I have some idea about trials. But a probation revocation? Never saw one on *Law and Order*.

"Put that file down, you'll be late," Jack says. We leave for court.

I haven't been back from court more than a few minutes when Denise buzzes. Ricky Florez is here.

"Who?"

"The client who has the probation revocation."

"Don't they make appointments?"

"Some, it's up to you. You can reschedule him if you want."

Might as well get it over with. "No, bring him to my office in ten minutes."

I make a bathroom run. Comb my hair, refresh my make-up and brush my teeth. Waste of time. I only have a few minutes to read the file. I flip to a petition filed by the probation officer, Dorian Johnston. She alleges my client has tested positive for meth and failed to report for appointments.

Before I know it, Denise hands over Florez. Ricky has tattoos on every visible part of his body, ugly, homemade ones with sexual imagery. He talks gang lingo and every other word out of his mouth is 'fuck'. All he wants to talk about is 'that whore bitch' of his who's fucking some other dude or that 'fucking-ugly-fat-bitch PO' who fucked him over.

He denies using meth or missing appointments. "I'm no fucking tweaker and don't miss no appointments with the bitch." I don't believe a word. The twenty minute appointment wears me out. Got no information that will help his case. As he leaves my office his last words are, "I'll show that bitch not to fuck with me."

His PO is an ugly fat bitch. She treats me like I'm no better than my client. I can't decide who I hate more, Ricky fucking Florez or Super PO Dorian Johnston. I don't know what to do about his profanity. I don't know if what he said about his PO constitutes a threat and if so, should I report it and to who?

How can I win Florez's hearing? He denies using, but his lab test is positive for meth. He denies missing appointments, but the PO has copies of appointment cards Florez has initialed next to the dates he was supposed to meet with her.

Beyond thorough she also sent copies of the reception log which verifies Ricky Florez has not signed in at all the day of his appointments. What's left to argue?

The hearing is twenty-four hours away when I freak. Jack isn't around. I decide to ask Barry Singer, my team leader, for help. He'd dropped by my office the first week, introduced himself and left. No 'come by if you need help'. Not even a grin. I walk over to his office. He's on the phone, motions me to sit. His office looks newly painted, uncluttered and is filled with pictures of bear, moose and deer. He quickly ends his call.

"What can I do for you, Molly?"

"I have a probation revocation tomorrow morning and I'm not sure what to do. I thought maybe you could, uh, give me some pointers."

After a couple minutes that last an eternity, he speaks "Have you read, Rules 27-29, Rules of Criminal Procedure, State v. Cummings and its progeny?"

"No."

"Come back after you've done that and we'll talk. Anything else?"

I try to hold back my anger as I leave his office. I should've read that stuff, but he's my supervisor and is supposed to help me. The hearing's tomorrow. Doesn't he care about the client? Is he so arrogant he's never needed help? I'll never ask him anything again. Asshole.

I'm reading the material Singer suggested but I'm still pissed at him when Jack appears. He has an uncanny ability to know when I need help.

"Hey what's the matter? Bad morning?"

"I asked Barry for help. He made me feel like a moron. He's probably right."

"One of the first rules you need to learn is never ask Barry anything unless you're an expert in the area. Then, of course, you don't need to ask. He's a great lawyer but a lousy colleague and worse supervisor. What do you need to know?"

"Everything about a probation revocation hearing. It's tomorrow. If what my client said is a threat, and if it is, what. . .? And how can I stop Florez's filthy mouth?"

"That's all?"

I felt better already.

"Did Florez threaten you?" Jack asks

"Not me, his Probation Officer, Dorian Johnston."

"In that case, nothing. Woman's a total bitch. Not an ounce of compassion. All her recommendations involve prison. She takes her unhappy life out on probationers. The good news is most judges don't like her. She acts like she's smarter than them. Even if a judge graduated last in his class and flunked the bar a couple times, the minute he puts on the robe he thinks he's Solomon. What did he say?"

"'I'll show that bitch not to fuck with me.'"

"Don't worry. If he said he knew where she lived and was going to set her house on fire then you worry. What's the filthy mouth problem?" Jack asks.

"Every other word is fuck or bitch. He even used the c-word."

"C-word?" Jack says with a grin.

"Shut up."

"You gotta put a stop to that." Jack continues. "Show him you're boss. Next time he does that say something like, 'Listen asshole, I'm not one of your worthless homeboys. I'm the person who's going to keep you out of prison. Treat me with respect, stop the cussing or I'm off your case. You may not care, but when I tell the judge why you need a new lawyer, he'll care and make sure you get someone worthless. Someone who hasn't opened a law book in years and couldn't care less about you.' Got it?"

"That's gonna work?" I ask.

"Most of the time. You have to say it like you mean it. And if he acts like a jerk again, file a motion to withdraw."

I check my phone for the time. "Jack, I've got mandatory training in ten."

"Public defender school?"

"Yeah."

"What's today?"

"Grand jury challenges."

Jack chuckles and looks at his watch. "Ten minutes is more than enough to explain probation hearings. You don't need to worry because they rarely take place. If they do you almost always lose. Everything's against you. The rules of evidence are relaxed. It's your client's word against the PO. What did you say were the allegations?"

"That Florez used meth and didn't go to his appointments."

"What's Florez going to say about the meth?"

"That he didn't use or more likely that he didn't 'fucking' use."

"And when the prosecutor asks, 'Isn't it true your drug test was positive?'"

I shrug. "I don't know?"

"Here's a sample of what I've heard them say.

> *'My girlfriend was pissed and put meth in my burrito.*
> *I got a cigarette from my roommate and there must've been meth in it;* or
> *That test's no fucking good.'"*

I laugh again. "What do I do?"

He checks the time again. "You make a deal. Have him admit to one allegation. It's easier for them to admit missing an appointment than using drugs. The state will drop the other one."

"The PO will agree to that?"

"If it was up to Johnston, probably not, but its up to the CA. He won't want to waste his time on this kind of crap. The judge has the same sentencing options whether he admits to one violation or a hundred."

"Thanks." I look him in the eye and give him my best smile, "I owe you big-time."

"No problem. Buy me a drink. Tonight after work."

And that's how we started.

Six

The freeway between Tucson and Phoenix is boring and ugly. The hundred-twenty miles seem longer every trip. Traffic's worse every trip. Why do I go? I long to have a conversation with someone who knew me before I was a defender of the oppressed. Even Emma. That's how desperate I am. After lunch I'll stop at my parents' to pick up some stuff for the condo and see Dudley. I wish I could bring Dudley to Tucson, but my parents would miss him, and they have the time to take care of him. When I'm home I wasn't even the one who walked him.

Near the Globe exit a car fire holds up traffic for about twenty minutes. When I arrive at the restaurant, Emma's drinking a glass of white wine. Her outfit, a teal blue tunic and black leggings, with matching jewelry and scarf, are fashionable. She's the kind of person who spends a fortune on her clothes but always looks dumpy and somehow wrong. She either needs a personal trainer for her wardrobe or an Aunt Margaret.

"Molly, good to see you." She gives me a hug.

"You too."

We order. I decline wine. Too risky with my disregard of speed limits.

"How's work?" I ask? Emma clerks on the Ninth Circuit Court of Appeals. She graduated in the top two percent of our class, snagged an Arizona Supreme Court clerking job and then moved up to the Ninth Circuit.

"I love it, but can't stay much longer. Because of the recession they've let some of us stay on, but unfortunately there's no open position for a career clerk. Someone has to die for that to happen. My judge thinks I should go to DC. He's got connections with a couple of federal agencies."

"Would you move?"

"Why not? My family's mostly back east and I hate summer. Seems hotter every year. Enough about me. Heard anything from Derrick?"

"The moron was in Tucson and called me all apologetic-like. All he wanted was to get in my pants. Derrick's history. I'm seeing a colleague, Jack Clarke."

"I don't think I know him, did he go to the U?"

"Yeah but a couple years before us."

"I can't believe you're a public defender."

"I can't either. You should see my office. It's disgusting. Small, dirty, ugly beige walls. They said I could paint it. I was going to hire someone, but that's not the culture there."

"Can't you sneak someone in on the weekend?"

"No, there's always someone there working. They work more hours than I did at BARF. And there's no extra pay or bonuses. I finally . . ."

"Would you like another glass of wine?" the waiter interrupts as he put down our meals. Emma always eats healthy in public. Today beet salad. She must really pig-out big-time at home. I have a burger and sweet potato fries.

"No more wine, but I'd like an iced tea, lots of ice, unsweetened, extra lemon," Emma answers. "What were you saying?"

"I hired a guy I said was my cousin and pretended he was helping me paint. My office still sucks but it feels cleaner."

"How about the clients? Aren't most of them guilty?"

"How about all of them? Worse than that they hardly ever show when they have appointments, they lie about everything, and they smell."

"Sounds lovely." She shudders. "How about your colleagues?"

I think about how to explain them as I eat a mouthful of fries. "That's the positive surprise. I had this idea most of them would either be the idealistic, 'everyone is innocent' type or they couldn't get a job anywhere else."

"Sounds about right."

"It's not. They're smart. Some are idealistic, but most seem motivated not because of their clients, but their hatred of the prosecutors and judges. And they're friendly, helpful . . ."

"That's good. Have you gotten into court?"

"Not a trial but I had a preliminary hearing the other day and got to cross-examine a victim."

I wait a moment as the waiter clears the dishes. "Any dessert?"

We both shake our heads no. "I'll bring the check. Stay as long as you like."

"She was in her eighties, poor health. The state wanted to make sure they had her testimony on the record in case she croaked before trial."

"What kind of case?"

"Purse snatching, but the prosecutors charged robbery because my client carried a pocket knife. He was nineteen, a business student at U of A. I almost believed he was innocent until the old lady testified she had $84 in her purse. My client gets all agitated and whispers in my ear, 'The lying bitch. She only had $16.'" Emma can hardly stop laughing and excuses herself to go to the bathroom.

I laugh too and for the first time since I left BARF, I realize I'm okay. I have a job, but contrary to what I told Emma and everyone else, I don't hate it. I don't love it. I can tolerate it till something better comes along. My parents are off my back. Derrick, the fucking weasel, is out of my life. I have Jack. He isn't the love of my life, but I can tolerate him till someone better comes along.

Love the one you're with.

Seven

enise phoned, texted and left me a note.

Ms. Elan wants to see you ASAP.

Denise is sweet, works hard, but trailer trash. Talks with a hillbilly twang. Dresses in out-of-style, old-fashioned tops. Pants too large for her skinny frame. She looks like someone who'd lost twenty-five pounds and wears her *before* clothes, or belongs to a religious sect that mandates *their women* be covered. Her dull brown hair is in need of a haircut. No make-up or jewelry except a cheap wedding band. Strange for a young woman in her twenties. She says little, but does whatever I ask, and does it right the first time. Unlike most staff, she is in awe of the lawyers and treats us with respect. Most act like we are a nuisance and we need them more than vice-versa. Denise is terrified of Elizabeth and refers to her as Ms. Elan even in private.

Jack likes her or, more likely, feels sorry for her. "She supports her family on a government secretary's salary."

"Doesn't mean she has to look like a bag lady. There are decent secondhand stores." At least that's what I've heard.

About time Elizabeth wants to see me. I know she shouldn't show favoritism, but we could've gotten together without the rest of the office finding out. I want to meet her husband and some of her prominent friends. People she knows can help you get ahead.

Double E's office is located one floor higher than the attorneys. We are housed on floors three through six. She's on seven with other county administrators and big-shots. I'd been told she was the first boss not to have an office among the lawyers. Lucy, Elizabeth's secretary, waves me into the reception area. Too bad she can't give Denise lessons in how to dress.

"Latte, cappuccino?" Elizabeth asks in lieu of a greeting.

"Sure, a latte with a couple sugars if you have the real stuff."

"Of course." She turns around and fiddles with an intimidating and spotless coffee machine. "I hear you bought a condo near Campbell and River. Not a bad area but I like the foothills better."

"Best I could afford now." No way I'd tell her Dad bought it.

"You know that's where Paul Terrazas lived?"

"Oh my god. You mean he died in my house?"

"No, calm down. I mean he lived in that complex."

Phew. I knew we'd bought a place where the previous owner had died, but I thought it was a woman. Yuck. I'm glad it's not Terrazas. That'd be too freaky.

"How do you like working here?"

"Fine. The lawyers are smarter than I expected."

"Denise working out okay?"

"She's competent."

"I know she dresses weird and talks like a character from the Beverly Hillbillies, but I've never had complaints about her work."

"If she were older I'd understand, but she's young, nice enough figure, not that you could ever tell."

She hands me the latte. Looks like a Starbucks barista made it. "Who's your team leader?"

"Barry Singer."

"You've lucked out twice. He's a great lawyer. Maybe best one in the office."

"He hasn't been very helpful."

"No one else has complained."

I decide to stay quiet. Take some sips of the latte which tastes greats. Elizabeth starts to speak, but first runs her fingers through her perfect hair. "Uh, rumor has it you're seeing Jack Clarke?"

Is that her business? It's not a secret. Gossip's rampant in the office. "I don't know if seeing is the right word. We've gone out a few times."

"You know I care about you, Molly. I wouldn't have hired you if I didn't. I need to give you a heads up. Jack's charming. But he's not someone you want to get mixed up with."

What the hell's she talking about? "I'm not sure I know what you're trying to tell me, Elizabeth. I'm not going to marry the guy. He's fun and that's all there is to it."

"Well, be careful. He's a womanizer, not to be trusted, and being with him won't help your future. Jack thinks working here's the zenith of a career."

"I appreciate your concern, Elizabeth."

"I don't want you to have another episode like—with Derrick."

How does she know what happened with Derrick? It's one thing for her to know about Jack, but I never told anyone here the truth about how Derrick and I broke up. If anyone asked, I said mutual boredom.

"Molly, don't get upset. I'm just passing on information. I'd love to chat longer, but I have a conference call. Let's do lunch. Lucy can set it up with Denise. Come and see me again. I want you to feel like you're welcome anytime."

Before I knew it I was out the door and in the elevator. WTF? This was not the person who reached out to me when she was my mentor. Or offered me a job. Who is the real Elizabeth? The power-hungry bitch or the compassionate caring human being? Has power changed her or did she put on an act to get that power. Maybe I'm the one who changed? I never got to finish the latte.

◆ ◆ ◆

The weekend's almost over. As has become our habit, Jack and I go out for dinner Friday night. We take turns choosing one of the new restaurants which have opened as part of the long planned downtown renovation.

"Let's go to La Caverna," Jack suggests.

"I thought we were trying new ones. Even I know La Caverna is old news. How about Relic's? Don't give me that look. Give it a chance."

"Okay." Jack says. I knew it wouldn't be his first choice. Or second. Or third. Relic's has fancy appetizers, salads, and pizza with gourmet toppings. Jack's the pepperoni or sausage pizza, hold the salad, type. I've heard raves about Relic's fabulous white chocolate martini. I want to try it.

The first time Jack invited me for a drink he ordered coke, told me he was an alcoholic--was in 'the program.' He proudly showed me a medallion representing five years of sobriety. I almost consider that a deal breaker. I enjoy a glass of wine or two with dinner, a beer with Mexican food, an occasional cocktail. I never have a problem knowing when to stop. "My issue has nothing to do with you. Feel free to drink whatever when we're together." I wasn't sure if his declaration was bullshit, but apparently it isn't.

After Friday dinner, we separate. Jack goes home, picks up what he needs for the weekend and comes to my place. Once in a while I go to his place. Either way when we get back together we head for the bedroom.

Jack seems totally comfortable with my body and knows how to turn me on. Lights on, lights off he doesn't care. Lots of foreplay. He knows how to use his tongue and unlike fastidious Derrick he couldn't care less if I don't shower immediately before sex. Derrick had all these hang-ups. Had to be dark. I had to have showered right before we started. No sex if I had my period.

Jack went to the office for part of Saturday, but otherwise we'd spend the weekend together. Except for the sex, we act like an old married couple even though we'd only been dating about a month. God, I hate that word, *dating*. It sounds so high school.

Saturday afternoon, after Jack leaves for the office, I feel at loose ends. I channel-surf, but Saturday afternoon TV sucks if you're not a sports fan. A copy of *Lincoln Lawyer* is on the night stand. I haven't read much except law in the past decade, but I'm bored and decide to read it. I must've dozed off. I awake when I hear Jack's car. He walks in, gives me a kiss and grabs a root beer.

"When did you first meet Double E?" he asks.

After my little chat with Elizabeth, I make no effort to challenge her nickname. He can call her the c-word for all I care.

"She was my law school mentor."

"Old girls network. And that's how you got this job?"

"Yeah. You don't seem fond of her?" A fragment of conversation with her makes sense in a different way. "You ever go out with her?"

"What do you mean go out?"

"Next thing you're going to say, I never had sex with that woman."

Jack laughs. "Okay, yeah, we hung out a few times."

"She's married and has been married since she started to work here. She doesn't seem the type to have an affair."

"And I do?"

"That's not what I meant."

"It was a long time ago." Jack say as he kisses my neck. "In law school." He didn't say anything further as he moves his kisses toward my mouth.

"Do I have to drag it out of you?"

He puts his arms around my waist. "Let's talk about this later."

I move his arm gently away.

"Okay, okay. Second year we were at a party and left together. It didn't last a month. She's not my type."

"What is?"

"A tall sexy red-head with long legs who never shuts up."

"One more question and I'll stop. How did it end?"

"It just did. Come on, Molly, let it go."

And I did, for now. Sex with Jack is easy. Maybe too easy. He knows how to please and doesn't want to do anything quirky. I think of him with Elizabeth. Did he dump her? Does he compare me with her? Her body with mine? Was she better in bed? Does it matter? It was a long time ago. My mind drifts to Paul Terrazas. I want to know the mystery behind his death, but three minutes after sex isn't the time to ask.

The rest of the weekend is pleasant, but I don't want Jack to stay tonight. I want to be ready for Monday. I need to take a long bath, tweeze, shave, and moisturize. Maybe watch what I want on TV. I'm afraid Jack will make a deal if I ask him to leave. Last Sunday night he'd gone home. Said he had a trial to prepare for. I'm trying to decide how to bring it up when Jack says, "I'm sure you've had enough of me. Unless you have something planned, I'm out of here."

"Sounds fine." Now that he made the decision, I'm irrationally miffed. I'm the one who decides when we're together, not him. Jack has a reputation for reading people. Maybe he reads me.

I barely finished my bath when the phone rings.

"Hi Mom. What's up?"

"Rose called, she's coming home."

"When?"

"I don't know. I could hardly hear a word she said."

"Bad connection?"

"Horrible. I hope she's coming back for good instead of squandering her life in some African wasteland."

"We can always hope."

Eight

Sophie Mercer had scheduled an appointment at ten. Three drug arrests in six months, two charges of possession of Oxycodone, and one of Percocet. Another junkie loser. I rushed through court to get back on time, but it's ten after ten and Sophie hasn't shown up. Her thin file revealed weekly meetings with Paul Terrazas, but little else. Seemed excessive to me. He'd logged in her visits, but made few notes. Maybe she was hot. Hadn't lost her looks to drugs.

I'm ready to give up when the receptionist buzzes. I call Denise to have her escort Sophie to my office, but she doesn't answer. Shit. I'm about to go get her when a young woman, in a wheelchair, an IV in her arm, wheels toward my office. More accurately is wheeled toward my office by a woman in blue scrubs.

"Hi, I'm Sophie," the woman in the chair says softly. "This is Maryanne," she adds as she smiles at the woman pushing her chair.

"Come on in, I'm Molly O'Rourke." There's hardly room in my small office for Sophie's chair and her companion. I study Sophie while Maryanne checks the IV bag, fiddles with the chair and smooths the blanket covering Sophie's lap. Sophie looks frail. She's bone-thin, pale and her eyes seem unfocused. She wears a turban-like thing on her head. Before I can explain to Maryanne she can't stay because the presence of a third party invalidates attorney-client privilege, she walks out of my office.

"I'll be in the waiting room Ms. O'Rourke. If you let me know when you're done, I'll come get her." I nod and turn back to Sophie.

Should I ask about her condition? Express sympathy. Best to play it safe. "I've been looking through your files. I notice you met with Mr. Terrazas often. I assume you understand your options."

"Not really. We didn't talk much about my case."

"What'd you talk about?" I doubt Terrazas was trying to get into her pants.

"I know this sounds weird, but we talked about dying, the afterlife, whether heaven and hell exist."

No shit, that's fucking-weird. Scary-weird. I decide to ignore it. "There's no plea offer in your file. Had you planned to fight your cases?"

"No, Paul was going to string them out. I don't have that much time left."

I look at her. Time for what and then I realize what she means.

"You're ill?" Of course she's ill, idiot.

"I'm dying. I have stage four lung cancer. It's inoperable. I've had chemo, radiation, but I'm out of remission." She points to a label on her wheelchair that reads **Valley Hospice**.

"Excuse me, but were you having cancer treatment and doing illegal drugs at the same time?"

"I wasn't partying if that's what you mean. I was in pain. Didn't have health insurance. I needed drugs to make it through the day." Who doesn't have health insurance?

"I'll write a letter to the County Attorney. I'm sure they'll dismiss your case when they find out your situation."

"Paul tried that. They refused."

"Are you sure? I don't see any letter Paul wrote to the CA." Or much else. The file was unusually incomplete.

"He gave me a copy of it. How is Paul? You seem nice, but why did I get transferred? Is that part of the delay strategy?"

I need time to think. "I'm going to get some coffee, can I get you some, or tea or something?"

"Tea'd be great."

"Relax, I'll be back." She's in hospice, talked to Terrazas about dying, heaven and hell. My head spins as I go to the first floor to buy drinks. As I pay I realize I could've gotten free stuff in the break room. Sophie had rattled me. How come no one told her Terrazas had died or at least that he wasn't here any- more? Other files had letters like that.

When I get back to my office nothing has changed. Sophie still sits in her wheelchair. I hand her a cup of tea, realize I hadn't asked about milk or sugar.

She takes the cup and says nothing.

"I'm sorry to tell you this but Paul . . . uh . . . passed away."

"Died? Oh no. That's horrible. What happened?"

"He had an accident. I don't know the details. He drowned in his hot-tub."

"Poor Paul." I give her time to process what she'd heard. I don't know what I expect her to say, but not, "Suicide."

"Why would you think suicide?"

"Uh, I don't know." She glances around the room. "I guess because most adults can swim. Forget I said that. It was stupid."

After that, Sophie seems to fall apart. She becomes even more pale and less focused. She answers my questions perfunctorily:

How far did you go in school? "A little college."

Tell me about your work history? "Waitress."

Did you have any other arrests, convictions, police contact? "No."

"I don't feel good. I need to leave," she says a few minutes later. I wheel her back to the lobby where Maryanne waits for her.

I can't stop thinking she is only twenty-six. Younger than me. The disease had aged her. Why did she think Paul committed suicide? I look through the file again. No letter to the County Attorney. No letter from them. I check with Denise.

"Paul's files are disorganized. I'm sorry."

Another one's sorry, but this time it isn't her fault. I consider asking what she knows about Terrazas, but it will probably be a waste of time.

The office begins to fill up as attorneys return from morning court. I walk down the hall to look for Jack but he isn't there.

"Looking for Jack?" a voice says. I turn and see an attorney I don't know. Carl, maybe?

"Yeah, I wanted to ask him a legal question."

"Jack, a legal question? Ask someone who might know the answer."

I have to backtrack. "It's not legal exactly, but it has to do with something my client told me."

"Come into my office." He points to the other window office in the corridor.

I walk in and sit down on a blue velvety couch that rests unhappily against the back wall. Out of place against the bare beige wall and parking lot view. The office is messy and cluttered, files and scraps of paper cover every empty space. No photos, but political posters for NORMAL and other pro medical marijuana groups. Isn't that against policy? Denise gave me a memo Elan had sent out spelling out what was appropriate to hang on the walls. Only two family pictures and nothing political. Most of the lawyers offices I'd been in ignored the policy. And why not? Since Elan rarely saw attorney's except in her office it seemed safe enough.

I sit down and wait for him to say something but he doesn't. He smiles and subtly checks me out. I verify his name is Carl F. Clinton from the law school diploma on the wall. I also verify he is damn sexy. "This may sound weird, but can you tell me what you know about Paul Terrazas' death?"

"He had an accident and drowned in his hot-tub." Same story, same flat affect.

"Everyone I ask says the same thing and acts like they're hiding something."

"I'm not hiding anything. I doubt anyone else is. Paul was in his 40's, in good health, didn't drink much yet he's found dead in his hot-tub with a .28 BAC. I think people are just confused and sad. What did your client say that had to do with Terrazas?"

"How do you know my client said anything about Terrazas?"

"Lucky guess. You came in saying your question had something to do with what a client said."

I'm not sure I want to tell him. "She used to be his client. She told me about a letter Paul showed her from the CA. It isn't in the file and other documents seem to be missing."

"What kind of letter?"

"From the CA about a plea."

"That's nothing unusual. Filing's always behind. Stuff gets misfiled or lost all the time. Ask Denise to look. And you can't always take a client's word."

"In this case, I believe her." I come at Carl a different way. "My client of is in hospice and very ill. She and Terrazas had discussions about dying and the after-life. Don't you think that's weird?"

He says nothing then shrugs. "Take a walk with me. I want to get an ice-cream. There's a great place down here hardly anyone knows about."

"It's not even lunch time."

"I have to meet a client at lunch. Come with me. You don't have to have one."

Several thoughts go through my head about why I shouldn't go. I'm dating one person I work with. How could I add another? I'd have to keep it secret. And that'd be hard. PD's are the biggest bunch of gossips. Wasn't I jumping the gun? We were having an ice cream cone not a drink at a hotel. Dad always told me never to get involved with people I work with although he put it more bluntly. "Don't shit where you eat." Too late to remember that advice. Way too late.

"Okay," I say.

Nine

I still taste the ice cream when Jack shows up in my office.

"How about lunch?"

I wasn't hungry after scarfing down a large scoop of strawberry. I spent an hour with Carl. I can't waste another with Jack. It would be worth it if he'd tell me about Terrazas. But it'd be easier to get him to talk when we were alone and relaxed.

"I've got to beg off. I've got a shitload of work."

"If you change your mind, I'm going with the group to Cora's."

The group. The attorneys that formed the heart and soul of the office. They shared triumphs and defeats. Relied on each other when they had trial jitters or when they were screwed by aggressive prosecutors, arrogant judges, mis-informed reporters or their own clients. Ate lunch together to share stories of morning court, irritated spouses or gossip. In the past, according to Jack, they argued daily over email about where to eat. "I hate the meatloaf," "I'm dieting," or "Why can't we try someplace different?" Someone suggested they choose a restaurant for each day of the week. Made it easy for people coming straight from court, but hard for those who wanted to try something new.

Frank, one of the appellate lawyers, champion of anal, sends out an email everyday to let the group know the lunch plan. He continues to do this even though the schedule hadn't changed for years.

I wasn't sure who was 'in'. I wasn't. During college, I always knew. Sororities teach you that. Lisa, Juan and Jack were in. Frank, Elizabeth wasn't. Neither was Barry. His arrogance didn't play. After my hour with Carl I sensed he was a loner. As for the other thirty-five plus lawyers. . .

The group suffered a loss when Anne Levy quit the office. Anne Levy, goddess of the public defender world. That's how folks acted when her name came up. "Anne could have won that case." "Anne would have made that client take the deal." "Remember when Anne's phone rang in court and . . ." Anne's trial skills were part of the office lore. So were her lack of organization, her penchant for misplacing things and profane language.

Jack adored her. They'd had a short fling. Jack had a short fling with everyone. He was usually the person who ended it. Anne dumped him. If I cared more, I'd be jealous. Or maybe I was jealous, but more for her office standing and what I imagined as her perfect figure and great looks.

Going for ice cream had been more than fun. Carl is witty, sarcastic and smart. He hates the prosecutors and loves the fight, but has no illusions about the clients. He'd asked me to dinner Friday. Jack and I haven't made explicit plans, but we'd spent the last several Friday nights together. I know Jack expects this Friday to be the same.

Carl is more my type than Jack. Jack's boisterous, warm, and everyone's big brother. Carl's tall, but wiry. He runs most mornings and is a gym rat. Jack had been athletic in his younger years, but has given that up. Jack lets people know who he is and accepts others at face value. Carl's more of a mystery. I know I can trust Jack. He's honest. As long as we're together, he won't cheat on me. I don't know if I can trust Carl. I don't know if he likes me or is playing me. Maybe that's part of the appeal.

I'm trying to figure out how to see Carl on Friday without letting Jack know when my cell rings.

"Hello, Molly O'Rourke."

"Molly, it's me."

"Rose, I can't believe it. Where are you?"

"At the airport. I'm renting a car."

"Here? You didn't go to Phoenix?"

"No, I wasn't ready for Mom's interrogation."

Shit, she's going to stay with me. Invade my space. Ask questions. Wait, she can be a perfect alibi. "I'll text you directions to my house, call the gate and make sure they let you in. Three rocks from the door there's one of those fake ones with a key inside."

"Okay."

"I can't get off work for a couple hours. Make yourself at home."

The day passes quickly. I'd planned on going to the jail, but that can wait. My clients aren't going anywhere. Unlike BARF, nobody tracks your comings and goings. You have to sign out if you leave the office, but that's for the receptionist to know how to handle calls.

Not for the boss to track you.

I finish what can't wait and take-off. At home I open the door to the smell of homemade food. How'd Rose manage to cook a feast with the few ingredients I have around?

"Molly." She throws her arms around me and doesn't let go until I pull away. I follow her into the kitchen. Everywhere I look there's food. Fruit, vegetables, bags of pasta, cans of god knows what and a couple of shopping bags she hasn't emptied.

Looks like enough food to feed a family of four for months. "Are you planning to live here indefinitely?"

"Of course not, but I haven't had a chance to eat like this in two years. The markets in Niger have limited selection and availability."

Rose is twenty pounds thinner than last time I'd seen her. Unlike me she was always on the edge of plump. But not now. She's tall too, but not as tall as me. We both have curly hair, but hers is long and in need of a cut. She's wearing faded jeans and a Doctors Without Borders T-shirt.

"What was Niger like?"

"Wonderful and horrible. I fell in love with the people, especially the kids, but the poverty, poor hygiene, lack of good food and medical care. . ." She rambles on. I pretend to listen. I can't stop thinking about Carl and wondering how long Rose plans to stay. I start to put the rest of the food away. The second bag has a printed flyer and a business card with a police logo on top.

"What's this?"

Rose turns and takes the paper from me. "A policeman came to the door. Very nice man. Asked me some questions. Did I live here? Was I at home on

March 11 last year? I told him I just got back from Africa and why I was staying here. He left the flyer and card and said if you knew anything at all about a hit and run that date to call this number."

"Today is March 11."

"No, last year. Detective Fajardo works the cold case squad. He says they've found talking to witnesses on the anniversary of a crime is a good way to jog memories. We chatted. Talked about all sorts of stuff."

"I'm surprised you didn't offer him tea."

"I did and he liked it."

I finish emptying the groceries. "Why are they're making such a big deal about this? Hit and runs are commonplace."

"Two people were killed. A mom and a young baby. A girl was seriously injured. It seems like a big deal to me."

I pick up the flyer. Mountain and Prince. Not far from here. I skim the rest of the details on the flyer----description of the victim's car, time of day, police looking for white male driver in his 30's or 40's driving a green, grey or blue sedan. Not very helpful. I pick up the card. Detective Alfredo Fajardo. Never heard of him. I put the card and flyer in the recycle pile.

"Don't throw that out?"

"I didn't live here then. I can't help the cops."

Rose grabs the flyer and card. "I'm going to keep that and pray for the family. And for Alfredo."

Alfredo, not Detective Fajardo? I don't know how Rose gets any sleep. The list of people she prays for gets longer every year.

Ten

Rose is awake and dressed when I stumble out of the bedroom. She cooks breakfast, multigrain pancakes and fruit salad. A pleasant change from a protein bar and as much coffee as I can get down. We'd talked late into the night about our parents, family trips, her work and men. She has a boyfriend for a change— Aaron. She'd slips his name in throughout our conversations, but when I press for details she clams up. I tell her about Jack, but not Carl. She's the faithful type.

Aaron seems like a normal American name to me, but I bet he isn't. Rose rarely had a boyfriend that I knew of, but if she did, the guy was from another country, usually a third world one. He's black, brown, Arab, anything but white American. He wants to save the world, is broke, and needs Rose to save him. Our parents freak out about her choices so Rose learned to keep her personal life to herself. In our family, it's often better to keep things to yourself. Avoid the interrogation.

I leave Rose engaged in cleaning the house. Unlike me she seems to enjoy it. I hate it and hired a cleaning service to come in every other week. I think the condo looks fine, but Rose mentions several projects one of which is to clean the grout on the bathroom tile. I never knew you were supposed to do that.

I almost call in sick. I have no hearings, client appointments, or pressing motion deadlines. But Rose isn't a good enough reason to put off going to the jail. I'd joked with Jack about my fears, but he saw through me. Knows I'm scared. He offers to go with me, but I know that would backfire. If my colleagues found out, I'd never hear the end of it, "Molly's such a wimp" or "What a chickenshit." PD's empathize with trial fears but not jail fears.

Jack gives me a copy of a memo that lists what you can and can't take into the jail. Firearms and anything that could be used as a weapon I understand. No food, sunglasses, or coffee. You can give your clients unstapled legal papers, nothing else. Not that I'd bring them gifts.

There's even a dress code. Apparently a female lawyer caused havoc when she showed up in tight pants, short skirts and low-cut shirts.

At PD school they explained you have to pass through a metal detector to get into the jail. I hate those damn things. What if you set the machine off? Does someone pat you down? (I'm afraid to ask.) In prison movies the guards are big, burly men. If you make it through the metal detector they can search whatever you take in except legal stuff. The lawyer who taught the class made it clear the jail staff wasn't thrilled with lawyers, particularly females. Lawyers make their jobs harder since we know our rights. As for women lawyers we should have found a more feminine career or done something decent like be prosecutors. As I drive into the parking lot I see a sign, **'All vehicles are subject to search.'** PD school didn't mention that.

Getting inside is the first hurdle. More obstacles follow. Long waits to see clients. Unexpected lockdowns. No matter how long you've been waiting, even if you are talking to a client, he has to go back to his cell. Lockdowns allegedly are called because of a security breach. The defense bar believes 99% are bullshit. Bored jailers want to harass lawyers or inmates because they can.

With trepidation, I approach the main entrance and walk in. I'm surprised to see a woman behind the desk. "Hi, welcome to the finest lock-up in the state," she says with a grin. "Lawyer?"

"PD," I say.

"New?"

I nod.

"I'm Mary."

"Molly."

"Have any contraband?"

"No," I step through the metal detector—expect it to buzz. Nothing happens. Mary haphazardly checks my briefcase.

"Feel free to ask me if you have questions. To get to Visitation, walk to the end of the hall. The CO's will buzz you in. Follow their directions."

Easier than I expect, but scary. Each hallway further from freedom. What if I get lost? What if a client realizes I don't know shit? What if there's a riot?

I make it without incident to the attorney visitation section, a series of tiny conference rooms with a table and a couple of chairs bolted to the ground. Did they do that so prisoners can't throw them? I thought I'd talk to clients on the phone like on TV. I can't believe they expect me to sit with my client in this tiny room. What if he attacks me? I'm sure most have BO and bad breath. Maybe lice.

The jail control booth is visible from attorney visitation. A woman and two men, armed and protected by large panes of glass, sit looking at screens. They're safe enough. They can see in here, but they can't see everyone every second.

I choose Booth #2. Booths on either side have people in them. Someone can see if I'm being attacked or raped. I wish I'd taken Jack up on his offer to come along.

I brought along police reports to read, but can't concentrate. After what seems an eternity a youngish man walks through the door. OMG he's not hand-cuffed. He stops at my booth, "Are you my lawyer?"

"What's your name?"

"Rick Fletcher."

"Yes, come on in. My name is Molly O'Rourke."

Before I can say a thing he begins to whine. "You gotta get me out. I've never been in jail. Bails $2200. Melissa, my girlfriend, has $1000. I can get more if I ask my parents, but I won't. They can't know I've been arrested. I'm missing class. No one in my family's ever been in jail. I don't know what . . ."

"Slow down. First things first. All you need is ten percent of the $2200 plus a title to property to cover the rest. Have your girlfriend call a bail bondsman. But you don't get the money back. If you put up the whole amount with the court, as long as you show up in court whoever puts up the bond, gets it all back."

"But the coke was mine."

"It doesn't matter if you're guilty, just if you show up for court." Do I have to explain everything to these idiots?

"What do you mean property? I'm a student."

"You can put up a car title. Most cars are worth more than $2000." I say feeling a little more confident. I'm not even scared of this guy.

"I have a Honda that'll cover it. I can't tell my parents. They'll kill me. I'm the first kid in my family to go to college. They've saved for years. They don't expect me to get into trouble. If they hear the word 'cocaine' they'll lose it." He talks so fast he can hardly breathe.

"You've got to calm down." I glance at Rick who avoids eye contact. His legs are crossed, his hands made into fists, his dark eyes intent on me. He's tall and thin. The orange jump suit hangs off him. His mid-length brown hair had been cut recently. He doesn't stink. He doesn't get it. I'm here to help with his legal problems not to deal with his parents, his friends and whether or not he stays in school. I'm not a fucking social worker. That's my sister.

"I can't calm down. What if my friends find out? I have a test tomorrow. A paper due end of the week. Am I going to get kicked out of school?"

"You're thinking too far ahead." And I don't know. "You sure your girlfriend will bail you out?"

"Yes. It was her idea to get the stuff. She feels terrible. She'll do anything to help me."

"Call her soon as I leave so you can get out. We can talk about the rest then."

"Okay."

"Don't talk to anyone about your case. Not your cellmates, not your friends at school, no one. It's probably too late to tell you not to talk to Melissa."

He doesn't answer.

"Okay, too late. Don't talk about it on the phone here. It's not safe. You understand that if you two break up, stuff you've told her could come back to haunt you."

"We're not going to break up. Melissa's awesome. Believe me I won't tell anyone else, I promise. I don't want anyone to know." Idiot Melissa has probably told half her friends. Posted it on Facebook.

"Here's my card. I've written down your court date. We need to meet before that. Call and schedule an appointment when you're released."

"How long will it take to get out?"

"Once your girlfriend gives money and the title to the bondsman, he has to do paperwork. I imagine its quick." Imagine is right. I haven't the faintest idea.

"How do I pay you?"

"Don't worry about that. The court will look at your finances and assess a fee based on that. Often it's less than $400 and you can pay in payments."

He looks relieved. "Thank you. Thank you so much." As he walks out he stands straighter. Gives me a smile.

I like Rick and want to help him. I feel like a real lawyer. It's only after I leave the jail I realize I should file a motion for his release. It's a first offense and he's a student. I'll get started in case Melissa doesn't come through.

Eleven

Rose is the perfect house guest. She cancels my house cleaner. Shops, cooks, cleans and washes my clothes. Provides me an alibi when I'm with Carl. Jack's not the suspicious type. He doesn't question I'd want to spend time with Rose. "If my brother had been in Africa for years, I wouldn't let him out of my sight."

Carl and I flirt for the next few days. I check the court schedule to see where he has hearings. Often we're scheduled in front of the same judge. When we have no courtrooms in common, I show up where he is and act like I'm confused or looking for someone else. Later, I find out Carl did the same thing.

I confirm the Friday night date. Carl's not the type to announce it in the coffee room. I drive to his house. Don't want Rose to see Carl. We go to a showing of a Coen brothers movie. I can hardly pay attention waiting for Carl to make a move. He doesn't. After the movie, he asks, "Coffee or a drink?"

I want a drink to calm me down but years of flirting have honed my instincts. I pick coffee. Carl nods his head and I know I've made the right choice. He chooses a locally owned coffee shop favored by students.

We talk about our clients and local politics. I look into Carl's eyes and brush my hand lightly over his, but he doesn't respond. After a long silence he asks,

"What's with you and Clarke? You an item or what?"

"Yes, and no," I say trying to buy time and figure out what to say. "We've been seeing each other for a while, but it's not serious."

"So I don't have to keep this a secret?" I look at him, wonder how much lying I can get away with. Before I reply he speaks. "Okay, I get it. We'll have an affair. It'll be more exciting."

"I'm all for excitement."

"We can have code names." He laughs. "Well, if we're going to have an affair let's get started. My house is around the corner."

By morning, I want to dump Jack. Soon as we enter Carl's house, he leads me to his bedroom, but instead of wooing me with his body he uses his mind. We talk for hours. His room unlike his office is neat and sparse. Carl's an astute people watcher and knows all sorts of esoteric facts about Russian literature, Italian opera and foreign films. He tells stories with funny accents. Every so often, he'd say since this is an affair, we have to have secret ways of communicating. Since this is an affair, we have to make sure not to go to public defender hangouts. Since this is an affair, I can't put my hands down your shirt in public. I haven't laughed so much . . .

By the time he touches my breast, I've been aroused for hours. It isn't like I can't initiate sex, I can, but not the first time. Carl turns out to be a great lover. I can't help comparing him to Jack. Jack is proficient but sex is sex. Talking is for another time. Carl never stops talking.

His alarm buzzes at seven. I want to stay and have breakfast, lunch and dinner. He goes into the bathroom and comes out dressed in shorts and t-shirt. "I'm going to the gym. You're welcome to stay as long as you like, but lock the door if you leave." He walks over to the bed, kisses me on the cheek and is gone.

His leaving's a wake up call, but not the one I expect. Didn't he like me?

Did he think I'm a slut? Surely he wasn't one of those guys who beg you to do it and drop you if you do. I dress quickly. Don't forget to lock the door.

Rose is awake when I get home. Cutting vegetables. I hate the smell of onions before I'm awake.

"Morning, Molly. Have a good night?"

"Yeah." Rose looks at me, but doesn't ask questions. Both of us had been interrogated too thoroughly and too often by Mom to do the same thing to each other. "I'm kind of tired." Rose smiles.

I fall asleep and don't get up till after noon. Nothing from Carl, but a text from Jack who asks me to get in touch.

I meet Jack at Wilbur Burger—his choice. He'd joined some guys there to watch basketball. Suggested I might like to come. I could think of few more boring ways to spend an afternoon so I don't show until shortly before the game ends. The bar's crowded and noisy. Everyone in Tucson is obsessed with their basketball team. Jack introduces me to his friends as 'my gorgeous girlfriend' and makes room for me to sit down next to him. The game ends in a win and high fives. His friends take off and we move into a booth.

"Great news, they caught the *Gentleman Rapist*." Jack says. This fiend's been front and center in the paper and on TV. Dubbed theThe *Gentlemen Rapist* by the press because he leaves flowers and candy for his victims. The victim's must love that.

"Why great? You're not usually a fan of someone being arrested."

"I got the case. Lisa covered weekend court and called to let me know. I went over to the jail before the game to see him. I want you to be second chair."

"In a rape case. A serial rape case. This guy must be a major sicko. Who ever heard of a rapist who leaves flowers for the victims, I mean 'alleged' victims. Alleged rapist. It's all too weird for me."

I'm saved for a moment by the waitress. "Hey Jack, good to see you. Want the usual?"

"Yeah. How's Maria doing?"

"She's been accepted at the U. I'm very proud." She smiles at Jack, scribbles on her pad and turns to me.

"What can I get you?"

"Bacon Cheeseburger no mayo, large order of onion rings and a coke."

"Thanks, Lupe." Jack says. Lupe was at least fifty and looks like she'd had a hard life. I wonder how Jack knows her. A former client?

"Molly, if you want to get ahead you have to take on more serious cases. That's what Anne did. Volunteered for the toughest ones." God I hate her. "Our client's name is Albert Weston, goes by Al. He's young and confused. Barely more than a kid. He's not a monster."

Do I want to get ahead? Do I want out? This case is made for TV. Getting my name out will help me find a better job. If I work the case, I'll probably have to stay with Jack till the trial's over. It'd be hard to try a case with someone you just dumped. Might be an excuse to string along Carl. Did Carl even care?

I check my phone once more. Nothing from Carl.

"Okay Jack, I'm in."

Twelve

promised Rose I'd go visit the parents with her. Even though I hate Phoenix. Two against two. Dudley never takes sides. He's a sweet dog. Rose drives. I'm exhausted—physically and mentally. Juggling Jack and Carl is stressful not to mention all the prep for my first big case. The media had dubbed our client 'The Gentleman Rapist' and it stuck in spite of victims' groups protesting. "No rapists are gentlemen,"; "It demeans the victims." The public can't get enough of him. A rapist who leaves flowers and candy. After the judge denies our second motion for a change of venue, he issues a gag order. Whatever that means. Jack explains we can't talk to the press, but the media can report on anything that's 'on the record'.

I still don't get it.

"I can't talk to the reporters, but if I want something to get publicity, I call Pam Hall at the Star and tell her where she can find the information or I send her a copy of the document."

"Isn't that cheating?" Jack doesn't answer.

"How do you know Pam anyway?" Again Jack doesn't answer.

"Did you date her?"

"No."

"Then what's the secret?"

"Had a short fling with one of her ex-roommates."

I don't even want to know more. Why am I with Jack? My mind turns to the case. What kind of moron breaks into a woman's home, terrorizes and assaults her, then leaves flowers and a box of candy? There are seven alleged victims, each generating hundreds of pages of paperwork that have to be read and reread, over and over. Motions have to be written, witness interviews have to be scheduled. Not to mention keeping up with other cases.

"Are you going to tell them about your big new case?" Rose asks.

"You mean that I'm representing a rapist?"

"What other big new case do you have?"

"Sure. Why not? They're adults even if they don't act like it."

I glance at the speedometer. "Rose, if you don't go faster, we'll never get there."

"I don't want to get a ticket."

"Just go seven miles over the speed limit. Everyone else will still be going faster than you." Lots faster.

"I believe there are speed limits for a reason. Dr. Laura says a good person does the right thing all the time even if no one is looking or nobody else does it."

"Yuck," I say with the hope if I don't argue about Dr. Laura that she'll change the subject. "Yes, I'm gonna tell them. Dad will be proud of me."

"Mom will go ballistic."

"Better over that than our personal lives. Speaking of personal lives, you haven't mentioned Aaron lately."

Rose is quiet for a moment. "We broke up."

"How come?"

"Six thousand miles between us."

"Didn't seem to bother you before. Aren't you going back to Africa? Lots of work to do."

"I'd like to of stay in Tucson. At least for a time. Don't worry, I'm apartment hunting."

"Tucson? What are you going to do here? No epidemics and we already have a food bank."

She ignores me. "I have savings. Not much chance to spend where I've been. Fredo says social workers are in demand. He has a good friend who's a social worker at the VA."

"Fredo? Who's Fredo?" No wonder she broke up with Aaron. Fast worker my sister. Fredo? "That wouldn't be Detective Alfredo Fajardo?"

"Yeah, Molly, he's the sweetest guy I've ever been with. I never thought a cop would be like that. Caring, interested in others. He wants to hear everything about my time in Niger."

I'm glad someone's interested. She proceeds to tell me in excruciating detail about their first date. I say 'wow' or 'ahhhh' and concentrate on my own thoughts.

I'll be a star. Every time we file a motion in the Weston case, the courtroom is more and more crowded. The first motion--to have the counts severed--the courtroom was nearly empty. A few lawyers, a court watcher or two. The second motion for a change in venue, only a few weeks later, draws media from Phoenix. Standing room only.

We luck out. Even with a serial rapist and salacious details, you don't get on CNN or in the New York Times, but the international press is covering the trial of Jared Loughner. Loughner is accused of the attempted assassination of Congressional representative Gabrielle Gifford and the shooting of sixteen others, six of whom died including John Roll, a highly respected federal judge.

The out-of-state reporters hear the buzz about the Gentleman Rapist. Federal District Court where the pretrial motions in the Loughner case are taking place have strict guidelines for media. No cameras or filming, only reporters and sketch artists inside. Cameras are allowed in state court. I'm not surprised to see a gaggle of reporters at Weston's hearing, but wonder why the sketch artist. Maybe she's bored with the formality of the Feds and wants a change. The following morning the local paper features her sketch of Weston and me at counsel table. She's made me look terrific. Over the next few days I keep running into the artist everywhere. At first it's cool, but it turns weird. Is she a stalker? She texts me.

How about a drink? I'd love to sketch you.

No thanks. First time a gay woman came on to me. I don't know whether to be flattered or grossed out. I worry she won't take no for an answer, but she does.

The press, being the press, soon loses interest in Weston. I hope they'll return if the case goes to trial. I imagine being interviewed by Anderson Cooper. Too bad he's gay. Appearing on Nancy Grace. Catch her in a legal error.

Once Jack gave me his seal of approval, I join the group for lunch. I'm originally accepted because of him, but once I become second chair in Weston things change. I'm treated like a colleague. I show up even when he doesn't. At first I join them because I have no one else to eat with. Soon I look forward to it. Conversations drift between gossip and legal questions. I learn which judges are fair and which think their job is to help convict. Which prosecutors are lazy. Who's sleeping with who. I don't know when it happened, but I'm in.

After I agree to be second chair my biggest concern is our client. I've gotten used to the jail. I can talk to lowlifes without a show of disgust—but a rapist? In college, I'd known a few drug addicts and once a friend's brother had gotten in trouble for a bar fight. Everyone knew or heard of someone accused of date rape. But a man who broke into women's houses, wore a mask and forced women to have sex?

Weston is not what I expect. He's ordinary. Short, thin with brown hair, brown eyes and a boyish look that belies his age of twenty-three. He treats Jack and me respectfully. Calls me ma'am, Jack sir, until Jack insists Weston call him Jack. He'd completed two years of community college majoring in computers. Wanted to be in the Marines, but was rejected. He has a girlfriend, Bobby-Jo, who doesn't look a day over twelve. Weston vehemently denies his guilt as does Bobby-Jo. The evidence says something else.

The first time I went to visit him at the jail I was nervous. I didn't think he'd hurt me, but I thought he'd expect me to be different. Older, more experienced, male? Jack asked me to explain court procedures to him. The case is going to trial. The county attorney assigned to the case, Eric Smithfield, is adamant there will be no plea. I haven't had any cases against Smithfield. He's in sex crimes. This is my first. The lawyers in the office agree he's an arrogant asshole and untrustworthy.

Jack has told me over and over about a murder case Smithfield tried against Anne Levy, the best lawyer on the planet. She kicked his ass. I am so sick of hearing about St. Anne. You'd think Jack won the case not her. He never shuts up about it.

I treat Weston as coldly and impersonally as I can. He keeps saying, 'Yes, Ma'am, no Ma'am' till I can't stand it.

"Don't call me Ma'am."

"I'm sorry. Don't be mad at me. You want me to call you Miss Molly?" Miss Molly. You're a rapist. I'm your lawyer not a Southern debutante.

We both sit there in silence and then Weston says, "Ma'am-sorry, Miss Molly. I'm so scared. I don't know how to fight or stick up for myself. Jack told me not to tell the inmates what I'm in for. If they push it, he says lie and say burglary. But they know. There's TV in here."

"Has anyone threatened you?"

"Not in words. They laugh at me, call me names, not the kind of names I can say in front of a lady. Say things about, about my, uh how I have to hurt people to have sex."

Shit. I don't know what to say.

"I'll talk to Jack."

My visit is unproductive. Weston is edgy and upset. He doesn't care about legal procedures. Nothing I say calms him down. I feel totally inadequate. At least I'm not afraid of him. He's scared of everything.

Jack suggests I move in with him to facilitate trial prep. A real romantic. I sense he hopes once I move in, I'll stay. I say no. Told Jack if we live together it won't be because of a trial. I sort of expect him to tell me he wants me to move in because he cares about me. He doesn't say that or anything else. I don't know if I'm relieved or sad. Between the trial and carrying on with two men I'm too busy to think about anything. Sometimes I feel like I'm in a movie. Someone else is making decisions about how I live my life. I don't know what I want to happen. I know I should break it off with one of them, but I don't know which one. I do nothing.

The case takes up more and more of my time as it gets closer to trial. It's like preparing for seven different cases. The CA has listed eighty-four witnesses on their pretrial statement. We need to interview all of them. The victims, the heart of the case, we aren't allowed to interview due to the passage of Victim's Rights legislation. I'd read about Victim's Rights laws in the paper. Sounded good to me. Victims needed to be protected from sleazy defense attorneys who would twist their words and pry into their sex lives. Now that I understand the consequences I'm horrified. How could you try a case if you can't talk to the victims?

Prosecutors argue the law doesn't preclude victims from talking. They can if they want to. How many do you think talked to us once the prosecutor explains, "You can talk to the defense attorney if you want to but you don't have to. It's your call. But keep in mind if you do, everything you tell them that's different from your statement can be used against you." Or, "You realize the defense attorney's job is to get the guy who raped you off." Or, "They'll try to intimidate you, put words in your mouth, twist your words."

What's happening to me? A few months ago I wouldn't have thought the system was unfair. I would have thought victims needed protection not defendants. Certainly not a serial rapist. Why was I pleased I was second-chair? I plan to leave this job. Soon. When I first started working here, I admired Elizabeth. Wanted to meet her friends. Now I hoped nobody finds out we knew each other. What's this place doing to me?

Thoughts of Carl still bring me pleasure, seeing him has become a problem. I have no time. Not only do we have to hide from Jack and our colleagues, but my sister. Like most women, she adores Jack. Hell, if she wasn't my sister, they'd probably hook-up if we broke up. I don't think she'd snitch me off, but I know how she feels about lying and cheating. Sometimes I feel like I live with Mother Superior or Dr. Laura. I wonder if either of them can cook.

"Molly, are you listening to me at all?"

"Sorry, I must have dozed off for a minute."

"Did you hear anything I've said the last half hour?"

"Of course, but I'm waiting to hear how Fredo is in bed."

"You're so… so crude."

"You think that's crude. I'll show you crude. 'Hi Mom. Hi Dad. Guess what? I'm screwing a public defender and Rose is fucking a cop.'"

Twelve

Dear A.K.
Can you meet for a quick lunch. Noon. Usual place.
V.

I hit REPLY. *See you there.*

I email Jack. "Tied up at lunch." Maybe 'busy' is better than 'tied up.' Good thing Jack's easy going. Good thing Carl lives close to the office. Good thing I always wear sexy underwear. Time and time again Mom had told Rose and me to wear clean underwear. 'In case you're in an accident.' Rose and I thought that was hilarious. Aunt Margaret told me to wear sexy underwear 'In case you have an adventure.'

The hours drag. 11:30. I can't wait. Luckily, Carl is home. I'd asked for a key, but he said no. We exchange small talk. It'd been over a week, almost two, since we'd been together. Carl, a typical defense lawyer, wants to hear about the Gentleman Rapist.

"Tell me about his arrest."

"Happened at his apartment. SWAT team. Ridiculous, he had no weapons and didn't resist. His girlfriend, Bobby-Jo, was there. White trash through and through. But she knows something about the criminal justice system. Yelled over and over at Al, 'keep your mouth shut,' and 'ask for a lawyer.' He listened. The only thing he said is 'I want a lawyer.'"

"So the police didn't question him?"

"No."

"What have they got?"

"Forensics, DNA. Remember the police said the rapist left flowers and candy at the victim's house? Bobby-Jo works at a florist shop. They had flowers all over their apartment. Several boxes of See's candy in the fridge. When he went to buy candy, the moron wore a big straw hat, large red sunglasses and asked so many questions, both the manager and an employee at See's could ID him."

"What's your defense?"

I look at my phone. It's 12:37 p.m. I have to leave by 1:10 p.m. at the latest. "It's almost 12:40 p.m. Do you really want to talk about the case?"

"You just want me for my body?"

I don't answer. Right now I want him for his mind, his body, forever. I think about him every free minute. I lust after him. Sometimes he acts like we're having a meaningless affair. Calls me ravishing and sexy, says he adores my body. Other times he acts like he cares. Wants us to be together. I didn't know which Carl is real.

He never asks me not to see Jack. He never seems upset when I don't have time to see him. He never mentions other women. His refusal to give me a key coupled with his rule I can't show up unexpectedly worries me. Makes me think he likes to see me a couple hours here and there, that's all. I've never seen signs of another woman being around— no clothes, errant earrings or an extra toothbrush, but he has advance notice of when I show up. Enough time to hide anything incriminating.

After our first date I don't hear from him for a couple days. After our second, he starts that stupid business of calling me 'A.K'. And himself 'V,' whatever that's about. If I break up with Jack, I don't know what will happen. He might dump me, treat me the same or declare his undying love.

"Okay, your case can wait." I follow him back to his bedroom. Twenty minutes later, we're back in our clothes and at the kitchen table. We both get back to the office in time for 1:30 p.m. court hearings.

Denise never found any correspondence between Terrazas and the CA or any other part of the file. Maybe the issue will be moot. Sophie hadn't shown up for her last appointment. Someone from hospice left a message, "Sophie's picked up an infection and has to cancel." I need to talk to her, but keep putting it off. How can people stand to work at a place where everyone will die?

Feeling guilty I call the prosecutor. "I've taken over Sophie Mercer's case. I know it's a little strange, but I can't find either the letter Terrazas wrote to your office about a plea nor your answer. Any chance you could send me a copy?"

"Not my case anymore. It's been reassigned to Julianna Dawson." He hangs up without a goodbye.

Good news. Julianna has a reputation as having some compassion. I call her and explain Sophie's situation. "I'd be glad to send you copies, but how sick is this woman really?"

"She's in hospice. She comes to my office in a wheelchair with an IV. Some kind of nurse or aide brings her."

"Can you send me her medical records?"

"Sure." One thing civil practice taught me is how to subpoena medical records.

"If they prove what you're telling me, I'll try to get her a deal, maybe a dismissal."

All my colleagues bitch about the CA's. "Not a hint of compassion"; "Don't think the rules apply to them"; "Only care about winning, not justice." I never say anything positive about the CA's, but I get along with most. I don't assume they lie. I know they have a job to do. My attitude helps me get results but I hide it from my colleagues who'd think I was naive or a closet prosecutor.

Smithfield's an exception. He is an unethical jerk He'd just sent over another packet of late disclosure in the Weston case. I'm reading it when Jack calls. "Judge Goldstone wants to see us in his courtroom. Now." Jack had been happy we drew Goldstone, but thought Smithfield would affidavit him. Smithfield had not only lost the murder case to St. Anne. Goldstone had chastised him in open court because of his poor performance. However, the ten day time limit for dumping a judge was long past. Smithfield hadn't.

Smithfield was in the courtroom accompanied by a female I hadn't seen before. She was about forty, fit with brown hair. She could be co-counsel, a cop, or a CA investigator.

Before I can ask Jack, Goldstone walks in. "All rise. State of Arizona v. Albert Robert Weston CR 20131090"

"Smithfield and Jacobs for the State." Smithfield says. So she was co-counsel.

"Clarke and O'Rourke for the defendant who is not present," says Jack.

"Good afternoon, counsel. You probably wonder why I've set this hearing. I need to let you know I've turned in my letter of resignation. I'll be leaving within the next three months. I'm convinced this case is going to trial. Even if the trial goes on the first trial date, which I find highly unlikely, I won't be here to complete it. My wife has booked a cruise and I won't disappoint her. I'm recusing myself from this case. It's being reassigned to Judge Quinn."

And he's gone. For a moment no one speaks. "Come on, let's get out of here," Smithfield says to Jacobs.

"One minute." The woman with Smithfield walks over to us. "Hi, I'm Beth Jacobs Co-counsel."

"Nice to meet you." Jack takes her hand and smiles at her. I follow his lead and do the same. We all walk out of the courtroom together. Smithfield doesn't say a word.

"Goodbye Eric, have a nice day." Jack says. Smithfield doesn't reply.

"What was that about?" I say when Smithfield and are out of earshot.

"Just to bug him."

"What do you think about losing Goldstone?"

"Goldstone isn't the most charismatic guy, but he's always given me a fair trial. Anne thought highly of him." If St. Anne thought he was great.... "I really don't know about Quinn. She's new. On the civil bench until a few months ago. I haven't had a trial in front of her. You?"

"Me neither." Has he forgotten I'd never had a trial or is that a subtle jab?

"Let's check around while we still have time to dump her. Sometimes judges without criminal experience can be great, but not always."

"Okay." A legit reason to call Carl.

"I haven't seen you much lately," Jack says as we walk back to the office.

"Busy time. Rose is job-hunting. Calls me constantly with questions about places she's applying. I practically wrote her resume. You probably won't be enthused, but she wants us to have dinner with her and Alfredo Saturday night."

"Why wouldn't I want to go? Cops are people. I'd like to get to know your sister better."

"Good. I forgot to tell you. I can't come over tonight till after dinner. Rose is cooking something special. She has something important to tell me."

Thirteen

I didn't expect Rose to go to so much trouble. The house looks great, more like date prep than dinner with your sister. Daffodils in vases. The table set with a cloth and matching napkins. Lit candles. Shit, maybe she isn't moving out.

Rose cooked all my childhood favorites: fried chicken, mac and cheese, corn on-the-cob, biscuits, and even pecan pie. Maybe Alfredo's moving in.

"This is delicious. Am I getting a bigger surprise than I expected?"

"Don't be silly. I got a job."

"Congratulations. Tell me about it. Is there more chicken?"

"Lots." Rose walks into the kitchen and comes back with another full platter.

I fish through the platter, look for the biggest piece.

"I'm going to work at Valley Hospice."

I wasn't sure what to think. I want her to get a job, but . . ." Isn't that kind of morbid? Everybody's going to die."

"People think that, but it isn't true. The first step when people arrive is to take them off their meds. Often it's drug interaction, not disease, that makes people sick. Some feel better and leave."

"But the rest? The name of your place sounds familiar."

"Maybe because I've talked about Valley. I really want this job. Helping people die without pain and with dignity is a privilege."

"If people go off their meds, aren't they in pain?"

"They don't go off pain meds. Hospice philosophy is to give people as much medication as they need to stay comfortable. They don't worry about nonsense like addiction when you're near death. And people can eat whatever they like.

"When they were showing me around I heard a nurse ask this gentleman what kind of ice cream he wanted for dessert. He answered, 'I can't have any I'm diabetic.' 'Yes, you can' she answered. You should have seen the grin on his face."

"You sure seem well-informed."

"I read up on the hospice movement to be prepared for the interview. I could tell you. . . ."

I interrupt her before she has a chance to tell me, in great detail, more of the principles of hospice. "I just figured out where I heard about Valley Hospice. One of my clients um, shit, Sophie, I can't remember her last name, lives there."

"It's hard to picture a hospice client getting in trouble with the police." Rose stares at me as I grab another biscuit. "I can't believe you can eat so much. I'd love to have your metabolism."

I start to reply, but stop. I'm sure she didn't want to hear a dieting lecture. She'd heard too many from Mom. "Sophie's young. Used illegal drugs to self-medicate. No insurance."

"They'd prosecute someone who's dying?"

"The CA's, County Attorneys, can be heartless, and they would, but lucky for her, her case got transferred to one of the decent ones. I might be able to get her a deal."

"Sophie you said? I'll make sure to take special care of her."

"Rose, I shouldn't have told you about her case. Don't say anything, promise?"

"Of course, promise. I'd never do anything to get you in trouble. If you're done with dinner, I'll get the pie. If you're not too full."

"Not even close. I'm going to open a bottle of wine. Want some?"

"With pie? I'll have mine with coffee. And I have more to tell you."

In a few moments we're back at the table, two large pieces of pie almost invisible under the whipped cream. Rose has a cup of coffee and I have a glass for wine. "Spill it."

She doesn't answer right away. Drinks some coffee and eats a few bites of pie. "I'm moving out end of the month."

"I'll miss you." I realize I will. "What's hard about telling me that?"

"Nothing."

"Where are you moving?"

"An apartment."

"Where?"

"Near River and Pontatoc?"

"That's a nice area. Can you afford it?"

"I have a roommate. Want another piece of pie?"

I want to, but I'm stuffed. "No, thanks. I'm full."

"I'll clear the table," Rose stands up and begins to stack plates.

"How'd you find a roommate?"

"I heard about someone looking for a place."

"I hope you know something about her. You have to be careful moving in with someone you don't know."

"I know, uh, this person." Rose says. She avoids looking me in the eye.

"Who is she? What's the big secret?"

"It's not a she."

"I don't care what sex they are, but I'm surprised you're okay with a male roommate."

Rose pours herself another cup of coffee but says nothing.

"I'm surprised Fredo doesn't care."

And all of a sudden I get it. "You're moving in with him?"

"Yes," Rose says blushing.

"Mom and Dad are going to be shocked. And what would Dr. Laura think?"

"Let me tell them." Rose shoots me what she considers her mean look.

"Don't worry, I won't say a word." Rose must be smitten. Unlike me, she takes her time getting into a relationship. She'd never lived with a man, at least that I know of. Maybe in Africa? She wasn't against living with a guy, but was slow to give her heart. At least she had been. Alfredo was another story. Every other word out of her mouth was Fredo this, Fredo that, Fredo's so, fill in the word . . . considerate, smart, giving.

"It's about time you joined the twenty-first century and lived with a guy. Can I help clean up?" I ask. She ignores my dig, declines my insincere offer and finishes faster than if I had helped .

"Molly, since dinner's over and cleaned up, I hope you don't mind, but Fredo wants to get together. He was helping his sister move some furniture but got done sooner than he expected."

"Go ahead, Rose."

Rose leaves the kitchen and comes back shortly with her hair combed wearing a clean polo shirt and baggy jeans. She seems so happy. I hope the two of them last, but I have doubts. Fredo comes from a large, traditional Hispanic family. Rose is Christian, but not Catholic. Our family was far from traditional. Mom had worked since we were babies. Rose wanted a career. I didn't know many Hispanics other than the ones I worked with. The few non-Anglos at BARF were carbon copies of the rest of us. The ones that worked at the PD or CA dressed stylishly, always wore high heels, lots of make-up and exuded sexuality. Rose is happiest in jeans, doesn't own a pair of heels or use make-up. Maybe if she prays enough it'll work.

My thoughts drift to Carl. He's out of town for the weekend. "I'm going to visit a friend who has tickets for the Final Four." A friend? I know the games are this weekend in Indianapolis. The office has a pool. I entered even though I don't know the first thing about basketball.

What did he mean by 'a friend?' He implied a male friend, but never said a name or even used 'he.' Was Carl really visiting a guy? Or some woman who liked basketball or pretended to? How can I tell if Carl's where he said he is? Asking him about the game wouldn't help. He could watch it on TV. Even if he didn't watch it, he knew more about basketball than I did.

Yesterday, after he left work, I sneaked into his office. No one left their offices locked. I felt panicky, my heart beating double-time. Don't think I'd make a good burglar. Lawyers and staff occasionally went into other people's offices to get a file or borrow things like, staplers. I had no excuse. You don't walk past several offices to borrow a stapler. Carl's desk was its usual mess. I picked up a file or two and then carefully replaced them the way they were. I opened the top desk drawer. Office supplies. I heard steps in the corridor. Shit, what would I say if someone opened the door? It was after five and almost everyone had left, but there was always someone around. The footsteps continued past Carl's office. I couldn't stay here. Too risky. What did I expect to find, anyhow? Carl was too smart to leave anything incriminating.

Only after I got back to Jack's do I manage to get Carl out of my mind. On Saturday, I do errands and in the afternoon come home to work on Weston. I spread the voluminous material on the kitchen table. I want to figure out how to make the information easier to access. I reread police interviews of the victims. The perp, whoever he is, must have spied on women until he found the right ones. Creepy. Each lived alone. Each was short, brunette and appeared fit. None were in serious relationships. Jack suggested I make a chart showing similarities and dissimilarities between the crimes which would help on our motion to sever counts. When Rose interrupts I realize I hadn't thought of Carl in more than an hour.

"You better get dressed. Our reservations are at 6:00."

"What time is. . .?"

"Almost 5:15 p.m. and we have to leave at 5:40. Fredo's meeting us there."

"Shit, I better move it."

The evening starts better than I expect. La Casa Rojas has good food and service. Kudos to Alfredo who picked it. Rose talks about him incessantly, but I haven't spent much time with him. He turns out to be intelligent, well-informed and a good conversationalist. I stereotyped him based on his job. He and Jack talk about Wildcat basketball and baseball. I kinda get basketball. The players are mostly young and sexy and the game moves. But baseball. I'd rather watch a cactus grow. My dad rarely misses a game. A lifelong Dodger fan even after Phoenix got a team.

Jack and I'd agree not to mention the Gentleman Rapist at dinner and Alfredo didn't bring him up. We steer away from our jobs except when Jack asks Alfredo how he and Rose met. "I was passing out fliers about a hit-and-run in Molly's neighborhood and Rose answered the door."

"Must have been serious, Tucson's the hit and run capital. Luckily it's usually old people hitting parked cars."

"This was serious. Two people killed, a child severely injured."

"You don't have any leads?"

"We've had some tips since the fliers went out but nothing concrete. A few people mentioned a small dark car driven by an Anglo male, but they describe him anywhere from being in his teens to early fifties."

I'd have called the evening a success except for a small incident. We'd finished dinner and are deciding whether to have dessert. I'm eyeing the flan, when an older couple walks past our table.

"Anne, "Jack practically jumps out of his chair. He hurries the few feet to the woman and grabs her in a big bear hug. I know instantly who she is. After the over-long hug, Jack turns back to our table. He points to the couple, 'Anne Levy and Jason Allen. Anne used to work at the PD with me. Jason's an ex-prosecutor.' He pauses and points at us. 'Molly O'Rourke and her sister, Rose O'Rourke. Alfredo Fajardo, he's a detective with TPD. Molly's a new lawyer at the PD. We're here celebrating Rose's new job at Valley hospice'" Jack hasn't taken his eyes off Anne.

So now I work with him. What happened to me being his gorgeous girl-friend? And this is the great St. Anne. Nothing much to look at. Short, brown hair, a decent figure, a little on the chunky side. She could use some help with her choice of clothes.

I pay little attention to what's said. Usual jabber when you run into someone one person knows and the rest don't. I watch Anne. In a few minutes Jason takes Anne's hand and they go to their table in another room.

Seeing Anne has put a damper on my enjoyment. No one notices. They're too busy listening to Jack talk about what a great lawyer Anne is, the murder case she won in front of Goldstone, and how no lawyer in the world can match up to St. Anne of Tucson.

Fifteen

Quinn set a 9:00 am status conference today, two days before the deadline to dump her. The lawyers who'd been in front of her have positive comments.

"Treated everyone with respect."

"Read all the pleadings."

And best of all, "Didn't let the state call the shots."

Her JAA called to give us a heads up that the judge planned to call our case last. I think that shows concern for our schedules. Jack's not sure.

I have nothing else in court so I decide to check her out. The courtroom is nearly empty except for fucking Smithfield and some staff. Why is he here? Panicking, I think Jack's wrong about us being last or that somehow Smithfield set us up. Then I realize Smithfield's covering morning court for the CA's.

The room begins to fill. As the clock strikes nine, the bailiff stands. "Oyez, Oyez, Oyez, All Rise, Court is now in session, The Honorable Judge Priscilla Quinn presiding."

Judge Quinn walks in, sits down. "You may be seated."

Quinn looks good for an older woman. Mid-length silver hair, unlined face. Make-up expertly applied. An expensive but understated necklace made up of brilliant blue stones. Her voice soft but commanding as she calls the first case.

"State of Arizona versus Crystal Kline."

I watch Quinn zip through the docket. The hearings are mundane until the sentencing of a young woman named Brandy who has a last name that sounds liked *Gipshitz*. She hardly looks old enough to have several felony convictions, numerous failures on probation and been in and out of rehab. Brandy's eighteen, but she could've passed for much younger. This is the third time the prosecutors have filed a petition to revoke her probation. "Does the state wish to make a sentencing recommendation?"

"Yes, Your Honor, State recommends the aggravated sentence of three years based on defendant's prior felony record, and three failures on probation." Aggravated sentence for possession? What an asshole.

The defense attorney makes the usual arguments but doesn't sound like even he believes them. "Brandy's barely eighteen, she comes from a dysfunctional family, and is in counseling." Didn't mention her parents saddled her with an embarrassing last name.

When Brandy's given a chance to speak, she mumbles "I'm sorry, I'll try harder," tears running down her checks.

No way the judge would give her three, but I expect she'd send her to prison. What choice do you have when someone screws up that badly?

"After I read the probation report and other documents I'd planned on sentencing you to the two year presumptive sentence. You have the most lenient PO in Tucson and she's sick of you. You haven't followed through with counseling, drug testing or even probation appointments. But as I look at you here today, I can't send you to prison. I feel sorry for Ms. Lewis having to deal with you again, and if I had the ability to do so I'd order her off your case. It is the order of the court you be continued on probation on the same conditions as previously ordered with the additional condition that you enroll in junior college next semester. . ."

This is our judge. I'm sure. A lot more sure than Brandy will make it on probation.

The judge begins the next case. I check my messages. Shit. A missed call from Carl. Maybe lunch. I hit voicemail. "Molly, don't dump Quinn till you talk to me." No time to call back. Anyway, it didn't seem like we had made a decision. There's still time. Did he have something to say about Quinn or is this a ruse to talk to me? Should I tell Jack what Carl said? What if Carl just wants to see me? How would I explain that to Jack? What if Jack wants to dump Quinn now and Carl knows something.

Jack walks in before I can follow up with Carl. "Jack," I whisper, "Quinn sentenced a young woman to probation on her third revocation. We should keep her."

"We can talk later. Let's not do anything now." Good. I'd have a chance to talk to Carl.

"Where's Weston?" Jack asks.

"He's not here or at least he hasn't been brought up yet."

"Shit, I hope we're not stuck here waiting for him." He joins me in the gallery I try not to think about Carl.

Quinn finishes her docket by again sentencing a defendant to probation instead of prison. Still no Weston.

"I'm going to take a short recess and check with the deputies on how long before they can bring up Mr. Weston." Quinn stood as the bailiff bellowed, "All rise."

"So you were impressed with Quinn?" Jack asks.

I tell him about Brandy's sentencing.

"Sounds good. Let's see how she handles our hearing. Did you hear Longoni's getting married?"

Before I can say anything, Quinn's bailiff, a young, kind of cute guy announces, "The Judge wants to see counsel on the Weston case in chambers."

I've never been in a judge's chamber. We follow the bailiff as he opens a door that leads to the hall behind the courtroom. There are a series of offices. We enter the closest one. A dumpy, matronly looking woman--likely the judge's secretary—speaks loudly on the phone and ignores us. The bailiff knocks on an inner door.

"Come in." Quinn sits behind her desk, her robe off. She gestures to two chairs and a sofa which face her desk. The room is cramped as the court reporter's equipment takes up much of the space. Jack and I take the sofa. Smithfield and Jacobs take the chairs. I check out Quinn's clothing. She has on a light grey pencil skirt, a turquoise shirt that matches her necklace. A matching jacket hangs on a clothes rack. Her chambers are decorated with desert landscape plus a couple of family pictures. Her husband's a distinguished-looking man and her two daughters slim, well-groomed and stylish. I want to puke.

My eyes move to the court reporter, a tall, leggy brunette. Her short black skirt is positioned so Jack and I get a peek of black bikini underwear. I catch her eye and she smiles. Neither Smithfield nor the judge can see her display. Not sure about Jacobs, but probably not, as her expression remains solemn.

"State of Arizona versus Albert Weston CR20131090. Present in chambers are Eric Smithfield and Jacobs for the state, Jack Clarke and Molly O'Rourke for the defendant who is in-custody, not present."

"Mr. Weston is in custody, and was not brought up by court transport. I called the jail and spoke with Lt. Reed. He advised me that Mr. Weston was jumped by several inmates yesterday evening and is currently in the infirmary. Mr. Weston has numerous stab wounds but none are life-threatening."

I'm afraid to speak out loud. Inmates getting stabbed at the jail. Did that happen a lot?

"Judge, how serious are the wounds? Maybe he should be hospitalized." Jack says.

"That's all I know, Mr. Clarke." Jack's about to continue, but Quinn gestures for him to wait.

"It is the order of this court that counsel be allowed to visit Mr. Weston at the infirmary any time as long as it doesn't interfere with medical treatment.

"I've also requested that the jail physician contact me within twenty-four hours to provide an update on his condition which I will forward to both counsel. At this time I think we should continue the status conference till a week from today. By then we should know if his injuries will affect the trial date. Does either counsel have anything they wish to put on the record?"

"Your honor, I'm concerned about Mr. Weston's condition. The jail infirmary isn't a hospital. Has he seen a doctor?" Jack asks.

"I've been told that he doesn't require hospitalization. I don't know who has seen him, but I'll speak to the doctor tomorrow. You can go see him right now."

"Your honor," Smithfield says in his slimy brown-nosing voice. "The jail deals with injured defendants all the time. It's their call, not Clarke's, how medical care is provided."

Jack rolls his eyes but doesn't respond.

"I think we've exhausted the subject for now. Does anyone have anything new to add?"

"No," we all say in unison.

"You may be excused."

Jack and I walk out of her chambers followed by the state.

When we were out of earshot I ask, "Does this happen often?"

"I wouldn't say often. The jail's well run. More often in prison. Inmates have less to lose."

"Is it because he's a rapist?"

"Alleged rapist? Maybe, probably not. Usually it's pedophiles who get attacked if the prisoners find out. They're often put in protective custody for their own safety. People get attacked for many reasons or none at all. Usually mental illness, gangs or too many violent men living too close together. We'll have to wait and see."

"Want me to go see him?" I ask, hoping he says no.

"No, I'll do it. I have to see another client anyway."

Jack and I part at his office. I walk toward mine, turn and hurry toward's Carl's office

"Hi Anna K."

"Would you stop that Anna K business? It's dumb."

"Tell that to Tolstoy."

"Who?"

"Never mind." Carl gives me an amused smile.

"I'm returning your call."

He laughs. "I was doing research on prosecutorial misconduct and came across a law review note written by Quinn. She analyzed a case where the Arizona Supreme Court overturned the disbarment of a Yuma prosecutor who put on perjured testimony in a murder case. The court said the sanction was too harsh."

"What'd her note say?"

"Basically that the Supreme Court was wrong and that prosecutors had to be held to the highest standard in order for our judicial system to work. Strong language. I think she's a keeper."

I tell Carl about this morning. Make small talk waiting for him to ask me to lunch. He doesn't. "Busy for lunch?" I finally blurt out.

"Sorry, but I have plans. How 'bout tomorrow?"

"Sure." I leave before I say something I'll regret. Who's he eating lunch with? He usually works through lunch if we aren't together.

I walk back to my office. Can this day can get any worse? Waiting for me is a note from Lisa. Although she's a colleague and friendly, she's never left me a note.

Anne Levy's joining us for lunch. You need to meet her. Will be at the Diner. Lisa

Sixteen

"Your sister, line two," Denise says.

"Feeing better?" Denise had taken sick leave the last two which was unusual for her.

"Yeah, I'm fine, thanks for asking."

I didn't realize how much I depended on her until she was out of the office for a couple days. BARF had 'floaters' to fill in. Not here. Some lawyers type their own stuff when their secretaries are out. Some type their stuff all the time. Claim it's easier. Not me. One reason I'm a lawyer is so I don't have to type.

"Molly, you there? Molly?"

"Jeez, Rose, don't be so impatient. I'm here. How are you?"

"Great. Fredo and I've been fixing our place up."

"How's work?" I'd rather hear anything but what a great job Fredo's doing.

"I told Mom and Dad we're living together." She says ignoring me.

"What'd they say?"

"They want to meet him. Since I didn't volunteer to bring him there, they said they'd come here and we could all go to dinner."

I make a face. "All" meant me. On the other hand, it might be amusing to watch them question him.

"What do your parents do?" Meaning—are they professionals?

"Where do they live?" Meaning—do they have money?

"Where did you go to college?" Meaning—if you didn't, what are you doing with our daughter, and if you did, why are you only a cop?

"How many siblings do you have? Meaning— did your parents plan their family or just randomly spill out children."

71

"They'll give him the third degree. He'll learn a thing or two about interrogation."

"I know they'll like him. How could they not?"

For a moment I say nothing. "Of course they will, Rose, I'm teasing. So how's the job?"

"Lots to learn. The people I work with are the best. Sophie's assigned to me. You need to come see her."

"Can't she come here?" I'm not paid enough to make home visits.

"Sophie's not doing well. Sleeps a lot. Wants to see you."

"I have nothing to tell her that she doesn't know."

"I wouldn't wait too long if I were you." Maybe if I string it out, I won't have to see her at all.

"Doesn't Sophie get visitors?"

"Not many. She hadn't been in town long when she got sick. She didn't have real friends. Started hanging around with druggies."

"She must have family?"

"Not much. A half-sister in Denver, but they're estranged."

A better person would be more interested in Sophie's life, but I'm not. I change the subject, we chat a few more minutes, and make plans to get together for dinner.

In one of those coincidences that sometimes happens, Julianna Dawson, the prosecutor on Sophie's case calls seconds after Rose hangs up.

"I hope you have good news for me. Sophie's taken a down turn. She's so ill she can't even come to the office."

"Sorry to hear that. My uncle's an oncologist. I had him review the records and he seemed surprised Sophie was still alive. Anyway, I got my supervisor to agree to dismiss all the cases in six months if Sophie doesn't have any police contact. We'll just continue the case."

I want to ask what kind of police contact she expects a woman in a wheelchair who lives in a hospice to have, but I keep my mouth shut. This is a good deal for Sophie. I don't understand why she cares about her case, but she does.

"Thanks, Julianna. Can you send a confirmation letter? I trust you, but you never know if either of us will be here in six months."

She laughs. "No problem."

I call Rose back. "Can I come to see Sophie whenever I want?"

"Yes, but earlier in the day is better. She's more lucid."

I call Jack, but he's not in. Neither's Carl. Might as well get it over with. I sign out and go to my car. A quick walk around. Still dent free. And the Camry still hasn't been washed.

The hospice is about ten miles from the office on the Northwest side. Once out of downtown, I enjoy the drive. My sense of unease disappears even though I feel like my situation controls me. One minute I know I should break up with Jack and try to have something real with Carl. The next minute I know I should break up with Carl and try to have something real with Jack. Sometimes I think I should dump both. Jack has been acting strange towards me lately. I'm positive he doesn't know about Carl, but he seems to sense I'm not totally there.

A few days ago, Laura Longoni, one of the lawyers in the office, announced that she and Jay, her long-time boy-friend were getting married. The whole office is invited to the wedding. A big extravaganza's planned, fancy dress, dinner and open bar. Jack assumes we are going together. Carl never mentions the wedding. I'm afraid to mention it to him. What if he brings a date?Maybe he won't go. Laura's one of the few women in the office Jack hasn't had a fling with. Maybe because she had been going with Jay since high school. Jack doesn't have flings unless woman are unattached.

One of our first nights together, Jack and I had one of those talks you have when you're with someone new. Explaining past relationships, the good, the bad and the ugly. Why they ended. I told him a funny story about a bad date.

"This guy asked me to dinner at a fancy steakhouse. He has a couple cocktails, the most expensive steak, a couple of sides, dessert. I have a glass of wine, a small steak and no extras. When the bill comes he says, 'Let's just split it, I hate squabbling over a few cents.' The cheap bastard left a minuscule tip. I never saw him again. Your turn."

"An ex-colleague mentions that a woman whose new at the PD is interested. She's not my type, but I decide to chance it. Haven't been with anyone for a while. We don't click, but we get totally plastered and end up at my place. She spends the night. I have a wretched hang-over. She leaves in the morning without saying much. I thought she was happy to get away from me. About an hour later she comes back with a suitcase. I ask her what the hell she thinks she's doing. She says something like I slept with her so I must love her. That's when I decided to stop drinking. Although it took awhile."

"What a psycho. What happened?"

"I told her to leave as nicely as I could. She went ballistic. Told everyone at the office I led her on. She'd come into my office and cry. It was horrible. She finally quit. I heard she met someone and they moved to California."

The conversation went on like this for a while and at some point Jack got quiet. "The one thing I can't tolerate is lying. If you want to see someone else or break up, just tell me. I'm a big boy."

And yet a few weeks later, I start seeing Carl. Big boy or not I haven't told him. What the hell's wrong with me?

"In one quarter mile turn left onto Thornydale, then make an immediate right, your destination will be on the left." My reverie was interrupted by the woman's grating voice. Wish she had a soft British accent like the lady in Carl's car. Almost there and I haven't figured out what to say.

It takes a few minutes to figure which building is Valley Hospice. On my left's a classy looking structure which looks like an expensive apartment complex not the drab, run-down institutional building I'd expected. The desert landscape of rocks, gravel, cactus and flowers could have won a contest. I finally see a plate with the words *Valley Hospice* placed discreetly above the door handle.

I open the door. Wait for the hospital smell and to see people lying in beds hooked up to IV's. Instead the place feels like a hotel. A couple of people in the living room watch TV and a few are talking. At the front desk, I ask for Sophie.

"She's in her room. Number 5. Not hard to find." She points to a corridor. "Fifth door on the right." I walk slowly. Most of the doors are open. The rooms have been painted cheerful pinks and oranges, not hospital white. Each has a desk and a couple chairs as well as a bed. Attractive art hangs on the walls. Some residents are in bed, others sit at their desk and one room is empty. I approach Room 5 and look in. Sophie's in bed, the TV on, but she doesn't seem to be watching.

"Hi Sophie," I say.

"Ms. O'Rourke? Thanks so much for coming. Please, have a seat."

If possible Sophie looks thinner. Her eyes are dull. Her voice weak. But her hair is combed and looks like it has been styled recently.

"How are you?" God, I'm stupid.

"Okay. I've been getting over a virus. Don't worry, I'm not contagious."

I smile. "Call me Molly."

"You know Rose is my social worker, Ms., I mean Mol-ly." She pronounces it hesitantly.

"Yes, she told me." She doesn't seem to have trouble using Rose's name. "I have good news about your case."

"Is that why you came?" Why else would I be here?

"Yes, I thought you'd want to know." She didn't reply so I went on. "After the CA, County Attorney, got your medical records, they've agreed to dismiss if you have no police contact in six months."

"I don't think that'll be a problem." She begins to cough and grabs a glass of water next to her bed.

"Can I get you anything?"

She shakes her head and after what seems forever the coughing stops. "You realize I'll be dead before then?"

My first instinct is to say, 'Of course you won't.' I don't. I nod, not sure I can find my voice. She's dying and soon. I didn't want to talk about death. Could I leave? I'd only been here a few minutes. I change the subject. "Is Rose here?"

"I don't know. She usually is. There's something I need to talk to you about."

Shit. "Sure."

"I told one of the women I've gotten friendly with I have a lawyer and she wanted me to ask you a legal question."

"Of course. I'll be glad to try and answer it." Legal question great, much better than talking about her dying. "Do you want me to talk to her?"

"No. She wants me to ask you. She's shy. She knows something about a crime. Does she have a legal responsibility to tell the police or the prosecutor's office?"

I start to focus my brain on when a private citizen has a duty to report a crime. Teachers, social workers might if it involved a child. "Can you give me more information?"

"Like what? She didn't tell me much."

"Did she find out because of her job, like was she a teacher who found out a kid got hurt?"

"No, nothing like that."

"And the crime already happened?"

"From the way she talks, a long time ago."

I thinks about the statute of limitations, but there are lots of exceptions and I wasn't up on it.

"Probably not. It's hard to answer without more detail. Maybe you could check with your friend."

"No, it's not that important. Forget it." Sophie begins to cough. The cough lasts longer this time. "My sister came to visit me this weekend."

"That must have been nice."

"I was surprised. Ashley and I haven't spoken for over a year."

"She must be concerned about you."

Sophie doesn't answer. We sit quietly. Sophie didn't seem to care if I talk, but I feel she wants me to stay.

I try to think of something to say. I can't ask her about what she's doing or planning. Everything I think of sounds stupid. I didn't want her to talk about death. That's what social workers are for. Where is Rose?

Sophie seems to have fallen asleep.

"Sophie" I whisper a couple times. No answer. I creep out of her room. I scan the corridor. Empty. Hoping not to run into Rose, I hurry down the hall and out the door. I don't breathe until I get to my car.

My thoughts are jumbled, but for a change not about men. Why can't I talk to Sophie about dying? Rose can, but she's a social worker. Paul Terrazas was a lawyer and he could. Everyone dies sometime. Jack would tell me if she wants to talk about dying, I should let her. Even Carl would. Of course they're public defenders and I'm just here for a while. Or was I? I hadn't checked to see who was hiring for weeks or was it months?

And what did she mean *someone* knew about a crime? Sophie is pretty ill to socialize. Why wouldn't *her friend* want free legal advice? She acted squirrelly when I pushed. Maybe there isn't a friend. Maybe it's her?

Seventeen

Jack's not in bed when I wake up Saturday morning. Not in the kitchen. I make coffee, read the paper. Alone, I can start with my favorite Dear Amy advice column. I love advice columns. Never miss Dear Ann or Dear Abby and even read, Heloise, queen of housekeeping. I don't clean, but every so often you learn some gem like about cleaning your jewelry. Best way to learn what people worry about. Only Rose knows about my advice obsession. She has the same one. Our sisterly addiction clash over Dr. Laura. Ann, Abby, Amy and even Heloise are kind, concerned about their fans. Aren't judgmental, like Laura. Don't demean folks who ask their advice. Don't think only they have the path to good living.

I put Jack's paper back together. He hates when I leave it 'out of order.' I go back in the bedroom and grab my phone. Shit. Still off. Jack has called twice. I check voicemail.

"Molly, you need to get in touch with Bobby-Jo ASAP. Al called early all upset. I couldn't sleep so I went to see him. Bobby Jo's waiting for your call. I'll text you her number." The second voicemail was short. "Molly, call me."

The text with her phone number had arrived. I can't believe Jack gave Al his cell number. He'd warned me to establish boundaries with my clients. Told horror stories about lawyers who got too involved.

A young lawyer *in love* passed drugs to a hot gangbanger at the jail. Disbarred. On probation.

A talented PD couldn't believe his client had raped a college student. The accused swore his innocence even after he lost at trial. The lawyer appealed to all the state courts and then federal court. After several years the prosecutor on the case retired. The newly assigned CA agreed he wouldn't oppose a motion for a new trial if the client passed a polygraph examine using a polygraph examiner of the state's choosing. The lawyer filled with excitement called the clients with the good news.

"I'm not gonna pass," the client said.

The lawyer couldn't believe it. "Why did you keep swearing you were innocent?"

"I didn't want to disappoint you."

I didn't want to spend one extra second with any client or witness. What was so important I had to talk to Bobby-Jo today? We didn't have a trial date. I wanted to shop for Laura's wedding before I met Double E for a drink.

"Hiya," she answers on the first ring.

"Hi, Bobby-Jo, it's Molly O'Rourke."

"I've been waiting for your call. Jack said it was real important I tell you about Al. I've been crazy worried. They won't let me see him till he's out of the infirmary. Is he gonna be okay? When can we meet?"

For a southern girl her words tumble out quickly.

I need to go home, shower and change. Eat breakfast. "How about 10 o'clock my office?" Fuck shopping.

"Can't we do it earlier?"

"No, I have business to take care of. That's the best I can do."

I drive home on autopilot reliving my conversation with Sophie. Something about the story of *her friend* who witnessed a crime was off. She seemed fearful, agitated. Like she was lying or hiding something. Maybe she'd witnessed a crime. Sophie'd bought drugs in the past. More than once. Had she seen something she wasn't supposed to see? A drug deal gone bad?

Home. Quick shower. Change. A stop at the bagel place down the street. Maybe I can get finished with Bobby-Jo and still have time to shop before I meet Elizabeth.

I hear laughter from inside the PD's office before I open the door. I follow the noise to the coffee room and run into Lisa and Juan. "Hey Molly. How's Weston?"

"Still in the infirmary. I think Jack's there now."

"We missed you at lunch the other day. I wanted to introduce you to Anne."

I lie. "Sorry, I got out of court late." Why did she want me to met Queen Anne?

"Too bad you didn't come. Big crowd. People who rarely show up like Carl." Carl? What was Carl doing at lunch with them? Why didn't he tell me who he was eating with instead of being mysterious? And what did Lisa mean? The way she had looked in my eyes when she mentioned Carl's name. Or was I paranoid? Could Lisa know about Carl and me? I'd heard she was proprietor of the office rumor mill, but still . . .

I'm saved from further conversation when I hear Bobby-Jo's distinctive accent. "I'm lookin' for Miss O'Rourke."

"Excuse me, guys. Got a witness coming in and I think she's here."

Bobby Jo wears wrangler jeans, and a red checked western shirt. Both have seen better days. Her dirty blonde hair is in a loose ponytail and looks greasy and in need of a shampoo and cut.

"Hi, Miss O'Rourke."

"Please call me Molly." She giggles, but I ignore her.

Bobby-Jo follows me into my office and sits down.

"Do you know what Jack wants you to tell me?"

"Sort of. He called me and told me what he wanted. Oh god. I've been praying really hard for him." She begins to cry. Shit, I hate criers. I hand her a tissue. When I get close enough I smell bubble gum. I'm relieved. At first I thought it might be booze.

"Tell me how you met Al." Maybe if I could get her to talk she'd stop sniveling.

"We lived in the same trailer park when we were kids."

"Where was the park?"

"West Fleming."

"Kentucky?"

"Yeah."

"How old were you guys when you met?"

"Maybe about five or six. He was bigger."

"What was his life like?"

"His mama drank. He'd hang out at my house."

"What did his dad do?"

Bobby-Jo looks perplexed. "For a living" I add.

"I don't know. He ran off when Al was a kid."

"He was raised by his mom?"

"I guess."

"What do you mean?" I ask.

"She drank all the time. People called her Big Betty to her face. She was fat. Boozy Betty the rest of the time. No one crossed her. She was mean."

None of this is a surprise. I hardly need to write it down. "Did she beat him?"

"When he was really little. Until his older brother Will got bigger than Big Betty and wouldn't let her touch Al."

"So Will protected him?"

She had stopped crying, "From his mom."

"What does that mean?"

"I need a smoke, more gum and a coke."

"You can't smoke in here and the snack bar downstairs is closed. Wait here." I go to the staff fridge, grab a coke make a mental note to replace it and hurry back to my office. At BARF sodas were free. I hand her the coke. "If you want to smoke, you'll have to go outside. Don't take too long." I show her the back stairs. "When you're done come up and knock on this door."

"Thanks, Molly," She giggles again. What's so funny about my name?

I google Nordstrom's and look under designer dresses. If I find something today, I can get it shipped in time for the wedding. I prefer to shop in person, but time's short. Sexy or feminine? It'd been a long time since dresses were in. And not just any dresses, but colorful, flattering ones. I'm wavering between a very frilly lime and a lo-cut print with different hues of blue and purple when I hear Bobby-Jo knock. I bookmark the page and retrieve her.

"You were telling me about Al's brother?"

Bobby-Jo sips her coke.

Get to it. At a seminar called something like 'Effective Deposition Techniques' the presenter discussed how to get the most information in the shortest time. Let them talk. Don't ask questions. I'm getting ready to disregard that advice when Bobby-Jo starts to talk.

"What Willie did to Al was worse. Al adored Willie. He was tall and handsome. Smart. Al bragged on him all the time. When Willie protected Al from Big Betty Al couldn't believe it. For a while he seemed really happy. He laughed, acted like a normal kid. Just for a while. Then things changed. Al started avoidin' me." Bobby-Jo has tears in her eyes, but keeps on.

"I'd see him around, but he wouldn't talk to me. Acted like I wasn't there. Then the cops came to Big Betty's. Arrested Willie. Dragged him outa there in cuffs. Willie was fightin' them. Real excitin'. For a while it was the same, but then Al and me started hangin' out again. Like the old days. He didn't tell me what happened for years."

I check my phone. 11:09. "He eventually told you?"

"Yep. We had a cop lady come to school. She talked about bad stuff adults do to kids. You know?"

"I think so, but you need to tell me."

She looks down. "Like when someone touches your privates. Or puts it in you."

I nod and she continues. "Al acted weird at lunch. We ditched school and went for a ride. He told me then."

She's quiet for a while. I hand her another tissue. "I know it's hard to talk about, but if you want to help Al?" She moves back in her chair and looks at the floor.

"He told me at first Willie touched him or made him touch Willie. After, he would buy him candy or Pokemon cards. Protected him from everyone else. But it got worse. He started doing him. He got meaner. Willie had friends over and they did him. Willie told Al if he told anyone he'd pour gasoline on him and set him on fire. Willie was really scared of him. Did whatever WIllie said."

"Did Willie do anything to you?"

"No, he ignored me. But I was scared of him before Al told. He was big and mean."

Oh god, poor Al. I didn't want to hear this stuff. If Jack wants to know more, he can ask Al or talk to Bobby-Jo. But I can't stop.

"What happened after Willie got arrested?"

"Big Betty was pretty sick by then. They didn't have no money. Al dropped out of school. Got a job as a line cook at a diner. He always cooked his own food at home if he wanted to eat. Then Big Betty died."

"What'd you do then?"

"We started savin' money so we could leave."

"Why'd you guys come to Tucson?"

"Al loved horses and the West. He watched cowboy shows on TV all the time. He wanted to go to New Mexico but we didn't know anyone there. He had cousins in Tucson."

I can't talk any longer. I open the file cabinet. One of the lawyers had given us a handout to help get to know your client. Maybe it'll work for a witness.

"Excuse me, Bobby-Jo. I need to copy this."

I return, hand her the nine page form. "Could you fill this out about Al?"

"It's real long." She browses through it. "Real hard too."

"But it will help us"

"Okay."

"Bring it back as soon as you get it filled out. If there's something you can't answer leave it blank."

I hand her another pilfered coke. "You've been a big help and I know you'll do your best." I walk her out.

The next few hours I shop, but find nothing better than I'd seen on-line. At Macy's, I buy capris and a top and change in the stores restroom so I don't have to go home before I meet Elizabeth. She'd chosen a fancy restaurant at St. Philip's Plaza that kept changing names but always had a cool bar.

Elizabeth's fifteen minutes late, on-time for her. She orders an expensive glass of white wine after talking to the waitress for a couple minutes and changing her mind several times. I order the house chardonnay.

We chat about judges, CA's and colleagues. Elizabeth doesn't seem to have any compunction about trashing colleagues in front of me. Then she changes the subject.

"Are you going with Jack to Laura's wedding?"

"Yeah."

"It's quite the do. Open bar, catered by L'Orangerie, valet parking."

"I spent all day shopping, but I think I'm going to order something from Nordstrom's."

"Shopping's abysmal here. Tom and I were in San Francisco last weekend so I bought something up there. Cost over eight hundred bucks, but it's stunning."

Bitch. I guess I'll get to meet Tom.

"He's a sweetheart, but I'm a tad irritated at him. He knows I don't like to socialize with my employees but his cousin, Chloe, is dating one of the lawyers in the office so we're all going together."

"Who?" I ask even though I don't give a shit.

"Carl."

Whatever else we talk about's a blur. I order another glass of wine. Carl's going to Laura's wedding with a date. Not any date but a cousin of Double E's husband. Worse, this isn't a one-time deal, they're dating. I want to believe Carl's only seeing me. I want to believe not giving me a key is pay back, since I can't give him one. I want to believe this is more than affair. What now?

Eighteen

I drive to Jack's in a fury. Fucking Carl. No wonder he won't let me have a key. Doesn't want me to catch him screwing Chloe or whatever her stupid name is. Does Elizabeth know about Carl and me? Do she and her husband sit around laughing about Carl's little piece on the side? Shit. I'm overreacting. I have Jack. But that's different. Carl knows about Jack. He should've told me about Chloe. I wonder what his code name is for her? MP. Miss Piggy.

Jack's car's in the carport. Damn I need time alone. Maybe I should plead a headache and go home. My feet have a mind of their own, get out of the car and go in. Jack gave me a key. Jack treats me the way a woman should be treated. Jack I'm cheating on.

Before I can put my purse down Jack begins to talk about Al. "Poor guy. He has eighteen stab wounds, but the knife wasn't long or sharp. Lots of skin damage, but none of the major organs involved. Might be better if they were. They'd take him to a real hospital. Al's more scared than before. Thinks the inmates are out to get him. And the guards. I told . . ."

"Aren't you going to say hello?"

Jack walks over and gives me a hug. I hug him back and hard try to hold back my emotions. I have a strangest fantasy where I tell Jack what's going on with Carl. Ask his advice. Jack's my best friend in Tucson. He'll comfort me. I come to my senses. I'll be out two boyfriends.

Jack, being a man, mistakes my hard hug as a hint. He starts to rub my back. I pull away. "Not now, my period," I lie. It's almost that time.

"Does Al know who attacked him or why?"

"He knows, but won't say. He's doing the right thing. Being known as a snitch isn't the way to stay safe in jail."

"What's going to happen to him?"

"The jail investigators know who did it, but unless they can find a witness willing to testify, there isn't much they can do. They put the suspects in disciplinary status, but it won't be for long. When Al gets out of the infirmary, he's going into protective custody which sucks. Twenty-three hours a day alone. He gets an hour out in the yard by himself or he can shower. Meals in his cell."

"It's like he's being punished."

"He is. Did you meet with Bobby-Jo?"

"She told me Al's mom beat him, his brother molested him and let his friends do the same. I'm sure I didn't get enough info, but it made me sick. I gave her a long questionnaire to fill out."

"You gotta get over being squeamish. Al doesn't want to go to trial. We need mitigation material to negotiate a plea."

"I'll meet with her again. I had drinks with Elizabeth today."

"How'd that go?"

"Same as last time. She was sort of friendly, but also snotty. Bragged about buying an eight hundred dollar dress for Laura's wedding."

"Eight hundred dollars—for a dress?" He shakes his head. "I picked up your mail when I was at the office. It's on the counter."

I go into the kitchen and grab a root beer. Jack and I both love root beer, especially A & W. I wish Jack hadn't brought the mail. I don't want to think about work. I rifle through the small pile. Junk until I see one with the county attorney logo. I contemplate leaving it but I can't. I open it. Shit. Kevin Walters, the CA on Rick Fletcher's case has rejected my plea offer. Shit.

"What's the matter babe?" I apparently spoke aloud.

"That fucking Kevin Walters rejected my offer. Rick's a U of A student, no priors, nice kid. Charged with possession. I was trying to get him a class 6 open."

"How much coke?"

"9 grams"

"Jerk. It's so fucked that in California possession is a misdemeanor and here you can go to prison or be on probation for years. Can ruin your life. What's the plea?"

"Class 5, at least 18 months probation. Rick's never gonna take it. He still hasn't told his parents. Claims his girlfriend wanted to try some and that he'd never tried it before."

"That's a shit load of blow for a first time. But if he's telling the truth, he'll make it on probation."

The weekend doesn't get better. In one of those weird ironies, I get my period accompanied by horrible cramps. Unusual for me. I want to go home. I can usually be with Jack and have my mind on Carl, but after what Double E told me I need space to think.

"I've got horrible cramps. I'll be more comfortable at home. I have pills and stuff I need," I say exaggerating. I knew Jack would be sympathetic and wouldn't ask questions. Men generally don't want to discuss periods.

"Want me to drive you?"

"No, thanks. I'll be fine. Call you later." Jack's a sweetheart and I don't deserve him.

As I drive home, I wonder what to say when Carl calls. How dare he not tell me about Chloe. Was she prettier, smarter, better in bed than me?

My cell rings as I step into the house. I grab it out of my pocket wish it was and wasn't Carl.

"What you doing?" Rose says. "Fredo's working all weekend and I'm bored. Wanna get together?"

"Come on over. I've got cramps."

"I'll bring over some fresh banana bread and make you some tea"

Rose had been skilled at taking care of people since she was a kid. Even when she played dolls, she pretended she was a nurse. Bandaged them. Fixed their broken parts. She was perfect for Hospice. If only she'd shut up sometimes about Fredo, super cop, super boyfriend. Can I tell her about Carl? I need to tell someone. I need advice.

Her banana bread's perfect. I'd tried to make it a couple times, everyone says it's easy. The first time it wasn't done in the middle. The second, and last time, it was uneven and when I cut it, it crumbled. I scarf down a couple pieces with the tea and feel better. My sister's changing. She's lost more weight and has a good haircut. Too bad her clothes haven't changed. Her jeans hang and her favorite Doctors without Borders t-shirt, the one she wears constantly, looks two sizes too big. She's kind of quiet.

"Rose, you look great, but you oughta buy some jeans that fit and that t-shirt's seen better days, better years, maybe better decades."

Rose sips her tea before she responds. "It's my favorite. I'd never throw it out. Fredo doesn't complains about what I wear."

"Just because he doesn't, doesn't mean he wouldn't like to see you dress better. Most Latina women care what they look like. I'd be happy to take you shopping."

Rose doesn't answer. Usually a comment like this would get a rise out of her. She'd call me materialistic, valueless, but she didn't.

"Something wrong?"

"Kind of."

"What?"

"You'll make fun of me."

"I won't, I promise," I say as I cross my fingers in my head.

She gets another cup of tea. "I don't think I should live with Fredo."

"What's wrong with him?"

"Nothing's wrong with him. He's the best man I've ever been with. He's my soul mate." Oh god not that. I hate people yakking about soul mates. That ought to be another ground for divorce, beside adultery and cruelty—we were soul mates. Did you need grounds to get a divorce these days?

"I don't see the problem if you're made for each other."

"I'm not sure people should live together if they're not married."

"Didn't you ever live with a guy before?"

"Yes, but I was listening to Dr. Laura the other day. She said more marriages end in divorce if people live together first, not to mention it's immoral."

"Please, don't tell me you listen to that nut-ball. She's rude, judgmental, and sexist. I've heard her call women who have trouble dieting 'pigs,' 'sloths,' and 'losers.' Why would you listen to her?"

"I listen to her because she's smart and gives good advice."

It takes a minute to figure out how to respond to that. "Nobody listens to her anymore. I'm surprised she's still on. What does Mom say?"

"She doesn't care if I live with *your friend of Mexican heritage.* She's worried I'll marry him, but too cowardly to admit she doesn't want a mutt for a grand-child. After all the lectures we got about tolerance and treating people the same when it comes down to it she's bigoted."

Any topic—even our parents—is better than Dr. Nut-ball. "What about Dad?"

"I don't think he cares that Fredo's Mexican, but he's bummed about the cop part. Wants me to marry a doctor or lawyer. I think being a cop is heroic."

I don't think she'd be sympathetic about Carl. Asshole hasn't called.

"Do you think Mom's a racist?" Rose asks.

"Probably, who isn't. Besides you?"

Both of us go quiet. Why hasn't Carl called? "Do you want to get married?" I blurt out, not aware I've been thinking that.

"I think. I love Fredo. I want to have a family with him. We haven't known each other long enough to make a decision like that. And he hasn't asked."

"It's the twenty-first century. You could ask him."

Rose laughs. "No way. I'm the romantic type. I want him to propose. If we had different parents, I'd like him to ask Dad for my hand." I crack-up as I try to visualize Alfredo on bended knee?

"Cramps better?" Rose asks.

And they were. "Yeah, you're the best."

"Speaking of health, Sophie's deteriorating. I don't think she's got much time. You should see her."

"First chance I have," I lie.

"And it wouldn't hurt to pray for her."

"That's your department."

"Thanks for reminding me, I'm going to pray that Dr. Laura's show becomes more popular."

Hope she's wrong about the power of prayer.

Nineteen

"I can't plead to a felony."

My meeting with Rick goes as I'd expected.

"You can go to trial, but you don't have much of a defense. At least you didn't confess."

"Can't the judge decide the whole thing's not fair and give me a misdemeanor?"

"Sorry no. A judge can't dismiss charges he doesn't agree with. A lot of judges would agree you should get a felony."

"What happens if I lose?"

"Pretty much the same as if you plead although you'll have a more serious charge on your record. Either way you'll get probation."

"Promise? I couldn't bear going to prison. Those days in jail were the worst in my life."

"I can't promise, but I'm 99% sure you won't go to prison." (Jack is 99% sure would be more honest.)

"If there's a trial, what do I say when I have to testify?"

"You're not going to testify. Can you think of anything you could say that would help your case?"

"What about I've never been in trouble and I was on the Dean's List last semester, stuff like that."

How about that your mom loves you or did before you were arrested. "If you testify about your good character, its called. 'opening the door.'"

"What's opening the door?"

How can I explain this? "The state can only bring in evidence about the crime. They can't say anything bad about you. Let's say you were on academic probation. They can't bring that up unless you 'open the door' by bringing in good stuff like you got a good citizenship award. If you do, besides academic probation it allows the prosecutor to ask questions like:

'*Have you ever smoked marijuana?*'

'*How many times?*'

'*How many times have you been drunk?*'

'*Have you ever driven after you've had a drink or two?*'"

Rick frowns. Tries to surreptitiously check his phone. "Can't the prosecutor make me testify?"

"No Haven't you heard about your right to remain silent in school? It's in the Constitution."

"I guess I've heard of it, but didn't realize that's what it meant. I never expected to be in this situation. Does Melissa have to testify?"

"I'm not calling her as a witness. I doubt if the state will either."

"Doesn't she have a right to remain silent?"

"No, she's not on trial. She has a right not to answer a question that would incriminate her, but her right to remain silent doesn't apply until she's accused of something. If they ask her if she had cocaine in her possession, she could 'take the fifth.'"

"The fifth? Isn't that what gangsters do?"

"At least in movies."

"She doesn't know that." Rick says as his eyes again dart to the phone.

"Since she's not going to be a witness, let's not worry about her. You two are still together?"

"Yes." I can tell the question pisses him off, but too bad.

"If I don't testify, how can we win?"

"I'll try and find holes in their case. Show their investigation was sloppy. The cop's an asshole. The state has to prove you're guilty by a standard called beyond a reasonable doubt. It's not that easy. The other option is called jury nullification. Even though you did it, you shouldn't be convicted."

"I don't get it."

"Some people think using drugs shouldn't be illegal. It's only a misdemeanor at worst in California. Some jurors might think you're a kid and shouldn't go to prison. The jurors aren't told what the sentencing range is. Most won't know you'll get probation."

"Doesn't sound good to me. My parents think you should go to prison for using drugs. They'd believe whatever the cops say."

I realize Carl wasn't on my mind since I started talking to Rick. "We need to pick a jury that's not like your parents. One of the lawyers who's good at reading people is gonna help. I'll want your gut reaction to the jurors. If someone reminds you too much of your parents, we'll dump them."

"What else do you want me to do?"

"Nothing at the moment. Make sure you dress up for trial. Do you have a suit?"

"I have a sports jacket and pair of pants I got for my cousin's wedding. My mom picked it out?"

"Does it fit?"

"I'm not sure. I've gained some weight this semester, but I've had no appetite since I got arrested."

"Try it on. Start dieting if it's small. A too tight suit will make you look like Porky Pig."

"I will."

"Have Melissa check you out." Like she would know the right way to dress. "She can watch the trial if you want her to. As long as she dresses appropriately for court."

"I'm not sure I want her there."

"That's your call."

I explain how the trial will proceed. By the time Rick leaves my stomach realizes his trial is scheduled in less than a week. I have to pick a jury, give an opening statement, cross-examine witnesses, make objections. Try to convince them the state hasn't proved their case.

With Rick's trial looming I should be able to concentrate. Ha. Yesterday, Carl had phoned, moments after Rose left. I was pissed about his upcoming date with Chloe. Subtly, I tried to let him know. He didn't get it. Maybe because he's not into small talk. He never chats, gets his business done and hangs up. I'm meeting him for lunch today.

I don't know how to get ready for trial. At PD school, they said we should prepare a trial notebook for each case. Lists of objections, a copy of the indictment, relevant law and a section for each witness. I'd done that. A few of the lawyers said to write closing arguments first. I couldn't. Too much anxiety. I reread the witness statements and police reports over and over. I'd rewritten my cross over and over.

"Isn't it true Rick never admitted the coke was his?"

"Isn't it true Rick had no drug paraphernalia in his possession?"

"Isn't it true Rick wasn't alone in the car where the coke was found?"

Shit. I have no witnesses so at least I don't have to worry about direct.

Lunch time finally arrives. I haven't decided whether to confront Carl about Chloe or not. He waits for me at the door. Puts his arms around me and kisses me. I don't kiss back nor do I pull away. We talk about our morning. I act cold. He acts like everything's fine.

As usual we wind up in his bedroom. Clean, bed made, masculine decoration, a contrast to Jack's room which is messy, even dirty and decorated only with dirty clothes. We lie naked on Carl's bed. He moves his hand up and down my back. I keep my hands at my sides. I don't move my hands or respond. It's not easy. I love his body. "Something wrong Molly?" he asks at last.

My big moment. "Am I as good in bed as Chloe?"

Carl sighs. "We better get dressed."

We put on our clothes and sit at the kitchen table. I try not to cry.

"When I'm with you, you're the only one on my mind. I could ask you the same about Jack?"

"That's totally different. You knew from day one Jack and I had a relationship."

"So you expected me to sit around at home when you were with Jack?"

"No." Yes.

Carl goes to the fridge, takes out a pitcher of ice-tea and pours me a cup. Then he passes me a bag from the Veggie Heaven. "Yours has the red toothpick"

I take my time unwrapping it. My favorite—mozzarella, tomatoes and pesto on cheese bread. Carl had listened when I ordered and remembered what I liked. Not that it mattered. Today was likely our last lunch.

"Are you going to explain why you're upset?"

"You could have told me you were seeing someone. Since you're taking her to the wedding, I was going to find out."

"I was going to tell you."

"When? Like when I saw you with her at the wedding?"

"Don't be ridiculous."

We continue to eat. I wait for him to apologize or tell me he asked her out to make me jealous or something.

"So this is it?" I ask.

"Don't be melodramatic. There's no reason for anything to change. I'm not moving in with Chloe or marrying her. It's a date."

"It's not 'a' date. You don't take just anyone to a wedding. I know you've seen her a couple times."

"I don't ask you about Jack and I don't want you to ask about Chloe or any-one else I date."

"Why not? What's the big secret?" I know I should shut up.

"You practically live with Jack. I only see you at lunch or if he's away." I don't argue or say anything about Chloe. We finish our sandwiches and drive back to work.

As we walk into the building Carl asks, "So will I see you again?"

"Do you want to?"

"Very much."

"Okay then, but knock off the A.K. crap," I mumble softly.

I'm such a wimp.

Twenty

I dread seeing Carl at the wedding. The whole office will be there. I need to be careful.

To make things worse Jack and I have been at odds. Something seems wrong, but I can't figure out what. As I had hoped when Jack saw me in the low-cut, clingy dress I can tell he's glad to be with me. Thanks to Aunt Margaret, I'd chosen well. Jack isn't the only one who checks me out.

Never have I attended such a spectacular waste of money. When Derrick and I got engaged, I imagined our wedding would be special, but not showy. What I can't understand is why, Laura, who always seems so down to earth, would choose this. This is an event to show off your money. Everything's lavish. Expensive. Sexy young men man the mandatory valet parking. In exchange for your car keys, the guy or the 'driver' (after all this is the twenty-first century) is handed a pen that says Laura and Jay with a number attached (for car retrieval). The women get orchid wrist corsages. I assume they'd figured out how to handle singles or gay couples. Perhaps two pens or two corsages?

Everything is in shades of purple. The food is delicious and plentiful, but I have too many butterflies to eat. Appetizers before the ceremony, dessert trays after dinner, and an open bar every few feet. A sit down dinner of numerous courses. Word like 'confit' and' infused' appear several times on the printed souvenir menu. I wonder how many people are invited. Jack and I are at Table 14 with six others. When I go take a pee, I hear someone grumble about being at Table 31 with a bunch of losers.

Laura and Jay chose one of the fanciest hotels in Tucson, but got the guests a reduced rate if they want to spend the night. The DJ keeps repeating if you're sloshed or horny and need a room it's not too late.

The couple, or the family of the bride or maybe the family of the groom, invited everyone they'd known since early childhood and everyone who was anyone in Tucson. I recognize the mayor, a Congressman and Jack points out a couple of philanthropists, a best-selling author, an Arizona Supreme Court Justice, and the Dean of the law school.

I'd hate a wedding like this. Mine will be small, only close family and friends. No friends of parents or in-laws. No politicians or rich people I don't give a shit about. If we can afford it, I'll have it at a resort in Maui. Half of Tucson might gossip about this wedding, but after mine people will ask, "Did you get an invitation?" It'd help to have a groom in mind.

I keep my eyes peeled for Chloe and Carl. Didn't see them at the ceremony. Maybe because Jack and I had snagged back seats. We couldn't see much except a sea of suit jackets and sexy backs. I'd been terrified the four of us would eat at the same table. I could imagine Double E arranging it. I relax when I reach Table 14. Mostly PD's, no Carl.

I get my first glimpse of Chloe as she passes our table. She reminds me of a popular high school girl. Petite, slender, long blonde hair and blue eyes. Her dress is off-white lace, short, but not too short, low-cut, but a waste. She's flat as a young boy. Her evening bag and high-heeled shoes shout pricey. Everything about her is today's fashion, no originality. She's a follower, a pleaser. The Carl I know couldn't want that.

My eyes follow Chloe as she sits down next to him. He turns around and our eyes meet. He gives me a thumbs up.

Carl's eyes return to his table as do mine. Jack introduces me to the one couple I didn't know, Don and Val Block. Don had been head of the office before Double E. Conversation turns to office gossip and cases. PD's loves shop talk. I watch Carl. He and Chloe are deep in conversation. She does most of the talking. He doesn't touch her, but he looks in her eyes and appears to listen to what she says.

After dinner there's a DJ in one ballroom and a band in the other. Jack isn't much of a dancer. He's happy to sit and watch. When the DJ announces a speciality dances that forces couples to switch partners I make Jack give it a try. As we change, I move away from Jack and after three moves, I'm with Carl.

"Hot dress." He pulls me close for a moment. I want to ask if he's having fun, if he likes Chloe, if he's going to sleep with her tonight, but I have enough brains to keep quiet. Being with Jack, I usually drink less. Tonight I let them refill my wine glass often. I have to be careful not to say or do something I'll regret. We dance for a few minutes until I notice Jack looking for me. When the song ends, we part.

Jack and I are one of the few not staying at the hotel. He doesn't say so, but I know Jack thinks it's stupid to waste money on a hotel when he's sober and can drive to his or my place. At first I'm irritated, but the thought of sleeping under the same roof as Carl and not being near him makes me glad.

"What do you think of the wedding?" I ask.

"Waste of money."

"They've been together over eight years. At least it's not one of those weddings where they hardly know each other." Why do I defend it when I feel the same?

"What do you think of Chloe?" I ask.

"Who's Chloe?"

"The chick that Carl brought?"

"Not my type," Jack says as he puts his hand under my dress.

◆ ◆ ◆

*M*onday morning, the day before trial is to begin, I'm greeted with three messages from Rick saying he wants to take the plea. Idiot. Last Friday was the plea deadline. I'd explained that numerous times. He's lucky the plea had been open several days. Often deals are only available twenty-four hours.

"Can't you explain I'm a college student and I have tests and stuff?"

"Rick, the CA couldn't care less."

"What should I do?"

"Do? Show up tomorrow at 8:30 a.m. dressed the way I told you." Another difference from BARF. BARF clients were bankers, financiers, corporate executives. If nothing else, they knew how to dress. Once or twice I'd heard a BARF lawyer tell a client not to wear his ROLEX or Armani suit.

One of the memorable days of PD school focused on client dress. Horror stories included: a transvestite who showed up for trial in a formal with gloves. A client wearing the same t-shirt he wore in the sting video. Women whose dresses barely covered their ass or boobs. A young man charged with date rape wearing a t-shirt with a slogan that touted his sexual prowess. A pimp in a yellow velvet suit and matching hat. And my personal favorite, a meth dealer whose shirt read, "Legalize drugs."

I never thought I'd have to tell clients to shower, cover their tats, take out their piercings, explain what professional dress meant or troll through the PD wardrobe room trying to find a decent suit coat. Rick's suit was too small. Freshmen fifteen. Not much to choose from. Most people don't want to donate used clothes to the public defender's office. Months ago the newspaper printed a story about how the public defender's office needed clothes to help their clients dress for trial. Derrick and I got hysterical. "Like I'd give my suit to a criminal."

Monday continues to be a nightmare. I call the County Attorney and ask, no beg, them to keep the plea open. A simple no would have worked, but after being on hold forever, the prosecutor comes back on and says, "No, it's no longer open but he wants to plead to the indictment that can be arranged."

Rick calls over and over, lamenting his choice and asking stupid questions about the trial. I can't sit still. I try to concentrate, but my body keeps sending me signals. I'm hot, cold, trembling, nauseous. Colleagues drop by, "Good luck tomorrow, kick ass." They made me more nervous. I read over my cross-examinations and can't believe how worthless they are. I have to show the jurors the police hadn't done a thorough job. That there's reasonable doubt. The drugs could have belonged to someone else. I'd reread the witness statement, reworked the cross. Had I missed anything? Should I bring a copy of the Rules of Evidence? I can't take every law book I might need.

I grab the trial checklist I'd put together after PD school. Yes, I've reviewed the indictment, read police reports. . . OMG. I hadn't viewed the cocaine.

"Jack, can you come to my office, now?" I say when he answers his phone

He comes in, shuts the door. "What's the matter, you okay?"

"I forgot to go to evidence and look at the cocaine. What should I do?"

"You're kidding me. You didn't look at the drugs in a drug trial. What kind of lawyer are you?"

I look at Jack and the tears roll down my face. "A horrible lawyer?"

Jack puts his arms around me and smiles. "Relax, I'm kidding. What possible good is it to look, unless your defense is it's baking soda. You're prepared, it's only pretrial jitters. Let's go take a walk."

Later I'd find out Jack knew I should've looked, but thinks its more important for me to be calm and confident. I'd never repeat that mistake. And it would turn out it didn't matter. I don't know whether to laugh, cry or go over everything again. In less than twenty-four hours Judge Jacobs will take the bench and announce "State of Arizona versus Richard Eric Fletcher. Is the defense ready?"

"Molly O'Rourke for the accused. Defense is ready."

Twenty-One

Buzz. I'm awake before the three alarms I'd set. What sleep I had was fitful. Countless times I awoke with an idea for cross or closing and jotted it down on the pad by the bed. This morning the thoughts look like they were written at 3:00 a.m. I shower, fix my hair and make-up and put on my most professional charcoal suit. Everyone at BARF owned a shitload of trial suits. Most of us never set foot in the courtroom. A PD is lucky if she owns enough suits to complete a week-long trial without wearing the same one twice.

Too bad Rose isn't here to cook me breakfast. Or maybe not. For the first time in my life I'm not sure I can eat.

Jack's supposed to drop by to discuss jury selection. He asked if I wanted him to be co-counsel. I did and didn't. I have to do a trial by myself. We compromise. He's helping with jury selection, his forte. He tried to persuade me to stay over last night but I hate his bathroom. I need a place with good mirrors, back-up make-up and clothes. And privacy. He got the hint.

The phone. I hope Jack didn't oversleep or something.

"Hi Rose," I answer as her name flashes on the screen.

"Hi Sis."

Sis, never heard that one before. "I start my first trial today, I'm waiting for Jack and I'm a wreck."

"You'll do great. I'll pray for you."

"Did you want something?" I steal another glance in the mirror.

"Yeah. I don't want to distract you, but Sophie's going downhill, fast. You need to see her." I think about telling Rose I didn't want to, but decide to stall not argue.

"No way until the trial's over."

"You could come at night. Just last night I heard Doctor Laura on the radio talking about how important it is … "

I lie. "Sorry Rose, got to answer the door. I'll call you after the trial."

Just what I need. More rules to live by from the doctor. Where's Jack? I pace. I want him to listen to my opening. Finally I hear a car in the driveway.

"It's about time."

"I meant to get here earlier, sorry." Jack eyes me up and down. "You sure look the part today."

I wish I could say the same for him. Same old suit, shiny at the elbows, a little tight. Boots that look like they haven't been cleaned since his first trial. Worn briefcase.

"What kind of jurors do we want?"

"Tough call. Boomers would be a good choice if they experimented with drugs. Some become more conservative as they age. Moms with sons. Rick has a boyish look about him. They may empathize."

"Rick said if his parents were jurors and heard these facts, they'd vote guilty."

"Yeah. We need to ask each potential juror as many questions as the judge will allow about their prior drug use and feelings about legalization. Not push too far. If the prosecutor believes they won't convict he'll dump them. Who'd you say was the judge?"

"Jacobs."

"Lucky draw. He treats us well and he's fair. He'll let you do a lot of voir dire."

"I feel like throwing up."

"You should. I always do. If you didn't there'd be something wrong. We also may want some millennials who don't see the big deal about some blow."

"How long do you think this trial's going to take?"

"Probably done Wednesday, maybe Thursday."

"I thought it would take longer."

"These cases go fast once you get a jury. The prosecutor's done a shitload of these and has it down to a science. All they need to do is put on the arresting officer and someone from the lab to show it's coke. You're not putting your client on?"

"No."

"Good move I'm sure. Let me show you the system I've worked out." He opens his briefcase and pulls out a folder. His 'system,' a combination of Jack's intuition and lots of post-its, seems like voodoo. But what do I know. Everyone says he's an expert at picking juries.

I practice my opening and it's time to leave. His approval makes me feel better.

As Jack reaches his car he calls out. "I have four hearings this morning I think. I'll meet you in Jacobs courtroom when I'm done."

"Don't be late. We start at 10:30."

"Don't worry. I'll be there."

On the short drive to the office I imagine everything that could go wrong: I forget my notes; Jack is late; my client is late; a witness I never heard of testifies; I spill coffee on my dress; I stand in front of the jury and forget what to say. By the time I get to work I'm a wreck. As I enter the office, Mabel the receptionist, calls out, "Denise is looking all over for you. Some emergency in your case."

Oh shit. I by-pass my office and go directly to Denise's.

"Mik Kennedy called and said he's taking over the Fletcher case. He wants you to call him ASAP." Denise passes me a pink slip. "Here's his cell number. And Rick Fletcher keeps phoning."

"Taking the case. He can't do that. It's not fair." I'm surprised to feel anger instead of relief.

Denise shrugs. "I'm sorry."

"It's not your fault." I walk to my office, try to calm down. I dial Kennedy who answers on the first ring.

"Hi Molly, appreciate the quick call back. I don't think we've met."

No, but I've heard of you. Tall, good looking, arrogant prick. Maybe the best defense lawyer in Tucson. "So what's happening?"

"I got a call yesterday morning from Rick's dad. He's hired me to take Rick's case."

"But the trial's today."

"No worries. I've called the CA and he won't object to a continuance. Neither will Jacobs. You need to meet me in court at 10:30 so your office can be relieved from the case. I'd like a copy of your file, but tomorrow will be fine."

I don't know what to say. "Okay, I'll be there." Rick's dad? How did he find out about the trial?

I call Rick. The phone rings and rings. I'm about to hang up when he answers. "Hello."

"Rick, it's Molly. What's up?"

"I'm sorry, Molly."

Another sorry. I thought Rick respected me, thought I was a good lawyer. I need to know what happened. "How did your dad find out you got arrested? I thought you didn't want them to know."

"I didn't. My mom called Friday night. Told me my aunt would be in town next week and I panicked. I kept saying it wasn't a good time because I had lots of homework, tests. She kept asking if something was the matter. I guess I'm not a good liar. Anyway my dad called Saturday. . ."

"And."

"He asked me all these questions. I could tell he didn't believe me. We got in an argument. I blurted it out. He hung up on me."

"Molly?" I turn and see Lourdes Velasquez. "Come to my office when you get off the phone."

"Sorry." I say to Rick, "Go on. Your dad hung up."

"My mom called back crying. She said stuff like 'I knew you'd get hooked on drugs in a place like that.' 'I never thought my son would be a drug addict.' I tried to explain but she kept crying. 'Your dad is so upset.'"

Part of me wanted to sympathize, but I'm still angry and confused.

"Go on."

"Anyway, Dad finally calmed down and asked about the case and my lawyer. Sunday he called early in the morning. Said he talked to some friend at work who said never trust a public defender, I told him I liked you and you were smart." Thanks for that.

"When he found out you were a woman he called me an idiot. 'You don't pick lawyers because you like them or because they're good looking.' Sorry, Molly."

If I hear sorry one more time . . . .

"Anyway, he called back again and told me he'd hired this Kennedy guy."

Rick gets quiet. I didn't know what to say. After a few minutes of silence Rick speaks again. "Thanks for everything. It wasn't my decision."

"I'll see you in court this morning."

"Kennedy told me I didn't have to go since the trial was continued."

"Okay, well good luck," and I hang up. I know Kennedy's a big shot. Did that mean he didn't have to follow rules? Clients always have to show up when trial dates are set. And how could he be sure he'd get a continuance?

What did Lourdes want? Could she know about Carl? Lourdes was an attractive soft-spoken woman. We'd talked a few times, but weren't friends. I'd never been in her office. When I got there I'm impressed. Two walls painted deep orange and two apricot. Several attractive landscapes. Later I find out her sister's the artist. She also has plants, fake flowers and family photos. Her hands full of files mean she's about to leave for court.

"Molly, do you have 9:00 a.m. hearings?"

"Yeah."

"Let's get your files and I'll walk with you."

She follows me to my office and indicates the back stairs with her hand. As soon as the stairwell's empty she begins to speak. "I heard that Mik Kennedy is taking over your case."

"That's what he said."

"I'm guessing you have mixed feelings. Half relieved, half angry. Especially with it being your first trial."

"You're right."

"You can't take this personally. Our office has great lawyers, but lots of people believe public defenders aren't real lawyers. Some think we're in it because we can't get any other jobs. Some think we couldn't pass the bar."

Geez, that's what I thought.

"My client and I got along great. He didn't want his parents to know he had drug charges. They didn't till last weekend. When they found out he had a PD, a woman PD, they hired Kennedy. They never asked my client what he wanted. Never talked to me."

Lourdes turns and faces me. I'm glad we stop. Walking down these steps is killing me. "God, I hate when men say women aren't competent. It's the twenty-first century. At least Kennedy's competent. Wait till you lose a case to someone totally worthless. My first murder case the client hired a guy who'd never tried a criminal case before. Charged the client a small fortune. Guaranteed an acquittal in a very difficult case."

"Isn't that unethical?"

Lourdes smiled. "This is the real world."

"Did he win?"

"Win? No, it was a slam dunk for the prosecution."

"He got death?"

"No, it wasn't a capital case. He got life, no parole."

I shake my head. "Kennedy seems awfully arrogant. He told the client not to bother coming to court. He assured me the CA wouldn't object to a continuance."

"The reason they won't object is they're all scared of him. The prosecutor probably wants some time to see if he can get off the case or deal it."

"It's not even a big case. Just possession."

"Just wait. If Kennedy's on it the press will cover it."

"Rick, my client, ex-client, will hate that. Didn't want anyone to know."

When I didn't say anything else Lourdes changes the subject to office gossip. "What'd you think of Laura's wedding?"

"A disgusting spectacle."

"Me too."

Maybe I have my first friend.

Twenty-Two

"Hi Molly, I'm Ruth Katzenbaum." She walks into my office, takes a seat. Who?

"The mitigation specialist."

"Hi, nice to meet you." A mitigation specialist? She looks like my grandmother except my grandmother's from the boomer generation and dresses and acts like someone half her age. More accurate to say Ruth looks like the TV stereotype of a grandmother. Her grey hair is medium length with no discernible style. She's short, chunky and wears pastel pink stretch pants and a knit top. Her face is wrinkled but she still applies blue eyeliner, eye shadow and pink lipstick—all too heavy. Even from a few feet away, she has an odor, no a smell, that I can't put my finger on. Something that makes me think of home.

Jack received permission to use Ruth on Al's case. Ruth's in great demand. Saved a client who sodomized, tortured and murdered two young men from the death penalty. Found out he had organic brain damage. Proved a woman who killed her husband had been beaten repeatedly.

I've never heard of mitigation specialists. When I ask I learn that like the title suggests their job's to find witnesses and evidence to show that the client isn't a monster. Usually an abusive childhood or mental illness.

Jack is obsessed with Al's case. He visits him almost daily since he was transferred from infirmary to protective custody. His obsession's a plus for me since it gives me time to be with Carl. I've seen Al once since his move. I wonder if Jack thinks I'm not much of a lawyer. Lately, he doesn't seem to think I'm much of a girlfriend.

My next visit with Al enhances my sense that Jack's obsessed. "I feel like I'm goin' crazy. All day alone. Bobby-Jo gave me money for a TV. That helps." Later I find out Jack bought him the TV, but it was unclear whether Al knew that or not.

"What can I do to help?" I ask Ruth

"I'm tracing people who've known Al over the years, especially when he was a kid. We need to verify the abuse he suffered."

"Okay. .."

"What's your impression of Bobby-Jo?" she asks cutting me off? I must have looked stymied because she adds, "Do you think she's being truthful or trying to help Al?"

"Truthful. She cares about him, a lot, but I don't think she'd make stuff up, she's not that bright."

"Molly, Molly. Don't be naive. Bobby-Jo might not be smart like you define smart: good grades, grad school, reads literature. There's a lot of people in this world with little or no education but they've learned a great deal about people in other ways. And believe me people don't have to be bright to lie."

I'm the lawyer. Who does she think she is, lecturing me? "I still think she's telling the truth," I say with a tad less conviction. "I'll tell her you'll contact her."

"Anything she likes I might bring to soften her up?"

"She's a smoker, drinks Coke and chews gum."

"Did she mention Coke as opposed to soda? Do you know what kind of cigarettes or gum?"

I scratch my head as if this physical act would help me remember. "She did ask for Coke. Since I've never been a smoker, I didn't pay attention. The gum smelled like bubblegum and I think she even blew a bubble."

"Good. Details of that sort are important. Smokers always have a favorite and with the cost of a pack these days they're always a great ice-breaker. I want Bobby-Jo to trust me. Bringing people even small gifts helps."

"One thing about Bobby-Jo that's weird is how she acts about my name. I say call me Molly and she laughs. What's so funny about my name?"

Without a moment's hesitation Ruth answers. "Maybe it's because Molly's another word for ecstasy."

I roll that around in my head. "Maybe you should bring her some ecstasy."

Ruth doesn't laugh. "I need her help to trace other witnesses which won't be easy. Jack told me Big Betty is dead, there are no other siblings or a dad. I need to find Willie. Bobby Jo's our best bet."

"You think Willie will help?"

"Don't know till you try. Maybe he's changed or feels remorseful about what he did to his brother. Lots of guys find God in prison."

I roll my eyes. "More likely he's worse." Ruth grins. Even though she thinks I'm a snob, I like her.

I have a rare free afternoon. My calendar's clear. I was supposed to be in trial on Rick's case. I should visit Sophie, but I can't make myself. I use the time to do some research and write motions in cases I'd let slide because of Rick's trial.

I'm proud of myself. I meet Lourdes for dinner when I could've been with Carl. He and I have settled back into our routine. A nooner a couple times a week and a night out when Jack is busy like tonight. Jack had gone to the state prison in Florence to visit a client and stayed to have dinner with a judge friend. Jack is so engrossed in Al's case, half the time he doesn't notice what I'm doing.

Carl isn't thrilled with me either. I ask him stupid questions like whether he's still dating Chloe or whose better in bed almost every time we're together. He refuses to answer. I know my behavior pisses him off, but I can't stop.

Thank god for Lourdes. Her reaching out changed my life. I'm lonely in Tucson in spite of Jack, Carl, and Rose. Double E's worthless. I can't discuss Jack with Carl or Carl with Jack. Rose and I are closer than ever but she wouldn't understand my boyfriend problems, and anyway, she spends most of her free time with Alfredo. Lourdes and I hit it off. We eat lunch together and get together most of the weekend. BFF's. I feel I can tell her anything. I'll find out tonight.

Like me, Lourdes is tall and slender and can eat like a horse and not gain a pound. Like me she's lonely. Carlos, her fiancé is in the military stationed in Iraq. Debbie, her best friend, had quit the PD for a job in Phoenix. According to office gossip Lourdes and Debbie had a squabble before Debbie left. Lourdes has never mentioned Debbie to me.

We agree on Caruso's, an Italian restaurant close to downtown. We split an antipasto and both order spaghetti and meatballs and garlic bread. Each of us orders a glass of Chianti, but the waitress reminds us it's happy hour and cheaper to order a bottle. We do.

"How long has Carlos been deployed?"

"Four months so far this time."

"That must be tough. You miss him?"

"Yes, and no," she answers. "I like being on my own. It's a first for me. I lived at home during school. I can work the way I want, go to the jail at night or on the weekend, eat what I want when I want. Let's get some more garlic bread."

We signal the waitress.

"You didn't answer my question?"

"Yes, I miss him, but maybe not as much as I should. Sometimes I think we're getting married because we've been together forever. Our families expect it. Mexican families always want daughters to get married. And it's too much work to try to meet someone." She smiles.

I want to tell her about Carl. I need to talk about him.

"Did you ever consider an affair?" I ask hope she won't get all offended and moral on me.

"Not really. How can you cheat on someone who's in a war zone?"

"Do you worry about him being disabled or killed?"

Lourdes laughs. "Carlos is pretty safe. He's a weatherman. In the Green Zone. Pretty much like being here. Hot today, hotter tomorrow."

"I didn't realize there were jobs like that in Iraq."

"Most people don't."

I grab another piece of bread. "Did you ever date Jack?"

"No. He's a great guy, but not my type. The two of you seem to have hit it off. How serious are you?"

"I don't know. As you said, he's a great guy, but we fell into a routine so quickly. Sometimes I feel like we're an old married couple."

"Speaking of old married couples I've known Carlos since high school. Our parents know each other. We all go to the same church."

"Some more wine, or dessert?" The waitress asks. I realize we'd finished the bottle.

"I'll have a cannoli." I look at Lourdes.

"Me too. How about a Brandy Alexander? I love 'em."

"Sure." I'm aware I'd drunk too much. I'd had most of the bottle. Maybe I'd need a ride home. "What do you think of Carl?"

"Strange guy. He's a good lawyer, but as a person I can't figure him out. What do you think of him?"

"He's okay." I feel myself blush.

"You like him, don't you?"

"Kind of."

"Kind of? What does that mean?"

"It means kind of."

"You're holding out on me, Molly."

"No, I'm not." I try to keep a straight face. "Oh hell, you're right. I do like him."

"You could break up with Jack and go for it. It's kind of awkward to date two guys who work together."

I say nothing. Lourdes looks me in the eyes.

"Speaking of affairs, you're having one with Carl? That's why you asked me about affairs."

I consider denying it, but don't. "Yeah."

"Oh god, Molly. How long have you been carrying that off?"

"A couple months. It's bizarre. It wasn't that long after I started to see Jack."

"What's Carl like?"

"He's smart, sexy, fun when we're together, but mysterious. Won't give me a key to his place even though I'd never drop by without being invited. He started calling me by this ridiculous code name, Anna K."

"He must know about Jack?"

"Yeah. Doesn't seem to mind. I think he's dating. . ." I hold myself back from saying bitch, "That woman he went to Laura's wedding with. Has he dated any-one at the office that you know of?"

"You're the first. He hardly ever comes to office parties, even the big Christmas bash. I was surprised he went to Laura's wedding."

"You think I'm horrible?"

"No. I wish I had the guts to do something like that once in my life. I've been dating Carlos since I was fourteen. A couple times I went out with someone else when we had a fight. He's the only one I've slept with. My friends' parents tell their daughters to be careful and not get pregnant till they're married. Not my mom. She wants me to get pregnant because she knows Carlos will marry me."

"Hard to practice law and have kids."

"My mom thinks law's a cute little hobby till I have a family which is the only worthwhile role for a woman. Even if you have to get pregnant to seal the deal. Your phone's ringing."

I dig it out of my purse. Rose.

"What? . . . Are you sure? . . . Shit . . . Now? . . . I can't I've had a couple glasses of wine . . . Caruso's . . . Okay, Okay." Shit, shit, shit.

"What's the matter?"

"My sister Rose. She works at that hospice where Sophie lives."

"Sophie?"

"My client. She's dying. Has to talk to me. It's an emergency."

"You shouldn't drive."

"I know. Rose's picking me up."

Twenty-Three

Lourdes and I finish the crumbs on our plates and settle the bill. Outside, the weather's cool, but not cool enough to account for the chill I feel. I'm glad Lourdes stays till Rose drives up.

I open the door to Rose's car. "What does Sophie want?"

"I don't know. She's gotten weaker and weaker. Stopped eating days ago and now she's not drinking. The doctor says she's dying."

I can't think of what to say. "I didn't know you could live for days without food."

"Weeks even. It's not drinking that kills you."

"You think she'll die soon?"

"Yes. She slept most of today, but when she woke up asked for me. I hurried to her room. She was barely awake, but kept repeating, 'I need to see Molly. It's urgent.' I tried to find out more, but she kept repeating, 'Molly.'"

Rose is driving over the speed limit. She must believe Sophie's dying. We're nearly there when Rose's phone rang. The opening bars of The Wedding March, oh my god.

"Aren't you going to get it?" At least the damn song will stop.

She pulls over. "Hello." After a few seconds she sobs. "Sophie's dead."

I wish I could feel sorry, but I'm relieved. What would I have said to her? I don't know how to act around a dying person.

"Where you going?" I ask as Rose starts the car.

"To Valley."

Shit. I want to go home. "Why? You can't comfort Sophie."

"I wasn't there for her when she died. Least I can do is say a proper good bye. Maybe for me."

I consider arguing, but I doubt Rose will change her mind.

Hospice has changed Rose. Before she'd have insisted I see Sophie. Now she says something like "everyone has their own way to grieve" and leaves me in the hall.

I feel buzzed, not grief.

By the time Rose finishes she's had enough time to pray for everyone she's ever met.

"I feel dreadful. Sophie's nurse told me Sophie got agitated after I left. Kept saying *the money*. Said it over and over. They gave her more morphine and she quieted down. Then she passed. I should have been there."

"You couldn't have known she'd die when you left." Rose says nothing. "What's going to happen now?"

"The doc has to sign the death certificate, and then we call the mortuary. Sophie left instructions that she wanted to be cremated."

"Doesn't Sophie have a sister?"

"A half-sister Ashley. She's supposed to come tomorrow."

"Tomorrow?"

"They didn't get along. Different dads. Ashley's dad died and her mom got remarried to Sophie's dad. Ashley resented her new stepdad and took some of that out on Sophie. Sophie tried to be friends."

"Has she been here?"

"Once about a month ago. Sophie was crying when she left, but she didn't talk to me about it."

"I feel sick. I don't want to stay here."

"I can't take you home now. I need to stay with Sophie till they take her away. I can't let her down again."

"Don't worry. I'll get a ride."

I call Carl without much thought. I probably wouldn't have if I wasn't drunk. "Hello," a woman answers?

"Who is this?"

"Who are you?" The woman asks?

Shit. "Is this Chloe?"

"No, who do you want to speak to?"

Oh shit. Does he have another girlfriend? I think about hanging up, but I can't it's too late. "Can I speak to Carl?"

"He's in the shower, can he call you back?"

For a moment I can't think of anything to say. He wouldn't be in the shower with a friend over. He's probably just had sex. Screw him. "Tell him Anna K called to thank him for the flowers." That'll serve the bitch right.

I might regret it when I sober up but now I think it's hilarious. Especially using his stupid code name. Can't call Lourdes. She isn't in any shape to drive. I check my phone. 11 p.m. I'm not sure how far the prison is from Tucson, but I doubt Jack's home. If I call and he is, he'll want me to come over. Might as well call Uber like I should have in the first place. Get my car in the morning. I scribble Rose a note. Call when you get home.

I barely remember the cab ride or how I got in bed. My phone wakes me. I'm in bed fully dressed. "Huh."

"Molly, it's Rose. You're not going to believe what we found."

"What time is it?"

"It's late, 2 a.m."

"Can't it wait till tomorrow?"

"You told me to call and it can't."

"Okay, wait a second."

I walk into the kitchen, drink some water "Okay."

"Guess what we found under Sophie's mattress?"

"Love letters?"

"Be serious Molly."

"I don't know. Just tell me."

"A joint savings account. In the names of Sophie Mercer and Paul Terrrazas. Who's he? He never visited Sophie that I know of."

"Paul Terrazas. He's an attorney, he was an attorney at my office."

"Did he quit?"

"Rose, I'm gonna puke, I'll call you back."

I run into the bathroom and lose the remnants of my dinner. I drink more water. Call Rose back. "It's me."

"You okay?"

"Yeah, better."

"Don't you think you're drinking too much if you have to throw up?"

"I'm fine Rose. Don't go Dr. Laura on me. It was a special occasion."

For a moment neither of us says a word. "Why did Terrazas quit?" Rose finally asks.

"He didn't. He died. Drowned in his jacuzzi. They always said it was an accident, but I thought there was something weird about it."

"You don't believe it was an accident?" Rose asks.

"I don't know. It seemed like there was something strange about the whole thing. How much is in the account?"

"Over $100,000."

"Wow. Why didn't Sophie use the money? I thought she was broke."

"She was. She didn't own much, had some clothes and knick-knacks. Hardly had money to buy extras. There's a letter with the bank paperwork. It got wet or something and it's not legible. I'm trying to dry it out."

I try to put my head around what she's talking about.

"I'm worried about Sophie's half-sister." Rose continues. "She's bossy and mean. I'm afraid she's going to want the money. She's Sophie's heir, right?"

"I guess. I don't know much about probate. Did you find a will?"

"Not that I know of. She didn't have anything to leave. There are forms we give people to fill out about their wishes. I've seen her file and there's nothing about a will. Just that she wanted to be cremated."

"For now, keep it. Don't tell anyone, especially the sister," I say.

"Couldn't I get in trouble?"

"We're not going to keep the money. Just figure this out and make sure Ashley doesn't get it."

"I don't know."

"Give it to me. I'll keep it."

"I don't know. Let me think about it."

"I'll talk to some of the PD investigators. They may know how to decipher the letter. One of the lawyers from BARF does estate planning and can tell me what happens when you die without a will. Probably her sister gets it, but I better check."

"Are you sure Molly? It doesn't feel right."

"Look. If it belongs to Ashley we'll give it to her later. Go home and get some rest. We'll talk tomorrow."

Twenty-Four

After I hang up, I turn my phone to mute. I need sleep. A wicked hangover's in my future. I toss and turn. My brain spins a mile a minute. What was between Sophie and Terrazas? Why did Sophie meet with Terrazas weekly? Her case was minor. It wasn't set for trial. Why was part of the file missing? Why'd they talk about heaven and hell? And the bank account. What was that about?

I finally sleep. When I awake, it's after ten. My mouth's dry. My head and body ache. I dread checking my phone. Had I really left Carl a snarky message? And my car. Probably ticketed if not towed.

Six texts. Lourdes, Carl, two from Jack, three from Rose.

LOURDES: *What happened last night? Hope you feel better than me.*

CARL: *Call me.*

ROSE: *We have to talk. Call me.*

ROSE: *Worried, get back to me.*

ROSE: *Call. Urgent ASAP.*

JACK: *Morning Gorgeous.*

JACK: *Wake up sleepyhead.*

Shit. Easiest first. I text Lourdes: *My client died. I feel like crap.* I want to talk to her about the bank account, but not until I see her in person.

I don't want to call Carl. He has every right to be pissed. I dial.

"Hello."

"Hi it's Molly. How's it going?"

"How do you think?"

"What do you mean?"

"Don't be stupid."

Carl's angry. I bite the bullet. "I'm sorry. I shouldn't've left the message. I was kind of buzzed."

"Blame the alcohol. What the hell were you thinking?"

"What do you think?"

"I'm asking you."

"I was with Rose at the hospice. Sophie died. I needed a ride."

"What are you talking about? Who's Sophie?"

"Sophie's my client who was in hospice. My sister Rose called. Said Sophie was dying and had to talk to me. Rose picked me up. On our way Rose got a call that Sophie died."

"Why didn't Rose give you a ride?"

"Rose wanted to stay with Sophie until the mortuary picked her up. Didn't want her to be alone. I wanted to go home."

"Your sister's a good person. Interesting how siblings can be so different. Why did you do it?"

I don't say anything for a few seconds. "Do what?" I finally blurt out.

"Leave the message. Don't play games."

"I thought some girl you were dating answered. I wanted to hurt your relationship."

"My sister answered the phone."

I relax a bit. "Good, no harm done."

"Wrong. I don't want to be with someone who would do that. What if I was with someone besides Chloe? You have no respect for me. All you care about is yourself."

"Wait a minute. Having an affair shows respect for me?"

"You agreed to it. I didn't force you. None of that matters. What matters is your behavior. We're done."

I don't know what to say. After a few moments of silence, Carl says, "Don't you have anything to say?"

"No,"

"You need to grow up." And he hangs up.

I want to be angry. Blame him, but Carl's right. I shouldn't have left that stupid message. Maybe it's for the best. My life will be simpler, more honest. Then why do I have a hollow sick feeling in my stomach?

I call Rose. Get my mind off Carl. "Morning Rose, you get any sleep?"

"Not much. I didn't get home until twoish." Her voice trails off.

"I can't hear you."

"I'm in the bathroom. Fredo's home and I don't want him to hear."

"You have the papers?"

"Yeah. I feel horrible not telling him."

"I'd come over and get them, but my car's at the bar. At least I hope it is. I'm worried it got towed."

"I'll come over and take you to your car. Fredo will understand. He wouldn't want you to drive impaired which you probably still are. We're sitting down to breakfast. See you in an hour."

"I need some time anyway. I feel horrid." But I'm not impaired.

"You hung over?"

"A little."

"Doesn't sound like a little. I'll see you soon."

I pull myself together as much as I can. Shower, eat some breakfast. Frozen waffles and finish Rose's banana bread. Curse Carl.

"Molly, you look terrible." Rose says as she walks in the door.

"You don't look so great yourself."

"At least, I'm not hung over."

"At least, I'll look better tomorrow." Rose gives me an angry look.

Shit, why did I say that. "I'm sorry. I didn't mean it. It's just that Carl dumped me."

"Carl? I thought you were dating Jack".

"It's a long story. Let's have some tea."

I put the kettle on. In a few minutes we're sitting at my kitchen table drinking Chai tea which Rose loves. Not my favorite, but I want to soften Rose up. I add a bag of Famous Amos cookies. How do I explain my life to Rose?

"I'm not Mom and I'm not totally naive, Molly. What's going on?" When I say nothing she grabs a cookie and makes a face. I can tell she's comparing it to her home-made stuff.

"I messed up. I started seeing Carl, a lawyer at the office."

"Seeing?"

"Sleeping with, having an affair with, screwing"

Rose looks at me quizzically and finally says. "I don't know what to say."

"I'm not you. You're lucky, you found this great guy."

"I'm not judging you. I'm trying to understand. Did Carl know about Jack?"

"Yes, from day one."

"He didn't care?"

"I don't know. Sometimes I thought he did."

"Did Jack know?"

"No, we were discreet."

Rose takes another cookie. I guess they aren't that bad. "Why did he break up with you?"

"Because I'm an idiot. I called him last night when I needed a ride. A woman answered. I said tell Carl thanks for the flowers or something like that. I'm not sure. I was pretty drunk."

"I learned a long time ago to be careful what I say when I'm high."

"You've been drunk?"

"Of course, I'm a normal person. I've made mistakes." Rose looks at her watch. "Maybe we should get your car."

"If it's still there."

"I forgot to tell you. I had Fredo check on it. He talked to some traffic sergeant and told them not to tow it."

"He did that for me?"

"I told you he's terrific. And you're family now." She grabs one more of my lousy cookies, her keys and we take off.

The ride to pick up my car might be best forgotten. Rose asks questions I can't answer about why I need two men and what I'm going to do. When I can't take it anymore I switch the conversation to Sophie's bank account.

"Are you sure Sophie didn't ever mention anything about the bank account or Terrazas?"

"No, I would have told you if she did."

"Or about a crime she knew about?"

"No." Rose sounds impatient which is unusual for her.

"You're going to give me the bank papers, aren't you?"

"I'm not sure it's the right thing to do but I can't keep them."

When I don't answer she starts back on my life. "Are you really done with Carl?"

"He said he didn't want to see me. I need to grow up. Even if I want him back, it's not going to happen."

"You're good at getting men to do what you want."

"Not this time."

"Are you going to tell Jack?"

"About Carl? Why would I do that? No way."

Thankfully, my car's in sight. No ticket.

"Thanks for the ride. Don't worry. You're off the hook. I'm entitled to her legal documents. I'm her lawyer."

Twenty-Five

Too much, too fast. Neither Sophie's death nor the end of my affair with Carl feels real. I need time. Alone. Jack wants me to come over. We were both busy Friday night, me with Lourdes, him with his judge friend. Saturday night Jack went to the basketball game. I tell Jack I don't feel well and need to sleep. My head is pounding. I take some aspirin and go to bed. When I wake up my headache's gone. I check my messages, wish for one from Carl I know won't be there. Only Lourdes.

Meet for coffee?

We agree to meet at Raging Sage, a local place with the best pastries. Small, expensive, but always crowded. We each get a pecan streusel scone and sit down at a small table. She has a drink with whipped cream and chocolate sprinkles on top. I choose their strongest brew.

"Carlos and I skyped this morning. Did you hear about that dust storm in Iraq?" I look at her without comprehension. "Of course you didn't. No one who doesn't have a personal interest ever pays attention to weather in Iraq. He was involved in helping rescue some civilians. The Army has great equipment and he was able to help find some people who were lost in the desert. More exciting than his day-to-day stuff. What happened last night?"

"Lots." I tell her about my stupid call to Carl.

"Wow. You think it's really over?"

"Yeah. I keep checking my phone for a message, but I know he won't get in touch."

"Maybe it's for the best," Lourdes takes a bite of scone. "You couldn't have kept up with both indefinitely."

"I don't want to talk about it." She refrains from asking why I brought it up. It's not that I don't want to talk about it. I don't want to hear it's for the best. "Sophie died before I got there."

"Poor thing was so young."

"Yeah. Anyway after I left, Rose stayed till they took her body away and then helped clean her room. They found a large bank account in Sophie's and Paul Terrazas name and a letter that was mostly unreadable."

"A bank account owned by your client and Terrazas. Weird?"

"He was Sophie's lawyer before me. They had a close relationship, but I have no idea why they'd have a joint bank account. I never met Paul. He died before I got hired at the PD. I have no idea what he was like. I was going to ask you."

"Hmmmm. I liked him and I think most people did. Big smile. Self-deprecating sense of humor. Had a traumatic break-up about six months before he died. His long-time girlfriend broke it off and he couldn't seem to get over it."

"Is she still around? Maybe she'd have some information?"

"Left Tucson shortly after they broke up. She was a reporter. Got a better job in Chicago. I don't think anyone in the office knew her well. Her name's Bethany Morse. Paul was never the greatest lawyer. His clients liked him, but he never had much passion. Better deal-maker than trial lawyer. One of the few that got along with the CA's, like you."

"Me?" Was that a slur?

"Don't be upset. I wish I could be more like you. I despise prosecutors. My Tio Andres, who I adored, committed suicide after being wrongly accused of kidnapping and molesting a young child. The child never ID'd his attacker. My tio, was the only Hispanic who worked at the school. He was the custodian, single, never married. The cop who investigated was a racist pig."

"Did he go to trial?"

"No, it never got that far. They fired him. The police kept taking him in for questioning. He got indicted. He lived with my abuela, my grandma. They searched her house. There was a story in the paper. The court ordered him not to have contact with kids, including cousins and nieces who were always at the house. One day he went into the desert and shot himself."

"That's horrible and sad and . . ."

"We lived in Nogales then. It's a small town. Everyone knew everyone. I think the newspaper story saying he molested a child was the last straw."

"How old were you?"

"Happened right after my thirteenth birthday. Tio Andres had bought me the new bike I wanted desperately. My parents said it was too expensive, my old one was good enough."

"I had an aunt like that."

Lourdes went on with her story as if I hadn't spoken. "All the cousins loved him. We thought he killed himself because he couldn't stand what it was doing to our family."

"What did the prosecutor have to do with it?"

"Said his suicide proved he did it."

Does everyone have a story? I need a breather. "I'm going to get some more coffee." I want to ask how she knew he was innocent, but I'm afraid Lourdes might take it wrong.

"You haven't asked how I knew he wasn't guilty," she says. "A couple weeks after he died another kid was kidnapped and molested. They caught the guy. He confessed to both. My tio never had a lawyer. I always thought if he did, it would've worked out differently."

"Wow." I look down at my plate. I'd finished my scone, but I don't remember eating it. No wonder Lourdes is such a rabid defender. I like this job better than when I started, but I don't have her fire. "I started to work here because I needed a job. I'd been at Barker Friedman in Phoenix. They laid off a bunch of us when the economy tanked. Being a PD was never my choice. I don't have your passion." I'll confess to my motives, but not to my friendship, ex-friendship, with Double E.

"Doesn't matter how you got here. You're here. Enough about me. Paul kind of changed after the break-up. Drank more. Lots more. With a different woman every week. Cheap, slutty ones."

"No one told me that. Everyone said almost in the same words that he had an accident. Carl said he was shocked his BAC was so high because he didn't drink much."

"He didn't until a few months before he died. Probably not that many people at the office knew what was happening. He didn't hang out with us much he was always with Bethany. They were one of those couples that are glued at the hip. My brother knew him from high school and they still hung out. You should show the stuff you found to one of the investigators."

"I don't want people in the office talking about this till I get more info. I'm not sure I'm legally entitled to have the stuff. Sophie has a half sister she's estranged from who's coming into town. I don't know if she knows about the account or not."

"Did Sophie leave a will?"

"No, she didn't have anything but her clothes and a few odds and ends. Can I trust an investigator not to open their mouth?"

"Ruth would be the best although she's always totally booked. Zoey's trust-worthy. Don't pick Kevin. He can't keep a secret. Lenny's too lazy."

"Ruth is working The Gentlemen Rapist case. When we meet tomorrow, I'll ask her."

Lourdes and I gossip for another half hour or so until I reluctantly decide it's time to leave.

Jack calls seconds after I get home. Not for the first time. I hadn't looked at my phone. If I thought I'd hear from Carl, I'd have checked. "I was having coffee with Lourdes."

"I haven't eaten. Meet me for dinner?"

"Sounds good, but I'm so tired."

"How about I bring over take-out and a bottle of wine for you? We can watch TV and just go to sleep."

"I don't feel up to it."

"You don't have to do anything except sit."

I didn't even have the 'I hate his bathroom' excuse. "I wouldn't be good company."

"I guess you were good enough for Lourdes. Never mind."

He hangs up.

Twenty-Six

Monday, Monday, so good to me. I wake to the Mama's and Papa's classic. This Monday is anything but good. Rose has a boyfriend who adores her and a job she adores. Carl's out of my life. Dumped me. Dumped me for no good reason. Jack's mad at me. I should've called him back, but I didn't have the energy. I feel bad about it. But the damage is done.

I walk to my office trying to avoid everyone.

On my desk is a small ceramic vase with a white rose inside. Maybe Monday won't be so bad. No note. Shit. What if it's from Carl? What if it isn't? If I thank Carl and it's not him, how embarrassing is that? Carl's done with me, isn't he? On the other hand, maybe he's changed his mind. I'd caused our problems by thanking him for flowers he never sent. Maybe this is his way to make up. A joke like A. K.

But it could be Jack. He'd been a jerk last night. Maybe this is an apology. He might not leave a note. He'd assume I'd know the flower was from him. If I thank him and they're from someone else, he'll wonder if I have someone else. That'd be the end if it isn't now. If I don't thank him, he'll be madder than he is now.

Shit. I need to focus on work. I check my in-box. Denise has left letters and motions to be signed and a flier announcing an office meeting on Friday. Oh god, Carl, Jack and I in the same room. Shit.

I get through morning court without seeing Jack or Carl, although Carl walks into one of the courtrooms I'm in. I'm in the gallery waiting for my client. He does his hearing and leaves without noticing me.

Ruth's in my office when I return.

"Should we wait for Jack before we get started?"

"Jack texted me he was held up in court, to go ahead." He texted her. Not good.

"I spent a lot of time with Al last week." Ruth says. "I'm worried about his mental state. Being in protective custody is taking a toll. I think he'd plead to anything to be with people."

"How's he doing physically?"

"Pretty good. All the stitches are out. He doesn't complain. I've arranged for someone from prisoner outreach to visit him weekly. It's a good thing Bobby-Jo's loyal."

Prisoner outreach? What's she talking about? I could asked, but I don't want to seem stupid. "You've talked to her?"

"Yes. She's given me some useful information on people who knew Al in Kentucky. I may have to go there. I've got a lead on Willie. He was released from prison two years ago and lives in West Fleming, Kentucky. Used to be a mining town. Small and poor. He was on parole but that's over. He's on a sex offender registry. Most important, I've got his address."

"Have you talked to him?" I ask.

"Not yet. Address, but no phone. I'd like to get an idea about his attitude before I travel there. I hired an investigator in Kentucky to try and make contact."

I half listen. I wanted to talk about Sophie. "Beautiful flower, you must have an admirer."

If she only knew. "I have kind of a half personal, half PD related thing I need to ask your help on. It involves an ex-client and a lawyer who used to work here. They're both deceased. Whether you help or not I need you to keep everything confidential."

"Slow down. Why don't you try a hypothetical?"

I laugh. "You've been around lawyers too long. I'll try. Assume someone died of natural causes and left a joint savings account. Assume the other account holder was a lawyer, also deceased, who. . . Shit this is ridiculous. The other account holder once worked here. A letter was also found. Damaged, I think from water. Is there a technique to figure out what the letter said?"

Ruth looks at me quizzically. I add "There's an issue about who the money belongs to and this might help, I mean hypothetically."

"Sounds mysterious. Who could turn this down. There's some kind of new technology. I forgot what it's called. Something like a video Spectrometer. I heard about it at a seminar. It can sometimes decipher water damaged paper. I don't know who has a machine or how much it would cost. There are less exotic methods that I can try."

"I'll pay you for your time."

"Give me the letter. I'll do what I can. Forget the money."

"And you won't tell?" I look her in the eye.

"You want me to pinky swear or sign my name in blood?" She laughs.

"Before we go further, I know this has something to do with Terrazas. He's the only lawyer here who died recently. And there's always been something strange about his death, at least to me."

"You think so too. I thought I was the only one."

"What link did Terrazas have with your client?"

"He was Sophie's lawyer before me. Her file's a mess. Documents missing. She met with Paul weekly, but when I talked to her about her case she has no clue. When I asked what she and Paul talked about she said heaven and hell, and death. My client was dying, but why was Paul so interested in those topics?"

"Do you have the letter?" Ruth asks

"I do—there's one other thing. Right before she died Sophie asked me whether a person had a duty to report a crime. She said a *friend* wanted to know. When I asked more questions, she clammed up."

"Wait, my phone." Ruth looks at the screen, doesn't take the call.

"I think the money had to do with a crime. I wish I'd pushed Sophie more."

"What do you mean?" Ruth asks.

"I think the friend was made up. Maybe she'd have told me why she wanted to know."

"What if Sophie or Paul committed the crime?"

Shit. I can't believe Sophie committed another crime. I know she bought drugs. But she was in pain. Paul was a lawyer. So what. Lawyers commit crimes. I hand her the letter I'd put in a plastic bag to avoid further damage. "That makes more sense. Maybe the money was compensation for a victim."

"When I got this job, I thought it'd be more exciting. This is like a real mystery. I'll need Sophie's case file. I'll have to get some information about Paul—the date he died, a copy of his obit."

"I'll have Denise get the file. What'd you think of Paul?"

"Eight years ago, after being a housewife forever, I got a job here. My husband had passed away. For months, I sat around being depressed. I realized I needed something to do. I'd taken tons of courses in criminal justice over the years. I applied for a job here and they hired me. My first case was with Paul. He treated me like a worthwhile person, not a useless old lady. We weren't close friends, but he made me feel competent. I liked him for that. You know what I mean?"

I shook my head yes, but I didn't. I probably would've treated her like an old lady. "I'm sorry about your husband," I say because you're supposed to.

"Paul was a compassionate man. At Christmas he made sure the janitors and receptionists got gifts, usually money. People here are good to their secretaries, but some less visible folks might have been forgotten without him. He changed totally after his girlfriend broke up with him. I was willing to listen when he cried. . ." Ruth stopped mid sentence and turned around. "Hey Jack."

Jack stands in the doorway. "We kind of finished with Al and we're just chatting." I ramble, flustered by Jack's presence, don't want him to know what we're saying. I look at Ruth, hope she understands.

"Good news," Ruth says. "I've got a lead on Willie. He doesn't have a phone so I hired a PI in Kentucky to contact him. I might want to go to Kentucky if he's willing to talk to me."

"I'll have to put in a request for funds so let me know ASAP."

Ruth gives Jack a big smile and glances at her watch. "I didn't realize how late it is. I've got another appointment. Molly can fill you in."

I tell Jack what Ruth said. He asks a few questions but I can't gauge his attitude.

"Nice flower," he says. "I guess you have an admirer."

"If I do, I don't have a clue who," I say.

Jack glares at me. Before I figure out what to say, he leaves without a word.

Twenty-Seven

TGIF. I'd been in a funk all week. The mandatory meeting this afternoon will send my funk on a downward spiral. I might never recover. I didn't want to sit in a room with Jack and Carl. I thought of skipping it. *Fender-bender, horrible headache, food poisoning.* I might've if Lourdes hadn't stopped by. "I came to get you." She had a white rose in her hand. "I figured the first one was drooping. Fresh flowers always perk me up."

Lourdes?

"Thanks. That's really nice," is all I could think of to say. Maybe it's a Mexican thing. I've never gotten a flower from a woman before. Thank goodness I hadn't said anything to Carl.

The meeting's anti-climactic. Double E announces that funding for an attorney position in appeals has been approved, but no merit raises this fiscal year. Only cost of living. No one grumbles. At BARF there would've been outrage. No raises? Funds are available for two attorneys to attend a week-long criminal defense seminar in San Diego. We should let her know by Monday at 5 pm if we're interested. She looks at me, when she states it's geared for people with not much trial experience. Thanks for the compliment.

The major agenda item is office security. Double E turns the meeting over to Tricia Goff, head of IT. I'd never met her, only seen her name on the office phone list. Every time I have a computer issue, a young man who fits the nerd stereotype shows up. I'd never have guessed this person is head of anything. Tricia's obese, with short dyed red and black hair, lots of tattoos and piercings. A tongue ring makes it hard to understand her. She wear jeans that are way too tight and a black t-shirt that reads, Eat Bacon. I can't stop staring.

"She always wears jeans and black t-shirts with slogans about food or music," Lourdes whispers.

"She barely looks sixteen."

"She's older, but not much. Skipped a couple grades, and in high school passed several AP classes. Went to college year round and graduated in two years. I think she got a master's on-line while she's worked here."

"Please give Tricia your attention," Double E says glaring at me. "Two attorneys had their computers hacked," Tricia says. "I don't know yet if the same person was responsible or who did it." Before she could say more several attorneys interrupt:

"It has to be the prosecutors."

"Assholes."

"Fucking CA's."

I space out the discussion. I don't care how to make my files more secure. I know when they figure it out, IT will send us an email. That's what they're for. I don't think the CA's did it, why would they, but it wouldn't help my office standing to say so. I panic for a second when I think Carl might be one of the hacked attorneys. Maybe his idea of code names wasn't so stupid.

I spend the rest of the meeting watching Carl and Jack. From their obvious lack of interest, I doubt they'd been hacked. Carl hasn't spoken to me since our last call. If we ran into each other at the office or court, he ignored me.

Not Jack. We talked, but only about Al's case or some PD gossip. He never brought up our quarrel. But he hadn't invited me over or acted like we had a relationship. I knew I couldn't act like everything between us was okay. I'd like to just walk up to him and say, "What are we were doing tonight?" But I was afraid he say something like, "Why would we be doing anything? We're done." Or worse.

Maybe a late Friday meeting would work to my advantage. Someone would suggest we go to a bar, have a drink and dinner. Carl'd never show up, but Jack might. Even though Jack wouldn't drink maybe the atmosphere would loosen him up. As I'd envisioned when the meeting ended Lisa suggested we meet at The Downtowner Hotel for happy hour and dinner.

"Lourdes, you want to go?" I ask as we walk back to our offices.

"Sure. I'll meet you in about fifteen."

My mood lifts a bit when I hear Lisa try to convince Kevin, one of the investigators, to come. "Big crowd. Juan, Janet, Marcos, Jack. . ." she went on, but I don't need other names.

By the time Lourdes and I arrive, there's a big crowd. We both order blood-orange martinis. Jack and Lisa look like they're engaged in a serious conversation. I tried to stand away from the others to make it easy for Jack to talk to me. He doesn't.

When our table is ready I sit across from Jack. I tell myself to talk to him, apologize, flirt. I order another martini for courage. I look Jack in the eye, he looks away. He doesn't say a word to me during dinner.

"I'm ready to take off, "I say to Lourdes. "What do you want to do?"

"I'm tired. Probably go home."

"Me too. How about a ride to my car?"

At home I pour myself a glass of wine and list the ways life sucks. Carl's out of my life. So is Jack. Ruth has left for Kentucky without any discussion about the Sophie letter. The state is adamant they won't plead the Gentleman Rapist case so Jack and I will have to sit side-by-side for weeks. Double E thinks I'm a lousy lawyer. I still work at the PD. I'm home alone on a Friday night. I'll never have another boyfriend. I can't imagine how life can get worse, but I'm about to find out.

The phone rings. Rose.

"Hi Molly, It's me."

"I know."

"I'm so excited. Fredo asked me to marry him. We're not going to get married right away or anything, but he knows I feel kind of bad living with him. He wants us to go pick out rings tomorrow."

I have to act pleased. "Rose, that's great. Have you told Mom and Dad?"

"No, I wanted to tell you first, I know how much you like Fredo. I thought maybe you could help me figure out what to do. Fredo says in his family, the boy asks the girl's father for his blessing, but he wasn't sure about our family."

This isn't fair. I've always been the popular one, the more attractive one. How can Rose be getting married, and I don't even have anyone to take to her wedding? I'll be the spinster sister like in one of those Jane Austen movies.

"Do you think Dad could handle that?"

"I don't know. He might be cool, but then again he might be Dad. What if he says no or not until he gets a better job?"

"Alfredo loves his job."

"I'm sure he does, but Dad wants more for you. Just tell 'em. Don't ask. Let them know it's a done deal. Are you going to take his name?"

"Why wouldn't I? His heritage means a lot to him. It'll help his parents be more accepting of our marriage."

"You never mentioned any problems with them."

"They're nice to me in person, but Alfredo told me they'd expected he'd marry someone like him."

"Like him?"

"Come on Molly you know what I mean. Someone Latina." I never thought Latinos would be prejudice against Anglos. I thought they'd think marrying Rose would be a coup for Alfredo. Don't minorities wish they were white? In college we'd read a book written by a black woman. I'd been shocked to learn lighter skinned blacks looked down on darker skinned ones. At least some did. I wondered how Rose fit in with the Fajardo's.

"You and Jack want to go to dinner tonight? Celebrate with us."

Shit. I'd neglected to mention Jack and I weren't seeing each other. No way could I be alone with the two of them. Their happiness would accentuate my misery. Worse Rose would try to comfort me.

I lie. "Sorry, Rose, Jack and I have other plans we can't change."

Twenty-Eight

"I've always pictured you girls getting married at the Club in long white gowns. Rose seems to want a glorified picnic. I'm not prejudiced against anyone. Mexicans are hard working people, but statistics prove mixed marriages don't last."

I put the phone on speaker so I can open a bottle of wine. "What does Dad think?"

I hear a football game in the background and picture Dad in the den watching TV, the volume turned up too loud. If it's Saturday in the fall, Dad is watching football. "He's not sure about a cop for a son-in-law. Wonders if he makes enough money to support her. We both thought you'd marry first."

I thought so too. But she didn't have to bring that up. I might have sided with Mom if she hadn't mentioned my marital status. I defend Rose's decision and talk up Alfredo. I wait for Mom to say, 'some of my best friends are Mexican' but that would be a laugh. I can't imagine any of her luncheon ladies are anything but white. I doubt many Latinos can afford private counseling with my mom. Most of her clientele are upper middle-class women who drink too much, take too many pills, think their husbands cheat, or are afraid their husbands will cheat if they didn't look anorexic. Not to mention the wives who cheat.

At the start of her career she worked at a state agency in Phoenix. Some of the employees had to be Latinos, maybe even her boss, but I don't remember seeing a Mexican in our home. Except to clean or do yard work.

Mom rambles on about how her concerns have nothing to do with Alfredo's background and I must know neither she nor dad have a prejudiced bone in their body. I'm about to hang up when Ruth phones through.

"Mom, got a work call, got to go." I pour another glass of wine.

Ruth pissed me off, too. "Hi Molly, I'm exhausted. How 'bout the three of us meet tomorrow to talk about my trip." She assumes Jack's with me. I agree to 11 a.m. Hopefully, Jack can make it.

"Any news about Sophie's letter?" I ask.

"I told you I'm exhausted. We'll talk tomorrow." I push, but she won't give in. Why bother to call? What a bitch.

Morning comes too soon. I feel hung over, but that doesn't seem possible. I didn't have much wine. But when I walk into the kitchen I see an empty bottle.

My head still hurts at 10:55 a.m. when Ruth walks into my office. Today she wears a green corduroy a-line skirt she must've bought at least twenty years ago. To say the lime green polo she'd pairs it with doesn't match is a vast understatement. Her eyes are ringed, as usual, with too much blue eye shadow.

"You have a cold or something?" she asks.

"Yeah," better than a hangover. My anger dissipates.

"I didn't get back to you sooner because I uh, a friend who works at TPD and owes me, has access to the machine I told you about. He had to find time when no one was using it and his supervisors weren't around."

"What did he find out?"

"Paul's letter appears to be sort of a suicide note. He thanks Sophie for her support. Tells her to use whatever money she needs and to give the rest to the Karinskis. Paul says several times he'd wronged this family, but never how. Last he says he knows what he plans to do is a sin, but he can't live with himself any longer."

Suicide. Not an accident. I'm right. Now that it's real I can't process it. To take your life. It's irrevocable. Getting fired or a divorce might be scary, but you have a chance afterwards for things to change for the better.

"Terrible thing, he was a decent man." Neither of us spoke for a few minutes.

"It's a good thing my buddy doesn't have much in the way of scruples." Ruth says, "I was afraid he'd show the letter to someone in the department, but he's a scientist first not a cop. He joined TPD because their lab is ultra-modern and there are all kind of machines he can play with."

"What do you think it means?"

"That Paul hurt this Karinski or his family. That giving them money might help fix it. If must have been really bad, if he killed himself."

"What could he have done?"

"Maybe Karinski was his client and he screwed up the case. Because of his fuck-up the guy's doing a long sentence. I've thought about this a lot. It's far-fetched, but what if he lost on purpose because he thought the client was guilty?"

"If he screwed up it'd be fixable. There's an appeal process. Worse case scenario he'd get in trouble with the bar. Get suspended. I doubt he'd get disbarred if he was remorseful. Doesn't sound like something you'd kill yourself over. I don't buy the on-purpose theory. PD's, even PD's who drink too much or are depressed or burned out don't throw cases."

"The letter explains Paul's changed behavior," Ruth says. "I told you he was drinking too much. I knew he was upset about his girlfriend, but there was more. A lot more."

"We need to find out if there is a Karinski who was a client. If that doesn't pan out, maybe someone with that name was a victim in one of our cases."

"Sounds reasonable."

"Ruth, would you have time to check the office databases? Try clients first and then victims."

"I'll do it tomorrow." She looks at her watch. "We better go meet Jack."

Ruth and I grab our files and head to the small conference room. Jack's already there a mug of coffee in front of him.

"Hi Jack," I try to keep my voice level.

He nods, gets up and gives Ruth a hug. The two of them chat about sports, and her rescue dog, Sadie. Ruth shows us some pictures. Sadie's black and white, appears to be some kind of shepherd. Jack always knows personal stuff about people and what's important to them. He looks good today. Was that a new shirt and tie? For a change the shirt fits him and isn't raggedy. What's the occasion?

They finish their chat, finally, and sit back down.

"Okay, Ruth, fill us in."

"Willie lives in a state-run home for the disabled. Before that he served seventeen years in prison for burglary and sexual assault. Never got arrested for what he did to Al. Got stabbed a couple times by inmates and received the usual horrendous medical care. He got *the cancer,* as he calls it, and doesn't look like he has much time."

"Hopefully enough."

"He says he found the Lord. Wants to help Al." She rolls her eyes. "Wants to know everything about him. He'll testify. He's broke. We'll have to foot the bill for travel, hotel, food, whatever."

"You think he'll make a good witness or just wants a free trip?"

"He's got jail tats, smokes, a hillbilly twang and he's thin enough to be a tweaker. Not to mention he refers to Jesus in every sentence. Lots to clean up especially if there's a jury. Add clothes and a haircut to the tab."

"You didn't answer my question." Jack says.

"Actually I think he will. He sounds sincere when he talks about what he did to Al."

"I hope we can use Willie's testimony to get a plea. I don't want to take this case to trial. Did he admit to the kinds of sexual conduct Al mentioned?"

"Yes. The details are in my report and they match Al's. He's adamant he's not a *queer* and that he never had sex with a man after that. He has no problem admitting he threatened Al. He almost acts like that's normal behavior."

"Any questions for Ruth, Molly?" Jack says.

I'm barely paying attention. Sitting this close to Jack makes me want him. Maybe after Ruth leaves we can talk. I can try to repair things. "Uh, no, I've read Ruth's report. Seems real clear. What do you want me to do?"

Jack looks at me. I can't read him. "We can discuss that later. I'm sure Ruth has lots to catch up on after being out most of last week."

Ruth gets the less than subtle hint, put her files in order and is out the door. For a moment it is all silence. I want to say something flirty or cute, but my mouth's dry. Something is up.

"So you have something to tell me, Molly?"

"No."

"No? I told you early on how I feel about liars and cheaters."

I say nothing. I should act innocent and outraged, but it's too late.

"You want to tell me who?"

Oh shit. Did he know or was he guessing? Did someone rat me out? Why was I such an idiot? Jack is smart, passionate about his work, funny, sexy. Is it too late to try and patch it up?

"I'm sorry. I never meant to do anything behind your back."

"I know it's someone who works here. Tell me."

"It wasn't his fault."

"I'm not going to have a duel with him. You're not worth it."

That hurt. My eyes start to tear. In spite of his calm tone, he's angry. This isn't a quarrel. We're done.

I may as well tell. It doesn't matter. "Carl."

"Fuck."

"I'm sorry Jack. Look, if it means anything, it's over."

"Did he dump you?" Jack no longer hides his anger.

"How'd you find out?"

"None of your business. I've given this lots of thought. No way can we be co-counsel. Make up a story about some crisis in your life that makes this case too time-consuming. Whatever you can think of, I'll back you." He takes a sip of coffee and sighs. "I've dated lots of women and you aren't the first one who cheated. I'm sure eventually we can be civil to each other, but I'd appreciate it if you stay away from me now. Have Denise give me any of the files you have."

"Of course." I pick up my papers and start out the door. Jack is staring into space.

Who told him? I'd only told Lourdes, but she wouldn't tell. Fuck Jack. I'll make up a story. A story about how I dumped him. Even if he talks, it's my word against his. No one will know for sure. I'll make him sorry he messed with me.

"Oh, and the boss wants to see you," Jack says. His parting words to me.

Twenty-Nine

I think my life can't get any worse. A few days ago I was worried about fitting Carl and Jack into my schedule. Now both are gone. The Gentleman Rapist Case, my ticket to a job at a big firm, is history. Without it no CNN, no interview by Anderson Cooper, no fame.

How can Jack be so unfair? Our relationship's over. Big deal. We can work together. We're professionals.

Soon as the other lawyers find out I've two-timed Jack, I'll be a pariah. Everyone likes Jack. People always blame the woman.

I hear Lourdes' car pull in the driveway. I finish my wine, grab my purse and close the door. No question I drink too much, but I can cut down anytime I want. Alcohol is supposed to improve my mood. It doesn't. Maybe I should get a dog.

"Molly, sorry I'm late. Last minute client emergency."

Tonight is Lourdes' turn to pick a restaurant. She choices a place in South Tucson, the mile square city surrounded by Tucson, famous for Mexican food. Friends in crisis have said, 'I'm too upset to eat.' Never happened to me. Lourdes pulls into a small parking lot filled with potholes, but jammed with cars. Good thing she drove. Wouldn't want the Miata here. This is the restaurant? The outside looks old and dingy. A sign that looks home-made reads Casa Ana.

"Best Mexican food on the planet except for my Mom's," she promises as she notices my reluctance to get out of the car.

The inside isn't much better. Noisy. Loud Mexican music. Maybe six tables all filled except the one Lourdes grabs. A waitress approaches immediately with menus and asks about drinks.

"I'll have a Dos Equis dark," Lourdes says.

"Me too."

"I'm ready to order, I know the menu by heart. You ready?"

"Go ahead. I'll figure it out."

"I'll have green chili carnitas with beans and calabacitas. And a side of guaca-mole." She looks at me. "Guacs enough for two."

The menu's in Spanish. "I'll have what she's having."

We nibble on chips and spicy salsa. When the beer comes I take a large gulp. I need to cut down. It'd be too easy to let my drinking get out of control in my state of mind. At least beer's got less alcohol than wine.

"So what happened? I can tell you're upset." I can barely hear Lourdes. That damn Mexican music.

"Upset doesn't come close. Jack found out about Carl. We're done. He kicked me off the rape case. Said some mean, nasty stuff."

"I'm so sorry. You okay?"

"I don't know. I'm humiliated. Who's going to actually believe any reason I make up to explain why I'm no longer on the rape case. Everyone's going to know Jack dumped me. And that I had an affair."

"Jack's not like that. He doesn't kiss and tell. He's had lots of breakups and unless the woman talks, no one knows why. He never trashes his exes. That's why he's friends with most of them. Try this guacamole."

I take a chip and scoop. "I didn't think I cared that much about Jack, but when I saw him yesterday I felt hot all over. I thought I could talk him into stay-ing together. I know how to handle guys. I was shocked when he started to attack me."

"I wish I knew what to say to make you feel better. It's a shame about the rape case. A couple months ago Lamar Loser took over one of my cases. I felt horrible. I liked my client and thought I could win her case. He pled it out the incompetent jerk."

That's precisely why I don't fit in. I don't give a rat's ass about Al except that his case will help my career.

The waiter brings our plates. I take a bite. Neither of us speaks. We scarf our food. Lourdes is right.

"How's Carlos?" I ask.

"Fine. We're going to Skype Sunday. I almost wish it was pre-computers. My mom has a stack of love letters from our dad. I read a few. They were so romantic. Now that we have all this tech stuff nobody writes."

At least you have someone that cares about you. I'm going home to my empty place tonight. No need to check my computer. I'm such an idiot. Why wasn't I content with Jack?

"You seem miles away Molly."

"I'm sorry."

We finish our dinner and Lourdes drives me home. The food was great, but I don't feel better. Maybe worse. Everyone has someone. Rose is getting married.

I change into something comfortable and am trying to decide what to do when the phone rings. I put my wine glass down. Rose. "What's up?"

"I made a dulce de leche cheesecake and I thought you might like some."

"How come you're not with Fredo?"

"He had to work. Some emergency."

"Come over. I need to talk."

Tonight's as good as any to tell Rose about Jack. I pour myself another glass of wine and begin to channel surf when the phone rings again. Ruth.

"You're working on a Friday night?"

"I guess I am. I checked the database and there is no client named Karinski. I went further and found no case in Pima County where either the defendant or victim is a Karinski."

"Shit. I really thought Karinski was connected to our office. What next?"

"I don't think going through the phone book will help. Even if we find a Karinski I can't think of anything to ask. How about if I drop by your office Monday twoish and we'll brainstorm?"

"Sounds good."

What connection did Karinski have with Paul? What did I know about Paul? He worked as a lawyer at the PD. He was single, but had a long-term girlfriend. The girlfriend broke up with him, and his life went to hell. He drank heavily. His work became shoddy, his files in disarray. He blew a murder case. His death seemed like an accident, but turns out was a suicide. He left a large savings account to a person unknown to anyone. Maybe Paul was doing drugs. Could Karinski have been a user or a dealer? He wouldn't leave a drug addict money. Even if he owed a drug debt it'd take a long time to owe that much. That's not it.

He spent a lot of time with Sophie. They talked about heaven and hell and punishment. He must have hurt someone. Felt he had to make amends. Maybe he came clean with Sophie. That would explain the question she asked, "If you know about a crime are you required to do something?"

My thoughts are interrupted by a knock on the door.

"It's not locked. Come on in."

"You can't leave the door unlocked, it's dangerous."

"I knew you were coming."

Rose walks in with a cake pan and a delicious smell.

"Fredo and I are going to look at rings tomorrow. I want something simple. I don't believe in spending a lot for jewelry. Fredo's cousin manages a jewelry store at Tucson Mall so I think we'll go there. He. . ."

God how long do I have to listen to this?

"How 'bout we have some of that cheesecake?"

Rose cuts large slices. She brought over a can of whipped cream. Knew I didn't have any. I slather my cheesecake with the whipped cream. I'm amazed how good she looks. Gone are the baggy jeans. Instead she wears a pair that fit well and a v-necked shirt with a sparkly design. Shows a little cleavage. No make up, but between her recent hair cut and new clothes. . .

"You look great Rose. I'm impressed you bought clothes without my help."

She blushes. "Fredo's cousin, Maria, took me shopping. She picked this out. I think it's a little over the top, but I didn't want to hurt her feelings."

"It's not anywhere over the top. It's stylish."

She changes the subject. "You seemed down on the phone. I'm surprised you were at home. You're usually with Jack Friday nights."

I sigh. "No more Jack. We broke up."

"What happened?"

What do I tell her? The truth? Not yet. "It wasn't working out. We weren't getting along."

Rose takes our empty dishes and puts them in the kitchen. "I'm sorry. You seem to be taking it hard. Doctor Laura would suggest . . ."

"Rose I don't care what she says."

"Sorry." I doubt she means it, but she's a peacemaker. "Did you care that much about him?"

"I'm not sure if it's losing him or the rape case. He decided it would be too awkward for us to work together."

"I guess that would be hard."

"I could've worked with him. I'm a lawyer, a professional." This time I change the subject. "One of my colleagues deciphered part of the letter you found. Paul wanted the money to go to someone named Karinski."

"Did he say anything else?"

"It was a suicide note. Lots of sorry's and goodbyes. Paul said Sophie could use whatever money she needed, but make sure the rest went to Karinski."

"Have you found out anything about who this Karinski is?"

"He's not a client or a victim in any cases in Pima County. We're not sure where to go from here."

"Maybe you should talk to Alfredo." Detective Alfredo Fajardo? Were we ready to involve the police? I wasn't sure.

Thirty

Saturday night is the meet and greet between the parents. Mom and Dad are coming to Tucson to have dinner with Alfredo's parents. "Molly, you've gotta be there. You know how they are."

"Please Molly," Alfredo echoes. "I'd be more comfortable."

I want to say no. I don't want to endure congrats to the happy couple, or my parents snide remarks. I've grown fond of Alfredo. He's a kind man and cares deeply for Rose. He'd protect her and by extension me. He'd kept my car from being towed. Had my back. I owe him.

I spend my few spare moments with Lourdes. We often eat dinner together, out or at her house. She's a terrific cook and doesn't consider it a chore. I can make basics and know how to fix either meat or vegetarian chili. Men always like chili. To help I chop vegetables or grate cheese. Bring a bottle of wine or pick up the restaurant tab. If Lourdes is swamped, I get take-out or order a pizza.

As far as I know Jack isn't seeing anyone, but Carl and Chloe seem to be an item. How could he switch from me to that Barbie doll bimbo? She's a receptionist for god's sake. No one seems to have blabbed about me and Carl. Jack is either too decent to slam me or doesn't want people to know I cheated on him. Carl wants to keep our 'relationship' quiet now that he's dating that slut. Lourdes acts as my extra set of ears. She swears she hasn't heard a thing. No one treats me weirdly. Maybe I'm not a pariah.

Lourdes suggests I tell the truth. Jack and I broke up and it's too hard to work on the rape case together. Why do I always think of a story, no a lie?

Last week Al's brother, Willie, came to Tucson for his deposition. Jack has chosen the depo route to insure the presence of a court reporter and more important a prosecutor. That way if something happens to Willie, his testimony can be used at trial. Normally defense attorneys prefer not to depose witnesses so they can keep their options open until trial. Depos also cost a mint; whoever sets the depo has to pay the court reporter. They can last days.

If I stayed at BARF, depos would be the closest I'd get to court in many years. Civil practice revolves around depositions.

Willie's depo is set for 9:00 a.m. Since it's in a courtroom, I can watch. Willie looks like he doesn't have much time—pencil-thin and coughs constantly. I can't abide people who mention Jesus every other word, yet I find myself sympathetic to Willie. He recounts how his life changed since he'd found Jesus. He sounds sincere. He answers Jack's questions straightforwardly and admits to doing terrible things. I want to stay and watch the rest of Jack's direct and Smithfield's cross, but I have hearings to cover. Later in the day I find out through the grapevine that the judge recessed early and Smithfield's cross is tomorrow at 9:00 a.m.

Smithfield had been one of the prosecutors in the Emily Nelson's case. Emily, sixteen years old, had been charged with first degree murder in the death of a prominent businessman. The case went to trial and Anne Levy, Emily's lawyer, had gotten an acquittal and fame. Smithfield had gotten a reputation as being incompetent and sleazy.

Smithfield's cross of Willie was typical:

Q. "You're related to the defendant, Al Weston?"

A. "Yes (cough) sir."

Q. "You don't want him to go to prison?"

A. "Course not." (more coughing)

Q. "You want to help him?"

A. "Yes sir."

Q. "You have a felony conviction for aggravated assault in the state of Kentucky?"

A. "Yes sir."

Q: "You haven't seen your brother in 15 years?"

A: "Sounds about (coughing) right.

Q "You don't really know what he's like today?"

A. "God tells me he's a good man."

That stopped Smithfield. Can't attack God.

I scribble a note to Jack with some thoughts and hand it to the bailiff to pass to him. Some bailiffs won't cooperate. They'd get all 'what do you think I am, the post man,' but Steve, Quinn's bailiff, is happy to help lawyers. He never misses an opportunity to ingratiate himself with the bar or spread gossip. Steve put it on the defense table, but Jack's too busy to open it. I hope he's not pissed I showed up.

On Friday, a crowd's gathers around him as he recounts the depo. As I pass by he nods at me, the most positive signal I'd gotten out of him since he dumped me.

Saturday morning I wake up with the now familiar hang-over. I go into hang-over routine. A normal person doesn't have a hangover routine. My parents want to stop at my place before 'the dinner'. I'd begged them to bring Dudley.

My place's a mess. I don't cook much, but dirty pans and dishes litter the kitchen along with empty bottles and take-out containers. I change out of my work clothes in front of the TV, another bad habit. My clothes are scattered around the room. Some are clean but all so wrinkly they need to go to the dry cleaner. A large bill. I don't own an iron and I haven't done a load of wash since Rose moved out. My mom sends me underwear anytime it's on sale. I finally got her to send the ones I like. Between her and Budget Cleaners on the corner I could go a long time without washing.

I'd had a cleaning service twice a month, but Rose insisted I fire them when she moved in. She thought paying someone to clean my house was 'an extravagant expense' and had some stupid idea that it was' immoral' to have poor people do your dirty work.

"Isn't it better they have a job?" I'd argued. "Dignified jobs are great, but if you can't get one. . ."

I'd planned to hire them back since Rose moved, but hadn't gotten around to it. I dust, pick up the clutter and mop floors. Luckily I remember how to operate the wash machine.

I'm tired, thirsty and ready to pour myself a glass of Chardonnay when I look at the clock. Too early. Only alcoholics drink before five. As the English say, it's five somewhere.

I spend the next hour in an attempt to houseclean myself. I wash and condition my hair, take a long bath and use a home facial kit someone had given me for something. I have a pedicure appointment at 2:30 p.m., but when I get there I have to wait. There's so much competition for nail services you'd think these people could be more competent. I want to make a nasty remark and leave, but where can you get your toes done late on Saturday? God knows what they'll do to my feet if they hear me complain. They all act like they can hardly speak English except when it's time to pay. Finally, god I need a drink.

I'm dressed, in a clean house and have only drunk one glass of wine when I hear my parents' car.

"Mom, dad, hi, Dudley," I pick him up and breathe in his soft shampooed hair. Mom probably spent more money grooming that dog than she did herself. Dudley licks my face and his body collapses into my arms.

"Place looks . . . decent," Mom said as she inspects.

"Want a glass of wine?"

"What are you drinking?"

"Chardonnay."

Mom frowns. "Do you have any red?"

"No sorry. I don't drink red." I lie. I could care less what color, but hadn't thought of wine for anyone but me.

"Got any beer?" Dad says as he walks in hands loaded with shopping bags.

"Dylan, don't start drinking now. This is a big occasion for Rose and you need to be at your best." Why is it okay for her, not him?

Dad glares at her but says nothing.

"I brought you a few things for the house. Nothing big." Mom opens one bag and hands me dish towels, blue place mats the color of my dishes (which she'd picked out) and opens another bag with a blue and white tablecloth with matching cloth napkins.

"Thanks, Mom." I say this with as much appreciation as I can fake. She'd shit if she knew I ate from containers, or on a special day, paper plates. Did she think I had dinner parties? Nobody had dinner parties these days. The few PD parties I'd been to had kegs and potato chips and, if you were lucky, bean dip.

"You've met this fellow's family?" Mom continues without waiting for me to answer. "You need to tell your father and me what we can expect. What we should talk about at dinner. Stuff like that."

"Geez Mom you've been at hundreds maybe thousands of dinners. The Fajardo's are no different from anyone else."

"Do they both speak English?"

"Of course. Their family probably came to the US before ours."

"Your sister can sure pick 'em. Why can't she choose someone like that kid Sean O'Connell she dated in high school. He seemed like such a nice boy."

"She dated him twice ten years ago. Anyway he's gay." I'd have to 'fess up later he wasn't, but she deserved it. Mom glares at me and Dad chuckles.

I finish my wine, open the fridge and look longingly at the half empty bottle on the top shelf. I couldn't. I put the glass in the sink. "Where you guys staying?"

"La Paloma," Dad says.

"I'm going to take Dudley for a walk. Rose should be here by then."

I put on Dudley's leash and leave. Rose is driving with us. Alfredo's coming from work. Mom will be in for a surprise. Mrs. Fajardo is extremely attractive and a stylish dresser. She'd been a stay-at-home mom, but after Javier completed sixth grade she went back to teaching. Manny was apparently 'a surprise' and Mrs. Fajardo again put teaching on hold. Mr. Fajardo is a honcho in the county. An administrator in charge of some important department. He's handsome. I hadn't mentioned that the Fajardo's weren't any happier about Alfredo and Rose's marriage than they were. I didn't want Mom to get on her high horse and ruin the evening.

By the time I get back it's almost time to go. Mom can't stop cooing over Rose.

"You've lost a lot of weight."

"What an attractive haircut."

"You look beautiful."

I run a comb through my hair. Put on some lipstick. I wait for Mom to compliment me. She doesn't.

Rose and Alfredo have chosen an old Mexican restaurant in a historic building downtown. When we arrive the Fajardos and their kids are seated. I don't see Alfredo.

Rose makes the introductions. "These are my parents Claire and Dylan. Fredo's parents, Olivia and Art. Alfredo's brothers Javier," she points to the older one, and "this cute one's Manny." The older boy, fifteen, is polite, but raises his eyes when Rose calls the four year old brother, cute. Manny's shy at first and later doesn't shut up.

We immediately order drinks. Great idea. As the waiter serves the drinks Alfredo arrives dressed impeccably in a suit. I've never seen him dressed like this. It's either his uniform or jeans and a polo. "I'm so sorry, I couldn't get out earlier. Accident with fatalities. I'm on call. I hope I don't have to leave."

Rose introduces our parents. Alfredo, as I expected, is ultra polite. He shakes dad's hand and kisses mom's.

Alfredo has done his homework. He asks my dad about his golf game, favorite teams, and his business. He compliments Mom on her outfit, asks about her job and treats her like she's the Queen of England. From someone else it might seem phony, but from Alfredo it works. Mom loves it.

The parents get along better than anyone expected. The Fajardo's are warm, welcoming and worldly.

By the time we're ready to leave, Dad has welcomed Alfredo and his parents into our family. Mrs. Fajardo calls Rose the daughter she never had. Everyone seems happy except me and Javier. He keeps fiddling with his phone. Mr. Fajardo threatens to take it away. He rolls his eyes but complies.

I want to go home and drink.

Thirty-One

Thank goodness for Lourdes. If she hadn't called early this morning my parents would have found me asleep.

Rose suggested we all have breakfast. The Fajardo's declined. They were going to church. Dad reminds us their room includes a free breakfast, not one of those cereal and make your own waffles ones, but the kind you can order from a menu. Mom tries to change his mind. He's adamant. Instead we're meeting at my place so the parents can pick up Dudley. Say good bye.

A shower, a couple cups of coffee. I'm almost okay when the doorbell rings and Mom comes in.

"Hi Molly, You feeling okay?"

"Just a slight headache, Mom,"

"You hungover?"

"No, leave me alone."

"Don't be so touchy. Can I borrow your phone? Mine's in the car."

"Why you would leave it in the car?"

"I packed it."

Who packs their phone? I hand her mine. "Who are you calling?"

"Rose. I want to remind her to bring the list we made . . ." I tune out. "Wedding stuff."

I grab Dudley, and put on his leash. A last walk before he goes. I should get a dog. I never was much for the outdoors, but there's something gratifying about walking Dudley. He seems so happy. His tail wags continuously and when he looks up at me he smiles. I love the thought of someone who waits for me at home and doesn't give me grief. Men like dogs. I don't have to get a poodle. A golden retriever or a lab — no a boxer. I could be safe anywhere alone.

I've never owned a dog. How hard could it be? Feed it, make sure it had water. Some toys. Vet checks. It'd be alone all day which probably isn't good. Maybe I could pay one of the kids in the neighborhood to walk it after school. Dudley chose that moment to look up at me. "Even if I get a dog, you'll always be number one." It's good to talk to your dog.

I walk slowly. If I time it right everyone will be ready to leave when I get back. I need a glass of wine. Now that our families have fallen in love nothing stands in the way of the wedding. Rose and Alfredo aren't flashy types. Rose told me she wanted a small outdoor wedding. Maybe at a park or our parents' back yard. She doesn't want a traditional wedding dress either. "Too expensive and I'll probably trip on the train. Something simple. Blue, my favorite color. Lots of flowers. Hire a couple food trucks."

I don't think my Mom or Mrs. Fajardo would agree to their plans. Dad might if it wouldn't cost much. Our family isn't religious, but Mom would want Rose to get married in a church. Alfredo's parents seem more religious and probably favor a Catholic church. I don't know if Mom would go for that. Will Rose have to convert? I've had girlfriends who marry Catholics. I think if they didn't covert they had to promise to raise the kids Catholic.

And food trucks. Mom would be apoplectic. How could she invite her friends to a wedding with food trucks? She'd want a fancy sit-down dinner with good wine. Shit, what did I care? Whatever they decide it'll be a miserable day for me. Other than some good wine and maybe wedding cake.

My timing's not bad. Dad's fidgety, ready to go. Mom and Rose talk intently at the kitchen table. Alfredo concentrates on the paper.

"Claire, Molly's back. Let's roll."

"In a minute, dear"

Dad sighs. "It's time to go," he says a few seconds later. "You know how bad traffic gets."

This time Mom gets up. "Rose, I'll call you tomorrow when I have more information. Think about what I said. You only get married once."

Rose smiles. Mom gives Rose a long hug. Alfredo walks over to Mom, but seems unsure of what to do. Mom spreads her arms and embraces him like a long lost relative.

"Come on already," Dad complains. He hugs me and Rose and shakes Alfredo's hand.

Am I no longer Mom's favorite? As if she reads my thoughts, she puts her arms around me. "Molly, I forgot. Your phone rang. I answered it. Hope that's okay. Thought it might be important. It was someone named Ruth. Thought I was you. She called about a guy named Kronski or Karinski. Said you'd know what it was about and to call her back."

"It's fine, Mom."

We walk them to the car. I carry Dudley and reluctantly put him in his bed on the back seat. I wanted to announce my dog plan, but Mom would probably trash it.

"That worked out better than I expected," Rose says as our parent's car is out of sight.

"I guess. I'm going to get a dog. Isn't that cool?"

"Sounds good to me. I always wanted a pet, dog or cat, but I've never lived anywhere long enough. Are you getting a poodle, like Dudley?"

"I was thinking of a boxer."

"Boxers are energetic and take time and energy to train."

"I'm not getting a puppy."

"I'll go to the Humane Society with you, if you want."

"Humane Society? Why should I get a reject?"

Rose stares at me like I said I'm going to kill a puppy. "There are so many dogs that need homes. Grateful ones that make the best pets."

Instead of answering, I take a half empty bottle of Chablis out of the fridge. "Want a glass?"

"It's awfully early."

"All you have to say is no." I pour myself one. "Are you converting to Catholicism?"

"I haven't decided. Fredo says it's up to me. He'd never force me to do something I wasn't comfortable with. Dr. Laura think it's important children are brought up with religion. That marriages have a better chance of lasting if the parents . . ."

I take a few swallows of wine. Dr. Nut-ball again. Why did I ask her? I didn't want to talk about their wedding or their life together. I pick up my glass and go into the bedroom.

I lie on the bed and wish Alfredo and Rose would leave. Wish I had a dog. Wish I had someone. Alfredo remained outside after he said good bye to my parents. Must have made a call or gotten one. I hear him on the phone. Maybe when he finishes they'll go. I turn on the TV. Nothing. I don't feel like reading. I start to drift off.

"Molly, we're leaving."

I don't hear the door close. After a few minutes I walk back into the kitchen. Rose and Alfredo sit at the table. Doesn't look like they're leaving to me.

We all look at each other. "Molly, I heard your mom tell you about a call. Do you know someone named Karinski?" Alfredo asks.

"Shit." I'm not ready for this. "It has to do with a case."

"Is he your client?"

"No." Was there an attorney-client privilege issue I could use to say nothing? Sophie's dead, but the privilege remains. I stall. "Why do you want to know?"

"Remember the day I came over with the fliers about the hit and run?"

How could I forget the day he and Rose met. She blabbed about it enough. "Yeah?"

"The accident that happened a couple blocks from here? The one that killed a woman, her eight-month-old and left another child severely injured."

"Yes."

"It was the Karinski family."

Thirty-Two

"Molly, tell me what you know about the Karinski family."

I guess there's no reason not to. "Okay. You know I have, had a client, Sophie, in hospice?"

"I think I remember you and Rose talking about her."

"She died a few weeks ago. Rose came to pick me up because she wanted to see me. She got a call she died . . ."

"Slow down, Molly, too many she's. Call them by name."

Isn't he supposed to be a detective? "Okay. I was having dinner with a friend. Rose called to tell me that Sophie had taken a turn for the worse and wanted to see me. I didn't think I should drive, I'd been drinking, so Rose came to pick me up."

Rose broke in, "I hated to leave Sophie, but she kept saying it was urgent, that she had to see Molly."

"Rose would you mind making me a cup of coffee," Alfredo asks. Rose probably doesn't mind, but I would. Get your own damn coffee.

"Sure." Rose walks over to the counter and fills the pot with water.

"Rose picked me up to take me to hospice. She, Rose, got a call while we were on our way back. Someone from the hospice called and told Rose that Sophie had died."

"What did you do after that?"

"Rose drove to the hospice anyway. I wanted to go home. Rose wanted to say a proper goodbye to Sophie. I left."

"Molly, you want some?" Rose says as she hands Fredo a cup.

"No, but I'm ready for more wine?"

152

Rose doesn't answer.

"Didn't you hear me."

"Don't you think it's too early to drink?"

"Never mind. I'll get it myself." As I walk over to the fridge I feel Rose and Fredo glance at me with disapproval. It's none of their business.

"Want to finish your story?" Fredo asks.

I sit down and take a few sips. "I got a taxi, went home and went to bed. Rose called later, told me they'd found a savings account book in the name of Sophie Mercer and Paul Terrazas. And a letter under Sophie's mattress."

"Go on."

"The account had over $100,000. The letter had gotten wet and was kind of unintelligible."

"I think I knew Paul Terrazas. He was a public defender?" Fredo asks.

"Yeah, before my time."

"He interviewed me on a few cases. I heard he died. Accidental, wasn't it?"

"That's what everyone at the office says. He had a high BAC and was depressed. Some people think he did himself in."

"Sad. Young guy like that, good job, great future."

That thought never entered my head. I knew he was only thirty-six, his girl-friend had dumped him, he was depressed. I'd found that out almost my first day at the PD. I didn't think much about his death other than in relation to his cases I inherited, and later the bank account. I'd never thought of him as a real person, not that much older than me, who died.

"How'd you tie all this to Karinski?"

"I had one of the PD investigators decipher the letter. You probably know her too. Ruth?"

"Everyone knows Ruth. Real character, but a good investigator."

"She made out the name of Karinski and the word 'victim' used several times. She's tried to tie Karinski to a criminal case, but hasn't been able to."

"Can Karinski get the money?" Alfredo asks. "He sure can use it. His wife and one of his daughters are dead. The other daughter's alive, but was badly injured. She's still having surgeries and its been well over a year. Karinski's a wreck."

"It's not quite that easy. Sophie had no will. Her only heir is a half-sister she doesn't get along with. I don't know if Paul had a will. Don't know if there were any beneficiaries on the bank account."

"We never closed the Karinski case. We had no suspect. Looks like Terrazas might be involved."

"I should have told you about the bank account, Fredo. I thought you'd be mad at me." Rose says. "I had no idea it had to do with a crime. I'm sorry."

Alfredo looks at her lovingly. "Rose, you can tell me anything." He hugs her. "I'd never be mad at you."

Go home and get it on there.

As if he can read my thoughts, "We got to get going Rose."

At the door Fredo calls out, "I'll call you when I find out anything. I might need to ask you more questions."

I'm relieved to be alone. I need to call Ruth back, although I don't want to. I promise myself a treat after the call. I dial and immediately hear her message. "You've reached Ruth Katzenbaum, Investigator Pima County Public Defender. Leave your name and phone number. If you're a client and it's an emergency call 520-325-5868." I try that number and again get a message.

"This is Molly returning your call. I've got news. Call me."

Do I still get a treat? I fill my glass, go into the bedroom and turn on the TV. *Law and Order* reruns. Always on one channel. The trick's to find an episode I haven't seen before or only seen once or twice. Success. I collapse on the bed. I must have fallen asleep because *Law and Order* has become *NCIS* which I hate. The clock says 4:06.p.m.

I grab my phone and dial Lourdes. She answers on the first ring.

"I found out about the bank account. Apparently Terrazas might've been involved in a hit-and-run. Two people killed including a small kid. Another kid hurt badly."

"Dios mio. To lose a child must be unbearable. Poor Paul must have been scared. He couldn't tell anyone. No wonder he drank. I wish I'd taken more of an interest."

"I'm not sure what's going to happen. It's ironic. Rose and Alfredo met when Fajardo stopped at my house to leave a flier about the hit-and-run on the year anniversary? Rose answered the door. Her first day back from Africa. Did I tell you that?"

"Yeah you did. Is this a secret?"

"For now. Except Ruth. Are you busy tonight? Thought we could do dinner."

"Can't. I'm going to Carlos parents' house. I haven't seen them for a few weeks. If you're bored there's a group going to the Shanty to celebrate Juan's 'not guilty' on a date rape case."

"Jack will probably be there."

"You can't spend your whole life avoiding Jack. Nothing's going to happen. He won't say anything."

"Does he have a new girlfriend?"

"Not that I know of. Usually he waits awhile before he's in a new relationship."

"I'll think about it. Have a good dinner. See you tomorrow."

I look in the mirror. If I'm going I have to shower, wash my hair, shave my legs. I empty the rest of the wine down the sink and make coffee.

I forgot to ask what time. Couldn't be too late on a Sunday night. Monday's a work day. I take a long bath. I'm famished, but the fridge is empty. I find a frozen dinner in the freezer. Check the expiration date. Still okay. It tastes like crap, but I eat it. Get dressed, fix my hair and make-up. Why am I going? Jack's not going to change his mind. Do I really want to get involved with another guy from the office?

I turn on the TV. *Law and Order's* on another channel. Maybe I should stay home and get a good night's sleep. I shouldn't drive anywhere. But I'm dressed, lonely and bored.

I open my phone and go to my Uber app.

Thirty-Three

The sun screams. I turn from the window. 8:30 a.m. Shit. Court at 9:00 a.m.

"Morning," a voice. What the hell? I look toward the voice. There's a strange, naked man in my bed. I check under the covers. I'm naked. I grab the blanket, wrap it around me and make a run to the bathroom. Grab my bathrobe off the hook and look in the mirror. My eyes are puffy and swollen. My makeup is smeared. My head is pounding. I'm sweaty and I stink of sex.

I leave the bathroom. The naked man is still in my bed. He smiles.

"Who are you?"

"Jeb," he says as he sits up. He's young, buff with blonde hair, blue eyes and a smirky expression. I want to punch his face.

"You need to leave."

"Chill out. What's the matter? You didn't want me to leave last night."

"What's the matter? I don't know you. I have to go to work. I want you out of my house."

Jeb gets up and searches for his clothes. I turn my back as he steps into a pair of briefs that looks like they have a fraternity logo.

"You didn't seem to mind me being here last night. I need the bathroom."

"There's another one in the hall." I point and he walks in that direction still wearing only briefs. I don't want him in my bathroom.

I gather his clothes, touch them gingerly. I throw them outside the bathroom door. "You clothes are by the door."

Part of last night floods back. I don't remember how we got here.

Finally Jeb comes out of the bathroom and starts to dress. He better not have used my stuff. Thank god my toothbrush isn't in there.

"I guess I can't kiss you goodbye," he says.

"Just go."

I open the front door as he walks out. I lock the screen and am about to slam the front door as he turns toward me "Bye Molly. If you want to get in touch me call SAE. I'm the only Jeb or show up at the Shanty." I slam the door. Like I ever want to see his ass again.

It's 8:45 and I don't know what to do first. I want to shower. I have to call work. I have three hearings. Clients wait for me. Judges . . .

I call Denise and feel relief when she answers "Denise, I woke-up feeling kind of sick and must've turned off the alarm. I wasn't going to come in, but I'm better. I'll be there in an hour. Can you get my hearings covered?" My voice breaks. I feel like crap and I can't concentrate.

"Don't worry Molly. I'll take care of it. You're not the first lawyer to get sick on a Monday morning. Take your time. If you don't feel well enough don't come in, it's okay."

"No, I'll be there. Thanks Denise."

I drink as much water as I can. A cup of coffee. I want some toast, but I don't have any bread. Turn on the shower as hot as I can stand it. I want to wash off every trace of Jeb. I'm going to have to wash the sheets. No, trash them.

I think back to last night. It comes back. I Ubered to the Shanty. As I leave his cab, JP, the Uber driver, gives me an appreciative glance. He's cute but wrong zip code. Inside, I spot the PD crowd. Before I can sit I'm handed a glass of beer. Walt, a guy who recently transferred to felony trials from juvie, recounts a story. "Rubin that piece of shit says they have a new witness. In the middle of trial. New witness my ass." The story goes on and on. I look around. About twenty lawyers, a couple investigators, and of course Jack. He isn't with anyone. Everyone talks the same old shit. Cases, lying CA's, chickenshit judges. I drink another beer, maybe more, then switch back to wine.

I feel sexy. The black knit top shows the right amount of cleavage. Why waste time with the PD crowd?

I sit at the bar, talk to a man and a woman. She has a dog who needs a home. I'm interested until I find out it's a pit-bull mix. They're not a couple. She leaves, maybe to find someone else who might want her dog. He buys me a drink. We move to a booth and Jeb sits next to me. We make-out. Oh god. Did the PD's see? Or were they gone? Lawyers are notorious gossips, especially about sex.

I can hear them now. "Molly picked up a college kid at the Shanty."

"Molly was making out with a stud she picked up at the Shanty."

"Molly left the Shanty with a strange guy."

I'd know soon enough. If they knew, someone would walk up to me, "Have a good time last night?" or "Hey, I heard you picked up a teenybopper." With a few it would enhance my reputation. At BARF no one would say a word to me, but forever more I'd be Molly the Slut.

Shit, I am a slut.

I drank so much. Three glasses of wine before I left the house. But over several hours and I ate. Beer and wine at the bar. Oh god. Did Jeb and I do coke? A faint memory of doing lines on the coffee table surfaces. My nose tingles. Or is it my imagination. I need aspirin. The coffee table's a mess. No coke residue.

My bra and panties are on the couch. I grab them, find my shirt and pants and throw them in the washing machine. There's a used condom in my pants. I've had sex on a first date, but never picked up a man, a boy, at a bar. Or anywhere. And this was no date. I grab my underwear out of the washer and throw it in the trash. At least, the moron brought a condom. I'm on the pill. Maybe he used the condom to make sure I didn't have a disease. Maybe he has herpes or chlamydia . . . ugh. Should I get a test? If it's positive and they ask for names, what should I say? Jeb someone at SAE.

The sex is fuzzy. We start on the couch in the living room and move to the bedroom. He's on top, his hands on my ass. He smelled of beer and manly soap. His body was smooth and hairless. He's probably going to tell all his frat brothers about the slut he picked up. Thank god I didn't give him my cell number. Did he even ask? I hope I didn't tell him I was a lawyer, but I think I did.

"Never seen you here before."

"Public defender party." The asshole probably thinks I'm a secretary.

My cell buzzes. For an insane moment I think it's Jeb. What a stupid name. His parents probably named him after an uncle who was the family loser.

"Molly, it's Denise. Don't worry about court. It's covered. I called your clients who are scheduled for appointments this morning and re-set them. I hope that's okay."

"It's great. Thanks."

"Like I said this morning you should stay home if you're sick."

"I'm better. Be in soon."

I have to go in. Can't have people speculate I'm hungover. I need to find out if they know I left with the stud from SAE. Lourdes will know. I call her. Voice mail. I don't leave a message. What would I say? Lourdes, I'm calling to find out if people at the office think I'm slut?

Coffee, aspirin and a shower help. The phone rings again.

"Molly I came by this morning and there was a strange car in the driveway," Rose says.

Shit, shit. Bluff it.

"So why didn't you come in?"

"I didn't want to interrupt."

"Nothing to interrupt. Friend from work. We're walking a couple mornings a week." Rose will never believe that.

"That's great. I'm a little surprised. You never cared about exercise."

"Times change. What did you want?"

She hesitates. "Just checking on you. You seemed a little down about Jack and that Carl person."

"Thanks. I'm fine."

Maybe it's not so bad. No one knows for sure what happened with Jeb. All I have to do is deny it and act fine. Politicians do it all the time. And stop drinking. I open the fridge. Quarter bottle of Pino Grigio. I dump it.

Thirty-Four

The drive to work feels like I'm on the way to the slammer to turn myself in. Most of the lawyers are in court when I arrive. I go straight to my office close the door, text Denise to let her know I'm here and wait. For what I'm not sure. Nothing good. My stomach curdles when I hear a knock.

"Yes," I say.

"It's Denise."

"Come in."

"You okay? You look pale. Sure you should be here?"

"I'm fine," I say, even as my eyes tear. "Who covered my cases?"

"Jack. He was fine with it."

Now I can't stop the tears. Great, Jack. First he dumps me and now he has to cover for me cause I'm hungover.

"What's the matter? I thought Jack'd be a good choice."

"Seriously? You haven't heard he dumped me? You two are thick. He must have told you."

"Molly, I'm so sorry. If I had known, I wouldn't've asked him. He's never said a word. Volunteered when he heard you needed help." She hands me a Kleenex. "I want to talk to you about something else." She looks at me. "It can wait."

"It's fine. Would you get me a coffee and then we'll talk."

"Of course. You like cream and sugar, right?"

"Yeah." I didn't want or need coffee. I need time to compose myself.

She returns shortly with coffee and a maple glazed donut. Did she know they were my favorite or a lucky guess? "I'm so sorry Molly. I'll get the files back from Jack and you two won't have to talk."

"No, it's fine. I'll take care of it. Please don't say anything about me—being upset."

"I'd never do that."

As I tasted the maple flavor my mood brightened. "Denise, what did you want to talk about?"

"My evaluation. Every year lawyers evaluate the staff. Ms. Elan takes these very seriously. I know I'm not perfect, but if you have anything you want me to do differently, please tell me. You haven't complained so I think I'm doing okay. Most of the lawyers I work for like me. I'm due for a raise to step four and it means a lot to me."

That's what she's worried about? "No worries. I'll give you a terrific evaluation." Something churned in the back of my mind and I caught it. One day at lunch the lawyers had a conversation about being evaluated. "Do we all get evaluated?"

"You mean lawyers. Yeah. By your team leader."

I grimace with the thought of an evaluation by Barry Singer. As if Denise reads my mind, "You have nothing to worry about. Barry thinks evaluations are stupid and gives everyone the highest ratings. Drives Double— Ms. Elan crazy."

"Call her Double E, I do."

"No, I couldn't do that."

"You almost did." I smile. "And you could. You were saying?"

"She complains about it and threatens to demote him as team leader, but he ignores her."

"Great." I take the last bite of my donut and finish the coffee.

"Molly, thanks, but if you don't mind I need to go. I've got lots to do."

"Sure. Take off."

I wish I only had to worry about a work evaluation.

Molly's a good lawyer but a better slut.

Molly flirts with everything that walks.

Molly's more interested in her colleagues than her cases.

The phone rings. It's Lucy, our great leader's executive secretary.

"Hi Molly, it's Lucy. How are you?"

Hungover, miserable, a mess. "Fine."

"Ms. Elan wants to see you?"

"When?"

"Now."

Had our discussion conjured her up? "Sure, I'll be right there." Shit. Why today? I stop in the bathroom, splash cold water over my face, refresh my make-up and brush my hair. Passable, maybe. I can plead allergies.

Big surprise, Elan isn't ready to see me. Lucy and I chat. We'd always gotten along, but I feel like she's staring at me. Do I look hungover? Am I just paranoid? Finally, Elan buzzes Lucy to let me in. Can't she walk fifteen feet to greet me? This is the public defender's office not BARF. I'd been told by someone, likely Lourdes, the past head of the office made coffee for everyone to show he was one of us, not the boss man. Elizabeth made her own because no one else knew how to do it right.

"Hi Molly, coffee?"

Why didn't she ask if I want a latte or a cappuccino like she does everyone else? "How about a vanilla latte?" I want white wine, but even to ask for fancy coffee is pushing it. She is my boss.

"Okay," she says with a frown, "but it will take a few minutes."

We sit in silence while she fiddles with the dials on her spotless machine. I'm surprised she doesn't ask Lucy to make it. She's probably afraid Lucy'll ruin her expensive toy. She hands me the latte.

"I've been looking at caseload stats. You're below average. It's time for a challenge so I plan to assign you a murder case that came in today. An old one. The Arizona Supreme Court reversed the conviction. Terrazas tried it the first time so I need to reassign it. The accused is a young woman who killed her husband in self-defense after years of alleged abuse."

"Why was it reversed?"

"Ineffective assistance of counsel. Paul tried it the month before he died. He wasn't himself. I'd like you to first chair. You can choose who you want as a second."

"Thanks, I guess." Wow. I can't decide if I'm pleased or terrified or both. A murder case is the ultimate test. Was I good enough? I didn't have much trial experience. The prosecutor would be one of their best. I'd be scrutinized by the press. This could be a big break or my undoing. I know one thing. I have to lay off the booze.

Now. Someone's life's in my hands.

"Good. It's State v. Warren. Have Denise get the old file."

"Okay."

She's quiet for a moment. "I heard a rumor I want to ask you about."

OMG. Could she know about last night? I feel like throwing up. The coffee rises in my throat.

"Is it true you're no longer on the Gentlemen Rapist Case?"

I draw a breath. "Yes, that's right."

"I also heard you and Jack are no longer an item. Is that why you're off the case?"

"Pretty much. We both thought it would be too hard to work together."

"I warned you about Jack."

I say nothing.

"What happened if you don't mind me asking?"

"As a matter of fact I do. It has nothing to do with my job."

"Not exactly true. If you're going to date guys in the office you have to be professional enough to work with them."

What a bitch. I want to tell her I know Jack dumped her, but I keep my mouth shut and hope she changes the subject.

"The other thing I want to talk to you about is the seminar in San Diego. I'm going to send you and Nathan Coleman from juvie. I plan on transferring him to trials. Lucy has the information and can explain about reimbursement for your meals and hotel." She stands up and opens the door.

"I keep tabs on murder cases so send me a status report every week. I don't want this case overturned again because another lawyer in this office messed up."

Thirty-Five

A murder case. Me. What if she's innocent? Lawyers want to win cases and try hard. Public Defenders work hard even if their client is likely guilty. But nothing is more stressful than when you think your client is truly innocent. Does Double E have confidence in me or is this a set-up. A chance for me to fail? I want this case. No, need it. I need to prove I'm not a worthless drunken slut. Maybe it's too late. I hope not.

I ask Denise to get the Warren file. Check the prison website to find out where Sarah Warren is housed so I can arrange a visit. 'In transit'. What does that mean? I walk to Lourdes' office. "I can't believe it. Double E assigned me a murder case. You think I'm ready?"

"Absolutely. Everyone's scared when they get their first."

"It's not a new case. The Supreme's reversed it for ineffective assistance. Terrazas tried it shortly before he died. The last thing Double E said was 'it better not get reversed again or some shit like that.'"

"She can be such a witch."

"I checked the DOC website and it read 'in transit.' What does that mean?"

Lourdes smiles. "It means what it says. She's being transported. Likely to Pima County Jail for the hearing to set a new trial. You need to read the remand statute. There are strict guidelines for retrials. For a change, it's usually more of a problem for the state. They don't have much time to locate witnesses and get prepared. You need to order the transcripts from the first trial."

"I need a second chair. Will you do it?"

When she doesn't answer I start to worry. Doesn't she think I'm competent? Were her compliments just talk? After a moment she replies. "I'm worried about my schedule. I have a gangbanger murder trial next month. I won't be much help till it's over. It'd be fun to try a case together. You'll have to prep by yourself. I'll be happy to guide you. See if Ruth will be the investigator. She's busy, so be persuasive. If she can't, ask Zoey. I want a woman. Have Denise get you the transcripts and start reading."

"You're the best."

Shortly after three, Ruth walks into my office. Today she wore a yellow polo over a long jean skirt and her usual over-done make-up. "I got your message about the Warren trial. I'll do it even though I'm swamped. I was the investigator in the first trial." She sighs and runs her fingers through her coarse hair. "Wish I could say the reversal was a surprise. Paul wasn't himself. Poor Sarah deserves another chance. Terrified of her husband for years. She told me she has more freedom in prison than living with him."

Wow. Ruth seems to think she's innocent. "There's a status conference set Wednesday. I'll get to meet her then if not before."

"I wanted to see you anyway. Give you an update on Al's case. Prosecutor offered to let him plead to all four rape cases but with a guarantee of concurrent time. Twenty to twenty-seven years. Al wants to take it. Jack's not sure. Thinks he can get a better deal."

"Sounds like a lot of time."

"It is, but if he's convicted on all the charges he's looking at more than two hundred years. Even if he gets twenty-seven he'll be out before he's fifty."

"Any news on Willie?" I ask

"He's ill. Could pass at any moment. How can the judge fail to take his testimony into account?"

"Judges can fail to take anything into account." I sound more like a PD.

Instead of a reply, she changes the subject. "You're not trying the Warren case alone?"

"No, with Lourdes. Don't you think I could do it alone?"

"No, I don't. No one should try a murder case alone. One of the reasons things went so badly was Paul's insistence on doing it himself. Wouldn't listen to anyone. I have some thoughts about why Paul screwed up that I want to tell you about. Let's talk after you've met Sarah."

A few minutes after Ruth leaves I look up and see Jack outside my door.

"Hey, can I talk to you for a minute?"

I nod not sure I can find my voice. "Did Ruth fill you in about Al's case?"

"Pretty much."

"Mind if I close the door, it's hard to hear."

I nod again although it doesn't seem noisy to me. What's this about?

"Did she tell you the plea?"

"Yes, twenty to twenty-seven?"

"Did she tell you Al wants to take it?"

"Yes." Say something other than yes.

"I think I can get them to come down. I heard some of the victims are reluctant to testify."

"How'd you hear that?"

"I was in Smithfield's office. He left to get some paperwork from his assistant. I could heard his paralegal talking on the phone. The guy has a loud voice that gets louder when he's agitated. And he was agitated. He was talking to, Mrs. Green, one of the victims,"

I'm about to ask how he knew who it was, but before I could, Jack says. "I heard him call her that. He was trying to convince her that she would be able to testify, that it wouldn't be that hard, that the prosecutor would do a dry run."

"That's only one."

"True, but Ruth found out that, another victim, Collins, is also reluctant. Collins is only eighteen. Her mother thinks testifying would be too hard on her. The woman's one of those controlling, over-bearing types. She's angry at the CA, wants him to plead the case."

I don't know what to say. Why is Jack telling me this? He's made it clear he doesn't want my input. He hasn't spoken to me since he found out about Carl. We both sit for what seems a long time. I can tell Jack is tense.

"Do you remember meeting Kevin Carlson? We were at dinner one night and I introduced him to you. Tall, gray hair in a pony tail, over sixty."

I think for a moment. "Looks kind of rough?"

"That's him. I told you he was an old friend of mine, but he's more than that. He's my AA sponsor."

"You still have a sponsor? You've been sober almost six years."

"Yeah, but if you want to stay sober it's a good idea. I know people sober twenty years who still meet with their sponsor."

Why's he telling me about his sponsor?

"I used to talk to Kevin almost daily. Now we meet for dinner the first Sunday of the month unless I'm in crisis and need him. You understand what sponsors do?"

"I think so." I surreptitiously check the time. I can't wait to go home and have a glass of wine. I don't know what Jack wants, but I'm certain it isn't me.

"You get a sponsor when you join AA. It's scary to admit you have a problem. Scarier to think about never having a drink again. That's why AA says, 'one day at a time.' Whenever you want to drink you call your sponsor. The concept behind sponsor is that they have been through what you're going through and know how to help."

Jack's quiet again. "Molly, this is difficult for me to say." Does he want to get back together?

I smile and look him in the eyes. "I know how to spot people having trouble with booze. I think you're in trouble. I care about you as a person. I think you need to go to AA."

"Are you fucking crazy? You think I'm an alcoholic? That's ridiculous? You're saying that because of Carl." I don't believe him. I never drink before five on weekdays. I never drink hard stuff except when I go out for dinner and other people are. Does he think they're all alcoholics? I've never been arrested for DUI. I don't throw up at parties.

"Molly, listen. It's hard to admit you have a problem. I want to help you before it gets worse. I'd go to AA with . . ."

I get up. "Get out of here, Jack. I'm not an alcoholic and I don't need AA. You're jealous because I can hold my liquor."

Jack stands up, looks at me and shakes his head. "When you're ready to admit you have a problem, get in touch."

Thirty-Six

Friday night without a date. Lourdes suggests or tries to, internet dating, "I'm not that desperate."

"It's not for the desperate. Times have changed. I know people who have found their soul mates."

Soul mates yuck. "All I've ever heard is horror stories about men who are married or in relationships who want a hook-up or weird sex or are too weird or grotesque to get a real date."

Not that I'd be home alone. Rose and Alfredo insist I join them and some of Alfredo's extended family for dinner at La Casa Cardenas, a Mexican restaurant, owned by one of Alfredo's uncles. Alfredo promises great chili rellenos and chicken mole to die for. They were even picking me up. Rose probably didn't want me to drive. I checked YELP. People raved about their house margaritas which sounded good to me.

On the ride to the restaurant she chatters about her engagement ring. She and Alfredo picked it out together. I'd probably've learned a lot about the pros and cons of ring choices if I cared. She never mentions how much it cost which is all I'm interested in.

You'd think Rose is a celebrity. Soon as the hostess recognizes Alfredo hordes of folks young, old, and in-between hurry over to meet Rose and welcome her to the family. It's hard to believe Alfredo has so many relatives.

"He doesn't. Some work here, others hang out. Live in the neighborhood." La Casa Cardenas is one of the myriad of Mexican restaurants in South Tucson that attracts tourists and residents alike. Later I learn many of Alfredo's family and friends live in the mile-square city.

Everyone acts thrilled Alfredo and Rose are a couple. I'd like to hear what they said when we're out of hearing range. *Anglo bitch;Won't last; Latina not good enough.* Rose believes every word. She looks great and acts gracious. She'd gone with me to get a manicure and pedicure. Something I'd been urging for months. She'd never be the kind of woman who wears the latest fashions, but gone are the t-shirts, sneakers and old levi's. Today she wears a pair of well-fitting stylish jeans with decorations on the pockets, low boots and a v-neck turquoise green sweater that compliments her coloring.

As long as they don't stop these excellent margaritas, I'm able to bear dinner. Everyone wants to propose a toast. As I drink, Jack's words floats through my head. I'm not an alcoholic. Drinking is something I choose to do, not something I have to do. I can quit any time. In fact, I'm going to. When the murder trial's done. The life of a criminal defense lawyer is stressful. Who can object if you have a drink after work or a few on weekends? I feel better. I've made a decision. As soon as State v. Warren is finished, I'll cut back.

Dinner lives up to its billing. I order chili rellenos, rice, beans and a side of guacamole. The waiter brings a cheese crisp with the works, and for dessert sopapillas, and a couple of plates of flan, compliments of the owners. Once again, I'm grateful I don't have to watch what I eat.

When we finish eating as much dessert as we can, our server brings the adults coffee and the kids Mexican hot chocolate topped with whipped cream. Javier, Alfredo's middle brother turns up his nose at the *baby* drink. I make sure his parents aren't watching and switch with him. He says nothing but drinks the coffee or at least tries to. Finally no more food. People begin to leave. Alfredo's parents are the last guests to go. Finally, only Rose, Alfredo and I remain.

Alfredo turns to me." I've waited till we had a few minutes alone to tell you what I found out about Terrazas. Unless you'd rather talk elsewhere?"

"No, here's fine."

"Terrazas died before you started to work at the PD?"

"That's right. I never met him."

"I'm glad. It makes it easier to tell you."

"It's fine. I know in the months before his death he drank heavily and acted erratically." Alfredo still hesitates. "Go on, I can take it."

"If Terrazas was alive we'd have enough evidence to charge him with manslaughter, hit and run, and DUI to name a few."

"What evidence do you have?"

"We were able to locate the shop where Paul took his Mustang for repairs a few days after the accident. He'd never used that place before. Damage was consistent with the accident report. Soon as the car was fixed he donated it to the Alzheimer's foundation. We probably could still get some paint chips, or maybe DNA, even, but there's no reason to."

"Why would he donate the car?"

"You don't keep evidence that ties you to a crime." Alfredo looks at me like he can't believe I'm that stupid but says nothing. "Alzheimer's was delighted to get a car two years old. Paul replaced it with a ten-year old Ford Fiesta with over one hundred thousand miles."

"I'm surprised no one at the office mentioned the car."

"It wasn't only the Mustang. He sold his treadmill, a computer, and probably other stuff I haven't found out about. Then he opened the bank account you found."

"You got all that information so fast," I say.

"It's not hard when you have someone's name, work information, Social Security number. It doesn't hurt that he's deceased. People are more willing to talk when the person can't retaliate."

"So what happened that night?"

"Best we can figure, Terrazas was driving westbound on Prince at least fifteen miles over the posted speed limit. He blew the stoplight at Mountain and collided with the Nissan sedan that was making a left turn. Both Karinski's wife, who was seated in the passenger seat and the eight-month-old baby in the back seat were killed on impact."

"Wasn't the baby in a car seat?" Rose asks. She had returned to the table.

"The accident reconstructionist thinks the baby seat wasn't properly secured. Karinski's eight-year-old daughter sustained a brain injury. In a coma for months. She's doing better, but her prognosis is unknown. The Karinski's had car and medical insurance, but still have a ton of expenses. The daughter's going to require years of special treatment."

"Are they sure Paul was drunk? People have accidents all the time when they're sober." When Alfredo answers I realized I've spoken out loud.

"As sure as I can be without a blood test. People don't pay attention when they drive for a myriad of reasons, but if he wasn't drunk why would he leave the scene?"

"Don't tell me everyone you've arrested for fleeing was drunk?"

"Not everyone, but the others had warrants, suspended licenses or no insurance. Terrazas doesn't fit into those categories."

I remembered Ruth mentioning Paul's behavior before his death. Heavy drinking. Poor lawyering. Bad judgment. I couldn't think of anything to counter the idea that he was drunk. And why should I defend him anyway? What started his slide? Was it all due to the girlfriend dumping him? I'm trying to figure out my next step . . .

" . . . totally against the backyard." Rose looks at me like I'm supposed to respond.

"Molly, aren't you paying attention. You agree, right?"

"Of course," I say although I have no idea what she's talking about.

"We've decided to get married the end of April." Rose continues. "The weather should be nice, there's enough time to arrange everything even though Mom doesn't think so. I don't want bridesmaids, but I want you to be my maid of honor. You'll do that won't you?"

"As long as I don't have to wear some god-awful pink dress."

"We can pick it out together. I tried to explain to mom, Dr. Laura thinks couple should pay for their own weddings, but she doesn't agree with Dr. Laura either."

Good for Mom. Rose chatters about the new plans all the way back to the house. As I get out of the car, Alfredo hands me a folder. "This is a copy of the accident report. I hope it'll help Mr. Karinski get the money. I haven't told him yet we might know who drove the Mustang. I don't want him to get his hopes up."

"For now the bank has a hold on the account. One of the bank's lawyers is looking into it. My concern is Sophie's half-sister. I'm sure Rose told you about her."

"Yeah. Said they didn't get along. Rose can't believe the sister would stand in the way, but that's Rose."

"I'll call the bank guy Monday. See if he wants the police reports."

After they leave I put on my sleep shirt, pour a glass of wine and study the accident reports. The accident reconstructionist believes Paul had to be driving at least twenty-five miles per hour at the time of the crash. A witness driving on Prince said the light on Mountain was red and Paul didn't stop. A couple walking their dog saw Paul speed up after the crash, but they'd have been lousy witnesses. They contradicted themselves and each other throughout their statements.

I've tried DUI's. Most are misdemeanors and those are handled by the City Public Defender. Felony DUI's are more serious usually involving accidents. Newbies are assigned most of these. One perk in being senior is you can refuse DUI's. (I'll be out of here long before that.) Clients charged with drunk driving are the hardest to deal with. Don't think they're guilty, always say they had 'two beers' at most. Always know someone with a much more egregious case who had gotten off. Complained the cops should arrest more serious criminals. Resented us because they felt they shouldn't have been arrested.

My first DUI client taught me a few lessons. She was an attractive well-groomed woman of forty. Claimed she had a fight with her husband, drank a couple glasses of wine and went to the mall. On the way, in the middle of a cloudless afternoon, on an uncrowded main street, she hit a couple of parked cars.

She swore she rarely drank because of meds she took. Drove so poorly because she had no tolerance for alcohol. I worked my ass off for her. She called every hour of the day to complain about the cops, the prosecutor, and the judge, when she wasn't whining about her husband. I got her a great deal with no jail time, but she refused to take it and started whining about me. She was found guilty. At the sentencing hearing, I found out she had three prior DUI convictions, two acquittals and had been in and out of rehab like it was a nail spa.

Clients charged with serious crimes like murder or rape are usually on their best behavior. They may say they didn't do it, but they don't argue it's not a crime. Most want our help.

Arizona has the strictest DUI laws in the nation. Fines around $5,000, at least a day in jail, license suspension, alcohol counseling, and driving with a breath testing machine in your car for a year. Not to mention sky-high insurance rates and attorney's fees if you aren't eligible for a PD.

I hate the thought of time in jail, even a day. Maybe losing my job. But I never thought about hurting or killing someone, maybe a kid or myself. I imagine the sound of a head hitting the windshield. I imagined a child bleeding, dead in the car seat. I thought about Jack's words.

I emptied the rest of my glass of wine in the sink.

Thirty-Seven

"*S*arah Warren's at PCJ," Denise texted at 7:30 a.m. What was Denise doing at work so early?

I need to see Sarah before tomorrow's hearing. Lourdes is too busy to join me. "You're first chair. I'll met her later."

Jail visits have become second nature. I know the rules. Inmates no longer scare me. Women's' housing is in a different building than mens, but still in the same complex. The visitation area is smaller and less crowded. Women commit a larger percentage of crimes every year, but are still way behind men. Rudy, a PD investigator comforts an attractive young woman who seems upset. I've heard Rudy had an eye for young, pretty ones. Otherwise no one is here.

I don't know what to make of Sarah. Most women in here are frequent fliers, young, minority, addicted to drugs or men. Sarah is thirty-five and anglo. She has no convictions, only an arrest for domestic violence. If the police think domestic violence has been committed, they have to arrest at least one person. If they're unsure who's at fault, they take both. Later, when a detective or prosecutor has time to sort it out, charges against one are often dropped. This happened in Sarah's case.

Like many things that sound good arresting both people turns out to be a bad idea. These arrests usually occur late at night or early in the morning. If both are in jail, who takes care of the kids? The police won't wait around while you call relatives or friends you primarily communicate with through Facebook. The cops call the Arizona Department of Child Safety, formerly Child Protective Services. Once they're involved it's hard to get them out of your life. Then there's that arrest on your record. Most employers assume an arrest means you're guilty. "The police wouldn't arrest an innocent person."

For a change Sarah appears in a few minutes.

"Hi Sarah, I'm your new lawyer, Molly O'Rourke."

She shakes the hand I offer, says nothing. Sarah's short and stocky. No visible tattoos. I wonder if she has always been plump or it's the starchy prison diet and lack of exercise. Her light brown hair is tied in a pony tail, her brown eyes neither warm nor cold.

"Is it true Terrazas's dead?"

"Yes, he drowned in his hot tub." I wasn't sure if I should mention suicide. I decide to save that for another time.

"He's pretty young to have an accident like that. Was he drunk?"

"What makes you say that?" I ask.

"I don't know."

"Yes." I still don't elaborate

"Were you guys good friends?"

"I never met him. He died before I started to work at the PD."

She says nothing.

I look through my notes. "Do you understand the Supreme court's ruling? Have any questions?"

"I'm not an idiot."

What's her problem? "Are you worried that I'm more concerned about Terrazas reputation than your case?"

"Aren't you?"

"No. I told you I never met him."

She doesn't look convinced. "What are you concerned with?"

"Doing the best job I can for you."

"Do we have the same judge?" she asks, ignoring what I said.

I've never thought about that, but since the status hearing is set in front of Judge Nichols, who tried the first case, it seems likely. "Yes, Judge Nichols."

"Same prosecutor."

"As far as I know."

Sarah gets up from the chair and paces back and forth in the small room.

She seems pissed off. Why hadn't I made Lourdes come with me or brought Ruth? "What's on your mind, Sarah? We have to work together if I'm going to win your case."

"Terrazas said he would win my case. I trusted him. I took his advice and got twenty years. I knew he was messing up in trial. He wouldn't listen to me. Just because I never went to college doesn't mean I'm stupid."

"Of course not." Am I supposed to be open with her. Let her know what was going on with Paul? Why not? It's not like he'll retaliate. "Look, this isn't an excuse but Paul was going through serious personal stuff. He was drinking too much, maybe using drugs, and had no business trying cases, certainly not a murder case."

"One afternoon at court I thought I smelled booze on his breath, but he denied it. Got totally indignant. I apologized."

"Look at the bright side. You have another chance to get a different result. Maybe plead to a lesser offense."

"I won't plead to anything. Ralph had been beating on me for years, threatening me, forcing me to do what he wanted."

"I can't make you plead. If you want to go to trial that's fine."

"Does Ruth still work there?"

"Yes."

"Why isn't she here? I like her."

"Ruth is going to work on the case with me. She couldn't make it today."

"How many years have you been out of law school?"

"Almost four."

"All at the PD?"

"No, I worked at Bellwood, Adams, Roth and Klein out of law school." She wasn't impressed.

"What kind of law did you do there?"

"Mostly real estate."

"How many murder cases have you tried?"

I think about a lie. Why not? I lie to everyone else, but I don't. "This is my first. But Lourdes Velasquez is second chair and she's very experienced."

We sit in silence. "I can't promise I'll win. No honest lawyer can promise that. I will promise I'll work as hard as I can. I promise I'll listen to what you have to say. And I promise you'll never have to worry about me being drunk in court." I wasn't lying. I never drink in the morning.

"You left a big firm to work at the PD's?"

"Yes." I try another tact. Don't want her to ask why I left. "Tell me how Terrazas screwed up."

"Where should I start? He seemed out of it all the time. He'd be late in the morning or from a recess. He didn't seem prepared. He pissed off the judge. Even I know he did a horrible job cross-examining the witnesses. I told him about medical records from Colorado that proved I'd been beat up. He said they wouldn't help because I never accused Ralph. I don't think he even got them. I kept asking to see them and he made excuses. His closing went on and on and I could tell the jurors were bored."

"I'll check the file and see if the medical records are there. I've read the transcripts of the first trial, and your right about his closing. It was awful. So were his cross-examinations. Make a list of what you want me to check out and give it to me at the hearing tomorrow. Be careful no one sees it."

"I told you I'm not an idiot. I've spent all the time I was allowed at the law library. I want to be included in every decision. I'll be in here for the rest of my life if you blow it. You'll go on to your next case."

We talk for over an hour, a long time for me. I usually see three clients in an hour. I'm convinced Sarah killed her husband in self-defense. She's bristly and doesn't trust me, but I'll turn her around. If I win this case I'll have a reputation as a good trial lawyer, not a slut. This case should help me stop drinking. I never want Sarah to think I have a drinking problem like Paul did.

Thirty-Eight

"State of Arizona versus Sarah Warren CR 20140003."

"Eric Smithfield and Nina Cohen for the state."

"Molly O'Rouke and Lourdes Velasquez for the defendant who is present and in custody."

"This court has received the mandate from the Arizona Supreme Court reversing Ms. Warren's conviction. The purpose of today's hearing is to set a trial date. As counsel is aware under the Rules of Criminal Procedure this case must be tried within sixty days unless the defendant waives time. Mr. Smithfield, is the state ready to proceed."

"State's ready Your Honor."

"Ms. O'Rourke is the defense ready or does Ms. Warren wish to waive time?"

Oh shit, I never discussed this with her. She must understand we need time. "Your Honor, may I have a moment?" Judge Nichols doesn't answer. I look up. His judicial assistant has entered the courtroom through the back door. I'd never seen anyone except the judge use that entrance. They confer.

"Excuse me counsel. Court will take a short recess. I need to take care of an important matter."

As the judge exits, a male says loud enough for the courtroom to hear, "Important matter my ass." Then another, "Probably his wife checking to see if she can get a quickie at lunch."

I try not to smile. Most of the lawyers laugh although a few women chastise the speaker. "I got a break there." Lourdes looks perplexed. "I never checked with Sarah about waiving time."

"You didn't discuss it with her yesterday?" I hear disapproval in her tone."Never mind. Let's talk to her while we have a minute."

Talking to a client in custody isn't easy in morning court. Judges often hear upward of twenty cases. Unlike at trials where your client sits next to you, defendants sit in the jury box handcuffed, chained together. Not much privacy. "Sarah, the Judge wants to know if you're willing to waive time, which means . . ."

"How many times do I have to tell you Molly, I'm not an idiot. No way I'm giving up my speedy trial rights. I've been in jail over two years. I want to get out."

"Sarah, no one thinks you're stupid," Lourdes chimes in. "It's just there's tons of work to do. Terrazas didn't do a thorough investigation. Molly checked last night and there were no medical records in the file. Terrazas's secretary confirmed she never sent out subpoenas. That can take time. What's a few months when you're looking at twenty years?"

"It's my life."

Before we could argue further, Nichols bailiff re-enters the courtroom. "All rise, Judge Nichols presiding."

Nichols sits down, looks at the files on his desk. "We're back on the record in State v. Sarah Warren. Ms. O'Rourke does your client wish to waive time?"

"Your Honor, could we reset this hearing for tomorrow. I need more time to talk to my client."

"Your Honor," Sarah interrupts."I'm not waiving time."

"You realize it may be in your best interest to do so. You're facing serious charges and your lawyers need to be prepared. Sixty days is not long."

"I listened to my lawyers last time and it got me twenty years. My new lawyer has the transcripts from the first trial so it's not like starting from scratch."

"Okay, Ms. Warren, your choice." She looks at what I assume is her trial calendar. "I'm going to set this case on March 29, which is fifty-eight days from now. I expect both sides to be ready to proceed on that date. I'll request seventy jurors. Motion deadline will be March 5. Anything else, counsel?"

"Please order that Ms. Warren be kept at the jail instead of returned to Florence. It's too hard to prepare if she's not close by."

"So ordered. Anything else." Neither side spoke.

I want to talk to Lourdes but we both have other hearings. By the time I get back to the office it's after eleven. I start going through the material in Terrazas trial file to put it in some kind of order. I make a list of things that need to get done before trial.

1. Re-interview witnesses. Will the state allow second interviews or argue we'd had our chance? I'd need to do some research on that.
2. Subpoena medical records.
3. Review case law on battered women's syndrome; shepardize cases
4. Read the police reports and other disclosure.
5. View the physical evidence.
6. Review the forensic evidence to see if it should be retested. Since the issue is self-defense it probably didn't matter that her prints were on the gun. Or DNA in the house.
7. Reread the previous trial transcripts
8. Find a new expert on battered women's syndrome
9. Find witnesses to substantiate Sarah's defense
10. Write opening, closing, direct and cross exams of each witness

These tasks will take more than two months and this is just a preliminary list. Lourdes is busy until her trial ends. Am I supposed to do this by myself? Do I care if Sarah's might be innocent? She brought this on herself. She doesn't care about me. And she's an idiot, if she refuses to give me time to do a good job

Almost lunchtime. Lourdes is busy so I decide to eat at my desk. I don't know how the groups feels about me. I've been avoiding them since I picked up Jeb at the PD party. His name makes me lose my appetite. I'd love a glass of wine. Too risky. If someone sees me, I'll be toast.

As if I'd spoken out loud, "Molly, why don't you join us for lunch?" Lisa asks as she passes my office.

"Okay, be right there." I guess I'm still okay with them. Maybe I'd lucked out and Jeb's my secret. By the time we get to Dizzy G's my appetite returns. The group energizes me. I work hard all afternoon.

It isn't till after five Lourdes returns from trial and we can talk. "Shit, Lourdes we'll never be ready. Why couldn't she waive time like everyone else?"

"Yeah, it's too bad. But I get it. She doesn't trust us. As to work, I told you I'd be swamped until this case is finished. Talk to Elan. She'll get someone else to help you till I'm ready. One of the new lawyers or a law clerk."

"I don't want anyone else. I'm comfortable with you." And I don't want to give Elan any leverage on me.

"Talk with Ruth then. She's almost as good as a third lawyer. Sorry I gotta run. My client's family wants to talk to me."

Lucky her. The family must be something else. Lourdes who sees the good in everyone dislikes her gangbanger client. Maybe this is for the best. I'll get up early, work day and night. I won't have time to drink. I'll start today.

I work till seven when I'm too hungry to continue. I put the boxes of files in my car. Drive to a gourmet market and buy salmon in lemon dill sauce, mac and cheese and a large piece of carrot cake.

At home, I change into comfortable clothes, eat dinner and get back to work. I can't concentrate. I'm all jittery. Maybe I'm getting sick. I read the same page over and over and don't remember a word. I consider hitting the bed when my cell rings.

"Molly, I'm at the door," Rose says.

What's she doing here? I open the door. She has several gift bags in her hands.

"I'm so excited. I think I found a wedding dress. I brought a picture." Rose takes out her phone. She fiddles around and finally hands it to me. It's light-blue lace with a tight bodice and a flared skirt. Beautiful but not a traditional wedding gown. Rose will look hot. Mom will have a fit. "It's beautiful. You'll look lovely. Have you shown it to Alfredo?"

"No. But he doesn't care. He just wants to get married."

"What are all those bags?"

"The women at work had a party for me. Totally unnecessary but everyone at Valley is so thoughtful. Looks like I interrupted you."

"I can't seem to concentrate anyway. The murder case I told you about is set for trial the end of next month. I'm worried I won't have enough time to get ready."

"I thought murder cases didn't go to trial for years."

"That's usually true, but this is a retrial. Unless the client waives time, it has to start in sixty days. My client refused."

"Is that unusual?"

"Yeah. Most waive. Defense strategy is almost always to delay. Police quit, evidence gets lost, witnesses forget or die."

"But don't . . ."

Rose starts to ask another question when her phone rings. She has a quick conversation which mostly consisted of yes and okay. "Fredo. He got home early. I want to show him the dress." She gives me a hug, and takes off. At least she didn't mention Doctor Laura.

I start to read the detective's report again. Maybe coffee will help. When I get up I see Rose forgot a gift bag. I peer in. Shit, a split of champagne and two glasses. I try to work, but all I can think about is champagne.

The bottle is beautiful green glass. Holding it feels good. *Drink me. Drink me.* I can't drink it. Rose would know. Or would she? Probably she didn't realize someone gave her champagne. Wouldn't realize she left it here. Rose doesn't care about booze. I can get a bottle to replace it.

If I don't drink it, I won't have to replace it. It isn't much alcohol. I can drink it and still work. It might help me concentrate. Calm me down. The Warren trial is the most important one in my life. Now isn't the time to make a life-changing decision. No one goes on a diet over Christmas. I can't spend the whole night obsessing over a small bottle. *Drink me. Drink me.*

I drive to Fred's liquors and look for the same brand and size. Shit $27. I don't even like champagne. I won't have to replace it if I don't drink it.

I buy a bottle of wine.

$9.95.

Thirty-Nine

Both Lourdes and Ruth have encouraged me to take a night off. "You can't work every minutes." Go out. Have some fun. With who? Lourdes is busy. Some family event. Rose is either with Fredo or wedding planning.

I've taken their advice. For once, the weekend night doesn't loom with misery. I don't want to tell anyone why. Lourdes says everyone uses the internet to find dates, but I don't believe her. She's never done it. None of my other friends have. I usually get together with her Saturday night, but that's when I'm going on my date. Even though she's busy, I lie and tell her I have plans with Rose and Alfredo. She'd never question me going out with family. I lie to Rose too. My conscious doesn't bother me. Not sure I have one.

I browse sites. I'm inundated with invitations to join eHarmony, *ChristianMingle, It'sJustLunch, EliteSingles* and even *JDate* and I'm not even Jewish. How do you chose? They all guarantee you'll meet your soul mate, some claim you'll be engaged in six months. I don't want a soul mate. I want to meet someone who's fun to hang with and acceptable enough to take to Rose's wedding.

I chose *Savymatchmaker*. $350 to join. No promises. At that price, it better be damn good. Some are free especially for women, but dad warned Rose and I that if you want the best you have to pay for it. You had to fill out a lengthy questionnaire, provide a *current* photo and a couple of references. References? I don't want anyone to know I'm doing this. "Don't worry we pretend it's a credit check."

Once accepted (I figure you're accepted on a combination of your looks and credit score), I'm interviewed in person by Michelle and Kumar who create my profile. Kumar's gorgeous and funny. He and Michelle seemed to be a couple, but I don't know what he sees in her. The meet-ups work through an app. Men they pick out for me can view my profile. If the men are interested, they log onto the app and contact me. I view their profiles and click *Yes* or *No.* For a few days nothing, and then, more than enough. I click *Yes* on five.

More info about the men I've chosen is provided.

Kent sounds too much like Derrick. Kelly looks too clean-cut, like he's going on a Mormon mission—tomorrow. Steve's allergic to cats and dogs. Not that I've gotten a dog yet, but I might. The two I like, Ted and Brandon, are good looking, have good jobs and don't seem creepy. I plan lunch with each next week. My sixth is the best yet. Louis is 32, a business man, has a dog. His passions are cooking and baseball. He's the third baseman on a city team. I'm hooked by his intense brown eyes and big smile. He suggests a drink Saturday night.

I resist the temptation to buy a new outfit which would make the date seem too important. I have no time to shop. Leggings and a tunic will do. He suggests BBQ Club or Relics. Relics is my favorite, but, I don't want to run into a gaggle of PD's. BBQ Club will have to do.

I leave work early on Friday burdened with Warren case files. There's more work to do than days left. I meet Lourdes at the jail Friday night where we spend a couple hours with Sarah. Saturday I work without a break except for lunch. Shortly after five, I call it a day.

I'm dressed and almost ready when I hear Rose banging at the door. Not now. "Hey Rose, what's up?"

"I need to talk to you. It's urgent."

Urgent? "Okay. Sit down "I'll make you some tea." I microwave water, add a tea bag. "Everything okay with you and Alfredo?"

"Yes, it's not that."

Rose sips her tea as tears fall down her cheeks.

"You're not sick, are you?" She certainly didn't look ill. Her face was glowing. She was wearing tight jeans and a top that emphasized her breasts which seem larger although that's weird.

"No, I'm fine."

"I don't have time to play guessing games. I'm going out shortly."

"You seeing someone new?"

"I don't know if seeing is the right word. I have a date. So what's happening?"

"I'm pregnant."

"Pregnant?" Don't you want a baby?

"Yes, more than anything."

"Then why are you upset?"

"I can't wait six months to have a wedding. Mom wants to rent the Botanical Gardens and we can't get a spot before then."

"What does Alfredo think?"

"He is totally, totally thrilled. He thinks we should go to the Justice of the Peace or a judge that he knows and get married ASAP." She has stopped crying.

"Why don't you do that?" I won't have to sit through a stupid wedding.

"Mom will be devastated. She wants this wedding more than I do."

"It's your life, Rose."

"I don't want to start with all the parents mad at us. Dr. Laura. . ."

"Rose, I'm sorry, but I need to go. Why don't we talk more tomorrow?" I scurry her out the door. I'm going to be an aunt and all I care about is being on time to meet a guy I don't even know. If Rose was anyone else she'd be pissed at me but she's better than that.

I get a late start. Traffic's heavy. By the time I get through the door I'm almost half an hour late. The place is busy. I scan couples, men too old, men too young.

"Looking for someone?" one of the waitstaff asks. "There's a patio outside." I walk outside and immediately knew Louis. Much like his picture, but less sexy. His face without a smile is less attractive.

"Hi Louis. My name is Molly. Sorry I'm late."

"No worries. I have two sisters and they're always late. What'll you have?"

Louis appears to be drinking draft beer. At least he isn't on the wagon like Jack. "I'll have a glass of red." He walks over to the bar and brings back the wine.

God the wine sucks. Did he ask for the cheapest? Or maybe he doesn't have a clue.

"You're a business man, what kind of business do you do?"

"I manage a high-class exercise facility. We employ personal trainers, nutritionists, people of that sort. We open at 5:00 a.m. I'm exhausted by the evening. But never mind that. Tell me about you."

"I work at the public defender's office"

"So you defend rapists and pedophiles"?

"Everyone's entitled to a trial."

"Chill, I'm just kidding. How about more wine?"

Besides the wine, Louis returns with a tall man with a beard. "Molly, this is Alfie, he's a friend of mine." The two of them talk fantasy football. Shit. It's like I'm not here. I look up as I feel Alfie's eyes on me.

"Where did you find Molly? She's a gem."

Louis doesn't seem to know how to answer. "We're not an item," I say. "We've never met before tonight. Excuse me, I need to use the bathroom."

I want Alfie. I know nothing about him, but he's ultra sexy. Louis has a seal of approval even if it's not from Good Housekeeping. But he's not my type. And the two of them are friends. Probably run in the same circle. I take a business card out of my purse and scribble my home number on the back. I'll pass it to Alfie when I have a chance. Then I'll get the hell out of here.

When I get back to the table there's another glass of wine and Louis is gone.

Forty

"What happened to Louis?"

"Do you care?" Alfie asked.

I don't. "What do you do?" I ask.

"Personal trainer. But I'd rather talk about you. How do you know Louis? He never mentioned you."

He probably works for Louis. I don't know what to say, I can't think of a lie that will work. My mind's fuzzy. "Met him on line..."

"You don't have to be embarrassed. Everyone does it."

"I guess, but this is my first."

Alfie looks like he doesn't believe me. "Wanna dance?"

"Sure." He grabs my hand and pulls me to the floor. It doesn't take long to see he's an accomplished dancer with the muscles of a personal trainer. I used to refuse to dance. Made up excuses, but the real reason—I'm self-conscious. I'm klutzy and have no rhythm. Always feel people judge me. Smoking pot, a few lessons, and liking my body changed that. But Alfie's out of my league. Way out.

"Wow, have you done this professionally?"

"No, but thanks for the compliment. Just relax and do what I do." I focus on him and between the wine and the music I relax. We move together like we'd practiced. Every so often he puts his hands on my waist or pulls me close. His touch becomes more intimate, but it's hard to tell if it's done purposefully or it's part of his dance style.

The band takes a break. "I'm going to get us another drink."

Instead of wine, he comes back with two cocktail glasses.

"Try this."

"Delicious, what is it."

"Vodka, tonic and some other stuff."

Must have been some heavy stuff. The next few hours are a blur. Later I wonder if he put something in the drink. I end up at Alfie's place. He must have driven. His place is awfully fancy for a personal trainer. His bedroom decor is more feminine than masculine. I'm naked. I don't remember taking off my clothes. My body feels sore and ill-used. I barely remember the sex. I wake to a man's voice.

I wish I could forget the morning. I wish I could forget what he said on the phone, "Drunken slut won't wake up." I wish I could forget the bathroom filled with women's cosmetics and monogrammed towels.

"Why do you go on dating sites if you're in a relationship?" I ask.

"I don't."

Oh god it was Louis who went on dating sites not him. "Why am I here?"

"Louis wasn't interested. He's prudish. Doesn't like drunk chicks so I stepped in."

I get dressed. Once Alfie sees I'm leaving he becomes pleasant again. He tells me called me a cab and while we wait he hands me coffee. What the hell's wrong with me? Why did I leave the bar with a man I don't know? I'm filled with excruciating embarrassment as the minutes drag on.

I'm a lawyer handling a murder case. How can I be in a strange man's apartment who can't wait for me to leave? "I'll wait outside, I need some fresh air," I say.

"Here," he say as he hands me a couple $20 dollar bills, "for the cab."

I throw the money on the floor. What does he think I am—a whore? And I realize that's exactly what he thinks. And a cheap one at that.

I can't wait to get home and into bed, but I shower and wash my hair first.

I'm woken up by a loud knocking on the door. Go away. I put my head under the pillow. More knocking.

"Hold on, coming." I slide on my robe and walk to the door.

"Rose, what are you doing here?"

"What do you mean? You told me last night to come and we'd to talk about everything. How could you forget?"

"I had a bad night."

"You look like hell. And you smell like a brewery. Are you sure you're not drinking too much?"

"Of course, I'm not drinking too much. That's ridiculous. You don't know what you're talking about. Just because you can't hold more than a glass."

"Should I ask how your date went?"

"I'm not seeing him again that's for sure. I don't want to talk about it. Give me a minute to wash my face and change." I hurry into the bedroom and put on some jeans and a t-shirt. Shit. I shouldn't have forgotten about Rose. And I've got to be at the jail. I check my phone. As long as we don't talk longer than thirty minutes I'll be okay.

By the time I get to the kitchen Rose has put the dishes in the dishwasher, put the teapot on, and arranged some cheese and crackers.

"I'm sorry Rose. You don't deserve a sister like me. I had a horrible evening."

"You want to tell me about it."

"I was too embarrassed to admit it, but I decided to try internet uh dating. I signed up with Savymatchmaker. Last night was my first date."

"He was that bad? Doesn't that cost a mint to join? I thought they were supposed to check the guys out."

"They do, but I fucked up. Really fucked up." I didn't want to tell her. "I met Louis, the guy from the website, at a bar. He was nice, but after a while his gorgeous friend showed up and sat down with us. His friend, Alfie, seemed so much more my type. Anyway, I went to the bathroom and when I came back Louis was gone and Alfie, the cool guy, was there alone."

"What happened to the guy you were supposed to meet?"

"I don't know and I didn't care." I didn't want her to know why he left. I take a bite of cracker and cheese. "We didn't click and he wasn't paying any attention to me. Alfie, the guy I left with seemed like someone I'd like. Great dancer. Charmer. Turns out everything he said was a lie. He's married or has a live-in girlfriend. She must have been gone for the night."

"That's awful. What a horrible guy. I'm glad I can trust Fredo."

What can I say? She probably can trust him. I wish I wasn't so jealous.

"You're lucky. Going off with someone you don't know. He could have been a rapist or a killer or both. You of all people should know that."

"Don't be silly. I can tell if someone is evil." I finish the cheese.

"No, you can't. I know you think I'm not very smart and kind of naive, but I saw evil when I was in Africa. Some bad people are obvious, but the most evil ones are often charming on the outside."

"Rose, I don't think that. I know you're smart."

She smiles. "So if I'm smart how come I don't know what to do about my pregnancy and the wedding?"

"What do you want to do?"

"Get married soon as I can with only family and a few friends there. Nothing fancy."

"And what about Alfredo?"

"Same. He's thrilled about the baby. He told me he'd almost given up on finding a woman that wanted a family."

"Then do it. Mom will get over it. She can save her money for my shindig. Not that I can see that happening any time soon." God, I make everything about me.

"Knowing you, you'll have a new boyfriend to bring to my wedding even if its next week."

"Listen Rose, Alfredo's family loves you. You think they'll love you less if you don't have a big wedding?"

"Not because of the wedding, but because I'm pregnant."

"Alfredo adores you and they want grandchildren. Don't worry."

"What about Mom? You think she'll forgive me if I don't have a big do?"

"There's northing to forgive. Don't let her bully you. When Mom finds out she's going to have a grandkid she'll forget everything else and start arranging baby showers."

"You think so?"

"Of course. She's always whining because her sister's kids got married first, had kids first. She wants a grandkid to brag about." At least I hope so.

"I don't remember her saying that."

"You were probably in Africa." She only said it once. "Dad will support you once he realizes how much money he's going to save."

Rose is quiet for a minute. "I feel better. I'm going to call Mom soon as I pick a date. You're the best."

Finally I'm the best at something. I don't deserve Rose. But right now I want her to leave. I need a glass of wine and didn't want to deal with any shit about my drinking. When the trial's over I'll cut down.

"Rose, I gotta kick you out. I'm meeting some colleagues at the jail and I need to change clothes."

"It's Sunday?"

"Jail's open 24/7."

"I'll be on my way then." She hugs me and says good bye.

I look at the clock. Forty-five minutes to change and get over to the jail. Sarah will be waiting.

Forty-One

Dressed, twenty minutes to go. I take a last sip of and go to open the garage. Where's my car? How could someone steal it from inside the garage? Did I leave it in the driveway? I open the garage door. No car. Shit. It's on Fourth Ave, in front of BBQ. Huge ticket.

I have to get to the jail. I call Rose. After all I'm the best sister. *"You've reached Rose O'Rourke. Please leave your name and number and I'll call you back as soon as I can. Have a wonderful day."*

Lourdes and Ruth would be on their way. If I call either I'll have to explain.

Uber again. My new best friend. Today he's older than the usual driver. Smells better. Today is the second time in as many days that I wait for a ride in excruciating circumstances. Maybe I should I've called Ruth or Lourdes? Told them I had a flat tire or something. Lourdes might buy it, but not Ruth. How many lies can I get away with? The driver wants to chat.

"You a Cats fan?"

"I guess."

"Great game Saturday,"

"I guess."

"What kind of music you want to hear?"

"Whatever."

He gets the hint and shuts up. We turn onto 4th Avenue. The street is empty unlike evenings and weekday lunch hour when you fight for a parking space. It should be easy to spot my car.

"Drive around the block again," I say as we pass the spot I thought I parked in.

"Someone stole my car."

"Are you sure this is where you parked?"

"Of course." Does he think I don't even know where my car was?

"What kind of car are we looking for?"

"Silver Miata."

We drive around again.

"Did you park at a meter?"

"Yeah."

"Did you pay?"

"It was after six you don't have to pay."

"You mean the car was here since last night?"

"Yeah."

"It's towed. Meters start up again at 8 a.m. The cops are tough in this area."

Shit, shit, shit. "Do you know where it is?"

"No. Tucson Towing is who the cops call. I don't know where the lot is. Cost you a mint."

"Can you wait while I make a call?"

"I guess," he smirks.

I try Rose again and she answers. I explain.

"I'll call Fredo and get back to you." I wait impatiently. This is going to cost me. I'll never get to the jail on time. I've probably ruined my career.

The driver gestures impatiently. Finally Rose calls. "It's towed. Get there as soon as you can because the fees mount up." She gives me the address of the tow yard. "Fredo said you'll need your driver's license and to call him if you have any problems."

I give the Uber guy the address and agree on his exorbitant fee. Like I have a choice. This time he doesn't talk.

I don't know what to do about Lourdes and Ruth. I'll never get to the jail before they leave. I can't face them. I decide to leave a message. They can't take their phones into the jail so they won't answer. I leave identical message. "*Had an emergency. I'll talk to you later. Sorry.*"

The tow lot is on the outskirts of town. It's filled with cars of all sorts, but mostly older, beat-up ones. I don't see mine. The Uber guy drops me at a small office that has a line reminiscent of Black Friday but it looks like no one's getting a bargain. Why isn't there more than one person assisting people? They have three service windows. The good news is every other person is sent away because they don't have a license or money. The minutes tick by.

"That'll be $260 and your John Hancock on the paper," says the guy at the window his smile and minty breath a surprise. I read the document which relieves them of liability if my car's damaged, if anything inside is stolen, or if there's a zombie attack.

"I can't sign this until I see the car."

"Fine. Don't sign it. Have a seat over there (he points to a group of people sitting in chairs in a corner). We'll bring your car down and you can inspect it. It will take awhile." The same few people had been sitting there when I walked in.

I sign.

My Miata's safe. A cursory search doesn't reveal any damage except dirt and dust. I rush to the jail in what I know is a futile attempt. It's too late. They're long gone. I go home.

I've barely opened the front door when my cell rings. Shit.

"Where the hell were you?" Lourdes says her voice cold.

"I had an emergency."

"So you said. What kind of emergency that you couldn't contact us? This was important. Sarah's trial's in a couple weeks. Don't you care?"

"Of course I care. I'm embarrassed, but my car got towed and by the time I picked it up. . ."

Lourdes is quiet for a moment. "My guess is you were drinking and left your car somewhere."

Now I'm quiet. I want to lie, but why else would my car have been towed? Who was she to lecture me. She drinks as much I do.

"Molly, are you there?"

"Yeah. Okay, you're right. I left my car. I didn't want to get a DUI." I didn't want to tell her about Louis or Alfie.

"I thought you were with your sister and her fiancé last night."

I could hear my mom, 'Oh what a tangled web you weave, when you practice to deceive,' a quote she attributed to my grandmother, but when I got older I learned some famous guy said it or something close to it. I wish I'd listened. "I was, but I went out later."

"You're supposed to be lead counsel. Sarah's innocent and deserves a good defense."

"I'm sorry. You're right. I fucked up. What can I do?"

"For starters go see Sarah. Stop at my place first and I'll bring you up to speed."

"Okay see you in a few."

How could I fuck up so badly? I'd trashed the PD's from the second I'd been hired, but I'd been wrong. The lawyers are smart, friendly and fun. They have my back. So what if my office is a tiny cubicle with old furniture. So what if some of the clients are smelly, guilty losers. Some are innocent, overcharged or never had a break. What I do here matters. I help people. Keep them out of prison.

At BARF I had great furniture, but all I learned was how to create large legal bills. Nobody had my back. The constant competition to see who made partner ruled out friendships and camaraderie.

Lourdes is one of the most decent people I've ever met. I value her friendship and I've probably've ruined any chance of continuing it.

And Jack and Carl. Why wasn't I satisfied with one? Probably half the place think I'm a bitch or a slut. Jack's a genuinely good man. Maybe not for me, but if I wanted to end it why didn't I just tell him the truth. Even after everything I've done, he offered to help me with AA. I don't need it but it was kind of him. Carl, I'm still not sure.

When I get to Lourdes' she's business-like and to the point.

"We got the medical records."

"Sunday?"

"No yesterday's mail. The good news, for us, is she had four trips to the ER in the last couple years. One admission for a head injury. When her husband was in the room she said she fell. In the doctors notes it says her injuries weren't consistent with a fall. Her husband rarely left her alone, but one time when he was out of the room for a minute she told one of the nurses that he'd beat her and it wasn't the first time. Admitted she was terrified of him. Good stuff if we can get it in. We can talk about that tomorrow."

"Does Sarah know?"

"Yeah we gave her a copy. Here's yours." For the next several minutes we discussed their visit to the jail. I get up to leave.

"Molly, there's something else we need to talk about."

I don't want to hear it. "I like you a lot and I think you're a good person, but you drink too much. We both do. I realize I have to cut down. I'm not going to have another drink until after the trial."

Half of me is seconds from tears and the other half hates her.

I mumble something and walk out the door. I hurry to the car and start to sob.

Forty-Two

I dry my eyes. Head to Starbucks. My face is puffy. I need something sweet and wet. After some indecision I choose a creme brulee latte and an orange-cranberry scone. Starbucks knows how to market what is basically coffee, milk and spices. I scarf down the scone as if I haven't eaten in days. As I sip the latte I outline a game plan for my meeting with Sarah. I feel better and am almost ready to go when I feel a presence behind me.

"I don't know if you remember me. Anne Levy, I used to work at the PD." She smiles at me.

"Of course, I inherited some of your cases." Who can forget St. Anne?

"Listen, um, this is hard to ask, I heard Sophie Mercer died, is that true?"

"Yeah, a couple weeks ago. How did you know her?"

"I covered arraignments the day she was on the docket. Hard to forget a young woman in a wheelchair. Later Paul Terrazas told me about her. I've never known anyone that young who died of cancer."

"Me either."

"What happened with her case? The county attorney's office was being typically unreasonable when I left."

"I worked out a deal to get her cases dismissed."

"That's great. Congratulations."

"I lucked out. A new prosecutor, Julianna Dawson, took over her cases from Eric Smithfield who as you know is a major jerk."

"He sure is. I only met Julianna once. She was doing division coverage. I'm glad to hear she remained decent. I don't want to hold you up. Looks like you're about to go."

"On my way to the jail."

"Sundays at the jail. Can't say I miss those. Here's my card. Give me a call and let's have lunch."

I fumble in my purse, found mine, hand it to her. "I'd love to, but I start a murder trial in a couple weeks." I say this with pride.

"No worries. I remember what that's like. Give me a call when you're done."

Lunch with St. Anne. Was I wrong about her too? I figured she'd be stuck up and full of herself.

The drive to the jail takes only a few minutes. "Hi Molly. The whole crowd's been here today. Don't you people ever take a day off?" Mary asks.

"Don't you?"

She smiles and waves me through. Maybe the crowd had been here, but the attorney booths are empty and Sarah appears in minutes.

"What are you doing here now? You missed our meeting," Sarah says. "I don't feel like talking to you."

"I can understand that. I'm sorry." Another sorry, but this time it's me. "Please sit and let me explain."

"Please and sorry. Wow. Go ahead and make something up."

"I'm not going to make anything up."

"I lived with a bullshitter."

"Just have a seat and listen. You can leave if you don't believe me."

"It's not like I have much else to do." Sarah sits her arms folded across her chest, her eyes on everything but me.

"I arranged a date with a guy I met through the internet. I'd never done that before so I met him at a bar. Wanted a public place. I drove my car there so I could leave if he was creepy."

"I thought you were with that lawyer, Jack Clarke?"

The jail grapevine.

"Not any more. We broke up."

"Did he dump you?"

Should I answer? Should I answer truthfully? "As a matter of fact he did."

"Why?"

"I'm not going to answer that."

Sarah says nothing for a few moments and then, "Finish your story."

"I had a couple beers with the guy and a friend of his showed up. His friend was gorgeous. I liked him better than the guy I went to meet. I left the bar with the second guy. We went to his place. I left my car parked in front of the bar. When I went to pick up it up today, it'd been towed. By the time I found out where cars get towed and finished all the forms and paid it was too late to get here on time."

"How much did that cost?"

"$260.00 to get it out, a parking ticket and cab fare to get down there."

"Well, at least you got a new guy."

"That didn't work out either."

She said nothing for a time. "Okay I believe you. I doubt you'd tell a story like that about yourself if it wasn't true."

Sarah and I spend about an hour talking about the issues that Lourdes and Ruth hadn't covered.

I put my files together to leave when Sarah says, "You and Lourdes aren't much different in age from me, but our lives our so different. You two are so stylish and smart with great futures. I'm a mess, fat, can't do my hair. I only have a GED and I'm probably looking at lots of prison time." I start to protest, but she won't let me. "Even before I was in prison, I never had my act together. I chose a terrible man who treated me like crap and stayed with him for years. I lost jobs cuz of him. I had no friends cuz of him." She stops talking, on the verge of tears.

I'm not sure what to say. I want to make her feel better. "It might look that way but we all have problems. My personal life's a mess." I start to tell her the last three men in my life dumped me, but decide that's going too far. "I was engaged once, but we called it off. I told you about Jack. How great could life be, if I'm looking for guys on the internet?" If I tell her about losing my job at BARF, I'd have to tell her how I wound up at to the PD. I thought further back.

"When I was in high school the kids called me the Molly Green Giant. I didn't have a clue about anything. All the cool girls were petite and curvy. I was tall and angular, but copied how they acted, dressed, everything. On me it was all wrong. I didn't get my life together until I spent a summer with my aunt who taught me to dress and helped me feel better about myself."

"I wish I had an aunt like that. There were four of us, three girls. My parents worked all the time. My brother was the family favorite. I used to be thinner, but it's hard here with all the rice, beans and potatoes they serve."

"It's obvious you're smart Sarah. Not many people can figure out as much as you have. When the trial is over, if it works out, you should go to college."

"I'm afraid to even think I might get out. It's like jinxing the outcome."

I let out my breath. I was still her lawyer. "Lourdes tells me you're adamant about testifying . . ."

"That was the biggest mistake Terrazas made. I wanted to and he talked me out of it." Sarah interrupts.

"Terrazas wasn't wrong about everything. There are downsides when you take the stand. I rarely let my clients testify." I've hardly had enough trials to make my statement credible, but I'm relying on my colleagues.

"What downsides? I don't have any prior convictions."

I'd always imagined having a well-informed client would make my job easier, but as they say a little knowledge can be a bad thing. Don't they say something like that? Whoever they were. She was right that if you had a felony prior the prosecutor could ask you about if, if you took the stand.

"'You lied to the police. That will likely by the first thing they ask you about. They can argue if you lied before how can anyone believe what you say now?"

"They lied when they questioned me. I can explain everything."

"Okay, let's go through some cross and you'll see what I mean."

I spend a half hour going over cross. She did a decent job. Maybe she's the one client we should put on. Lourdes and I will have to talk more about that. We don't have to decide till the state puts on their case. As I walk out, I feel I'd made headway on our relationship. I want to win the trial for her.

On the way home from the jail I make a mental list of how I need to change my life. Stop drinking. Not after the trial. Now. Spend all my time preparing. No more internet dating. Cancel lunch with Ted and Brandon. Goodby Savymatchmaker. $350 down the drain. But think of all I could save on booze. I can live life without a man. Apologize to Lourdes. Show her she could depend on me. After the trial I'd get that dog.

And Rose, I need to be the sister she thinks I am. Somehow I have to lose the jealousy over Fredo. Concentrate on being helpful during her pregnancy and being a good aunt. Like Aunt Margaret was to me.

At home I empty all the bottles and put them in the recycle. I google alcoholism. Quiz: How to find out if you have a drinking problem:

1. Have you ever had legal trouble due to drinking such as being stopped for a DUI? No.
2. Do you spend a lot of money on alcohol? Not a lot, some.
3. Do you need a few drinks to face certain people or situations? No.
4. Are you ever late for work, school or other functions due to being drunk or hungover? Yes, I guess.
5. Do you ever suffer from loss of memory or blackout from alcohol? No. Maybe.
6. Have your ever lied or found you needed to lie about drinking. Ummm Maybe?
7. Have your family mentioned they are concerned about your drinking? Mom, Rose, Jack, Lourdes shit.

Why waste time on Google? I wouldn't diagnose a disease this way. I push the red dot and it goes away.

It's still early. I call Lourdes.

"I just got back from the jail. Everything went well. Sarah was angry at first, but I was there almost two hours and we worked it out."

"Good."

"Also I want to apologize. You're right. I drink too much and I'm going to stop. Now. No more wine when we go out. I'm going to work as hard as I can on Sarah's case." Tears fill my eyes. "I've never thanked you . . . for all … you've … done . . . ."

"Molly stop crying. I accept your apology. You don't have to say more."

"No, I have to. Your friendship has meant so much and I don't want to lose you."

"I'm sorry. Who I am to judge you. I drink too much, too. And your friendship's just as important to me. I haven't been close to anyone since Debby moved to Phoenix." Lourdes sounds like she's in tears too.

"You stop crying. You were right."

"We can stop together. People exercise together, diet together, we can be sober together."

Forty-Three

It's a good thing my metabolism hasn't slowed. I fill the house with chocolate chip cookies, powdered sugar doughnuts, all sorts of candy bars and bottles of Starbucks coffee drinks. When I feel like wine, I grab a cookie, a candy bar and a sweet drink.

Lourdes and I stick to our bargain. We don't order drinks when we go out to dinner nor does she serve wine when we eat at her house. She never asks if I have stopped drinking, but sometimes mentions she'd like a drink.

Rose starts to crave sweets. Snickerdoodle cookies, Ben and Jerry's Chunky Monkey. Not pickles. As I predicted Mom and Dad are on board once Rose announces they will be grandparents. Fredo works any overtime he can to make sure Rose can stay home with the baby as long as she wants. The wedding's scheduled right after Sarah's trial. No food trucks.

On nights she's alone, Rose comes by and bring treats. When she's not too tired, it's homemade. She reads books about pregnancy and motherhood while I work on Sarah's case. She worries that her doc will tell her to cut down on sweets, but so far it hasn't happened.

I never told Rose I'd stopped drinking, but she seems to know. Maybe it's obvious since the fridge isn't filled with wine and I don't have a glass in my hand all the time. She spends lots of time with me. When I'm restless, she tries to distract me. Asks my advice about something. Talks me into going to the store to buy baby stuff. I don't really give a shit what she buys and I thinks she knows, but she still asks, "Molly, tell me which ones you like best."

I work hard. I read and reread every police report, witness statement, every case that's relevant. I role-play cross examination with Rose playing the witness, but she's so damn kind at heart. I'd explain she's role-playing a prosecution witness and not to volunteer anything that will help me, but she can't drop her persona of sisterhood. I write and practice, and then rewrite my opening and closing. Lourdes will likely do one or the other, but I want to be ready.

I feel good. Wake up without a headache, alone in my bed, not with someone I barely know. Dinner with Lourdes is as fun without alcohol. I know after the trial I'll want to date again, but I feel strong knowing I don't need to. Jack treats me like a colleague again. We might even be friends. Carl ignores me, but it no longer hurts as much. No drama is good.

Then Walter Paterson, a classmate of mine, who works at a large Phoenix firm calls. "I'm coming to Tucson to argue a motion next Wednesday. Any chance we can meet for lunch? On me."

"Sure but I'm getting ready for a murder trial so it'll have to be quick." I hear the pride in my voice. Murder trial.

"Perfect, I need to get back to Phoenix as early as I can." We make plans to meet near the courthouse at an upscale hamburger joint.

Walter and I had sat next to each other first year. Most profs had seating charts arranged alphabetically which meant O'Rourke and Patterson were seat mates. Under different circumstances we may not have been friends, but first year angst creates strange bedfellows. Between classes and study group we spent many hours together. Walter started law school at age thirty after a stint in the Marines. He married his high school sweetheart. He'd known her since first grade. Did that mean she was his elementary school sweetheart? Jennifer, a stay-at-home mom, invited our study group over often for much-appreciated home cooked meals. She wasn't the jealous type and seemed delighted that Walter had a study group. I was single, a liberal Democrat and Walter, a married conservative Republican but these distinctions didn't matter.

I graduated in the top 15%, but Walter was a star. He was on Law Review. Graduated in the top 2% and won writing and speaking competitions. After graduation he clerked for an Arizona Supreme Court Justice and the following year for a Ninth Circuit Court Judge.

We tried to maintain a friendship after graduation, but we no longer had much to share. After I lost my job, Walter emailed to express his concern, but I was embarrassed and ignored him. Thought maybe he was mocking me. Why did he want to meet? Odd, but I was to busy to think about it.

Days pass. I've never worked so hard. Ideally, Lourdes and I, and even Ruth would sit in at all the interviews, at least the important ones. Because we had so little time we split them. Lourdes and I took the key witnesses. In typical prosecutor fashion, Smithfield filed a motion to deny us interviews on the grounds that Terrazas had interviewed the witnesses in the previous trial. This was a decision in which a judge could go either way and not get reversed. Quinn denied the motion. So far she had lived up to my expectations. A ruling on the use of medical records was the next hurdle.

I'd sent the records to the CA. He immediately filed a motion to preclude the use of the records at trial. His motion wasn't unexpected, but I thought he'd offer a plea after he'd read them. Sarah was adamant she wouldn't plead, but clients sometimes change their minds. She might be willing to do a year or two more if she was guaranteed release. But nothing. Why did we have to deal with one of the most hard-lines prosecutor in the office?

Lourdes and I were still unclear whether Sarah would testify. I thought she should.

As the trial date gets closer I feel more and more scared. There's so much to do. We'll never finish it all. We decide that whoever interviewed the witness would do the cross-examination. As first chair I have more responsibility and am in charge of the expert witnesses. We hire Dr. Adelstein, an expert in battered women's syndrome. Dr. Wellman, the state's expert/whore is going to testify that battered wives syndrome is a sham diagnosis, and even if you believe in it, Sarah didn't fit the criteria. I'd have to do the cross on him. To carry this off, I have to become an expert in battered women's syndrome. I'd never taken a psychology class in college.

Dr. Wellman has testified numerous times in Arizona and California almost always for the prosecution. I can show his bias, but after reading several trial transcripts including the previous Warren trial I can tell he's a believable witness. Doesn't talk down to the jury or mock the defense attorney, answers questions clearly. When I interview him I find him good looking in a fatherly, not a sleazy, way. How can I discredit him other than showing he's a whore for the prosecution? I can't undermine his credentials. But his denial of battered women's syndrome is out of line with most of his younger colleagues. Dr. Adelstein can help me with that.

Wellman's other Achilles heel is laziness. He didn't read newer articles about battered women's syndrome. His excuse was 'why read about something you don't believe in.' I can make him look less credible, but it means I'll have to do a lot of reading myself.

Dr. Adelstein hadn't testified in the previous trial. The expert Terrazas used was a defense whore and a jerk. Young. Full of himself. He made his living testifying. Charged public defenders less so testified often. Dr. Adelstein is young, attractive and hasn't testified before. She's a recent hire in the psychology department at the University who believes Sarah's innocent. I hope her work ethic and belief in Sarah will trump her lack of experience. At first Lourdes is dubious, but I win her over. I hope I'm right.

Always a sound sleeper, I've started to wake up every couple hours drenched in sweat. I dream I'm in the courtroom in my pajamas. I dream a witness I've never seen before takes the stand. Worse, I dream Sarah's found guilty.

I almost forgot about lunch with Walter. He calls again and suggests the restaurant in the Marriott, but I insist we go to the up-scale burger joint we'd agreed on. I can't waste time.

He's at the table when I arrive even though I'm early. Walter has always been fit and reasonably attractive, but now he smells of success. He looks hot with his expensive hair-cut and well-tailored suit and it's clear he's a man on the way up. I wonder if he cheats on his wife. I hope not. Jennifer's special.

"Made partner last year and I'm head litigator on a class action against an international drug company. Fascinating case."

"That's great. Congratulations. How's the home life?" I want to steer the conversation away from me.

"Three kids, youngest six."

"I remember when you and Jennifer talked about having a dozen."

"That's before we had one. Jennifer wants to go back to school. Nursing. You and Derrick ever get married?"

"No, we broke up after I lost my job. He moved to Seattle."

"I always thought he was a jerk."

I signal the waitress for more iced-tea. Had everyone thought Derrick was a jerk?

"How do you like being a public defender? I was shocked when I heard. You never struck me as the type."

"I'm trying my first murder case in two weeks. First chair. It's scary. This is the second trial. First was overturned for ineffective assistance. She killed her husband in self-defense"

"You sound like a defense attorney."

Both of us take a few minutes to eat. I'd ordered a burger and fries and Walter, always disciplined, a salad. "I'd like to hear about your case, but we don't have much time, so let me get down to it. I didn't ask you to lunch to chat. I've been checking you out. Your bosses at BARF gave you excellent recommenda-tions. Between your stint there and your trial experience, you have a lot to recommend you. If you're interested, we'd like to have you interview with us."

Are you fucking kidding me? Now. "Well, this is a surprise. I don't know what to say."

"Molly dumbstruck. That alone's worth the trip and cost of a meal. This isn't a guaranteed partnership offer, but we'd put you on an expedited partnership track. The starting salary is more than twice what you're making now." How does he know what I make? "We have our ways," he answers my unspoken question.

"Tell me more," I say in an effort to give myself time to think.

Walter continues to fill me in although I not sure I take much in.

When the waitperson put down the check, I ask. "You sound like this is a done deal if I say yes. When you first mentioned the job you said interview."

"As far as I'm concerned if you want the job, it's yours. My partners will have a say, but when one of us vouches for someone it's rare to have one of the others nix it. Unless you have a secret life, trouble with the bar or are about to get indicted. . ." he chuckles.

He grabs the check. "We have expense accounts. 'Another perk.' Any per-sonal reason you couldn't move to Phoenix —a husband with tenure at the U or one who's a rabid Cats fan?"

Now I chuckle. "I'm single and no serious significant other. How long do I have to decide? I have to try this case. Even if I wanted out, which I don't, the judge would never let me withdraw. I expect the trial will take two weeks. It starts a week from Monday. If we lose," it hurt saying that out loud, "I'll have to be down here for sentencing."

"No problem. You can always come to Tucson if you have a hearing. It's only two hours away. We need you soon, but I think two months notice to the PD would be fair. We want to know your answer soon, because if you're not interested we need to find someone else." He pays the check and we both get up.

"Let's say two weeks. If you can't say yes by then you're probably the wrong person anyway."

Forty-Four

A job offer at Kavanagh, Cather. Salary in the six figures, a partnership in a few years and no money worries ever. No matter how long I worked here it I'll be a miracle if I make $80,000. I grab the bar directory and look up the firm. None of the lawyers had any reason to blackball me and a few had been friends in law school. I'd never slept with any of them.

Kavanagh, Cather's address is on the 44th floor of the Territorial Bank Building in downtown Phoenix. I imagine a large office with a window, new furniture, classy rugs. No Salvation Army rejects. My own secretary and paralegal. Fancy lunches and firm dinners. 'Lots of drinking' a small voice murmurs in my head. There's always club soda. But you have to be strong. It's one thing to say no to a draft beer or cheap wine at a PD party, but $100 bottles of the best wine or blood orange martinis. My mouth waters. I can almost taste them. I need advice, but who? Rose would listen and tell me to follow my heart. Mom would tell me to take the job at the civil firm where I'd make a big impact on the world and she'd no longer have to tell her friends I'm a PD. Dad would tell me to follow the money. Lourdes would—I don't know. In her mind she'd say stay here, but might not say it out loud.

The afternoon passes slowly. It's hard to concentrate. Lourdes is busy with her gangbanger case. It wouldn't be fair to bother her. I call Mom.

"Mom, I've got some good news."

"More good news. Can't believe I'm going to be a grandma. Your room will make a great nursery for the baby."

"My room, why not Rose's room."

"Rose will be a married woman. She and Alfredo need their own room when they visit."

"Where do I sleep? On the kitchen floor?"

"Don't be such a drama queen. I'm going to get a new sofa for the Arizona room. One that opens up into a bed. It's a lovely room. Looks out to the back yard." She could drive me to drink. "So what's your news? Are you engaged too. You and your husband will need. . ."

I interrupt. "No, I'm not engaged." Trust Mom to put a damper on things. "I got a job offer at a fancy firm in Phoenix. More than double the salary I'm making now. Good chance to get a partnership."

"That's great, honey. I can't wait to tell your dad. And you'll be moving here. I'll get to decorate another house."

"I haven't decided to take the job."

"What's to decide? You never planned on making a career of the public defender."

I get off the phone. Plead work. I feel deflated. Mom seems happier about my salary and a chance to decorate than understanding what an offer like this means. It wasn't as great as having a husband in her eyes.

The afternoon passes slowly. I decide to go to the jail and visit a few new clients and Sarah. Even while you prepare for a murder trial you have other clients who need your attention. A typical case load might be as many as forty or more depending on how many serious or complex cases you have. Some things could wait, but not motions to get people released from jail, not discussions with clients about plea offers while they are still open, and not hearings. On the other hand, if I was going to Kavanagh, Cather my cases would be reassigned. I had files and purse in hand when Lisa walked into my office.

"Molly, you won't believe what I just found out. To be honest Juan found out. He was on one of his gossip-finding missions and went to chat with Double E."

"I didn't realize you could go uninvited unless you're one of her admirers and I didn't think he was."

"Juan can put on the charm when he needs to. And her door was open for a change."

"They were shooting the shit and she got a call. Acted very secretive. She wanted him to leave, but he pretended not to take the hint. She has an appointment with a real estate agent and he put two and two together."

"I'm not sure I get it."

"She has a lovely house in the foothills. Why would she be looking for a different house unless she's going to move?"

Lisa loves to tell stories especially if they're juicy. She also can take a long time to get to the point the same way she took forever to order a meal. "So get to it already."

"She's leaving. Took a job with a firm in San Diego."

"What kind of job?"

"Civil litigation with a big salary is all Juan found out."

"Didn't she move from California because her husband had a job here?"

"Yeah, but rumor has it the husband is history."

"I'm shocked but not sure about which."

"She told Juan not to tell anyone till she announces it, but everyone will know by tomorrow. Can't keep something that great to yourself."

I need time to digest this. "It looks like you're on the way somewhere but I had to tell you." Lisa says. "She never had the stomach to work here. She'll be much happier around a bunch of snobs who think lawyering's about writing contracts and billable hours."

I weigh the pros and cons of the job offer as I drive to the jail. Never have to come here again.

For once Mary isn't at the front desk. I'll miss her. When I get to the attorney booths I hear Jack and Kelly Wendell, a private lawyer complaining about some judge or another. "Have you heard about Elan," I ask Jack when Kelly's client is brought down.

"What are you talking about?" he says? I repeat what Lisa told me.

"Great day for the office. I'm surprised she hung around as long as she did."

We spend a few minutes speculating about possible new bosses. Jack naturally thinks Anne would be perfect. Then he changes the subject. "I want to show you something." He puts his hand in his pocket, rummages around and pulls out an object I recognize as an AA token. "Six years clean."

"Congratulations."

"I don't know where I'd be without AA. My sponsor saved my life more than once. When I was in trial once I skipped our dinner. Wrong. That's when I needed it most."

Again with AA. I have a feeling Jack is trying to tell me I need AA. I've stopped drinking. I don't need AA. I don't need a sponsor. I have everything under control. I'm not an alcoholic. Jack's client finally walks into visitation which ends our conversation. A few minutes later Sarah arrives.

I had planned a short visit to go over loose ends. I've seen Sarah almost daily over the past weeks. Sarah verifies her mom had sent a couple dresses to the PD's office. Except during trial, in-custody defendants have to wear ugly orange jumpsuits. Clothes for trial can't be sent directly to the jail. They go first to the PD's office. Then someone from the PD's office has to bring them to the jail to be checked for contraband before they're given to the defendant. Big waste of time.

A client's appearance matters. A hair-cut, shave, and a professional outfit can make a difference to a jury. So does hiding tattoos and piercing. Many jurors have this idea they can tell if someone is guilty by the way the person looks. They are dead wrong.

Sarah is one of the few clients who doesn't need to be dressed up. The out-fits her mother sent make her look like your maiden aunt or introverted sister. Someone you wouldn't think belongs in jail.

I'm about to leave when Sarah says, "I appreciate everything you've done. I know you've worked very hard. Thank you, whatever happens." No BARF client had ever thanked me. How could they? I rarely saw them. Just worked on their contracts and other documents.

I'd planned to see two other clients, but I'm too antsy. Sarah's praise makes me feel proud, but is that enough reason to turn the job offer down?

Forty-Five

As I reach the parking lot, I get a text from Lourdes: *Quick dinner. Rosa's 6:30?*

I hit reply. *See you there.*

I beat Lourdes and order a cheese crisp. A few minutes later she arrives. We both order chicken chimichangas with green salsa and iced tea. I want a beer, but I know I'm not allowed.

"Did you hear the great news about Double E?"

"I did, but you were in trial all day. How'd you find out?"

"A few people were still at work, when I got back to the office. Mostly celebrating. I haven't seen the office so happy since we got our last raise —a very long time ago."

And that's not about to change. "I saw Sarah today. Her mother sent some trial clothes."

"Terrific. One less thing to worry about."

"It was a strange visit. Instead of the usual hard time Sarah gives me, she thanked me. I was shocked."

"Molly, you're an excellent lawyer. You've got to stop second-guessing yourself and talking about leaving. You haven't been here that long, but you've got what it takes." Wait till she hears I might leave.

The waiter brings our food and we dig in.

"Lourdes I have something to tell you."

"You have a new boyfriend?"

"No."

"I'd be surprised if you did. You've spent every minute the last several weeks on this case as far as I can tell. Let me think. You got a dog."

"No, not that either."

"I give up…"

"I was offered a job in Phoenix today. Kavanagh, Cather."

"Prestigious firm. Probably a huge salary."

"Over double what I make now and two years to partnership."

"I don't know what to say." Her voice seems cold.

"They gave me two weeks to decide."

"It's a good opportunity if making money's your main purpose in life."

For a few moments neither of us speaks. I look at my chicken chimichanga like it will tell me what to do. Lourdes is angry. I can tell even if she tries not to show it. She thinks I'll take the job. Who's she to be angry because I have a great chance. Maybe she's jealous. She's always worked here and probably always will.

"I wonder who our new boss will be?" Lourdes says. "They always searched nationwide, then picked from within the office until Double E. No one could believe someone with her lack of criminal experience got hired."

"Who's they?" I ask glad the topic isn't me.

"The usual hiring committee. Defense lawyers, a law professor, some prominent community folks. They decide who gets interviewed, usually five to ten lawyers depending on the size and strength of the list and narrow it to three. Then the County Manager picks."

"Double E probably knew exactly how to play it. Blow job."

Lourdes bursts out laughing and chokes on her food. When she regains her breath she says. "I don't think she and Tom have been married very long. At least they don't have kids."

Sweet Lourdes. She's worried about the personal part of Double E's divorce. I doubt anyone else will. Rose will probably pray for them. "How's the trial?"

"Almost done. The prosecutor hates my client, the judge hates my client, the jury hates my client. Even after he put on a decent shirt and tie, the tats on his neck and hands show. He glares at prosecution witnesses. A couple times he shouted out, 'fucking liar.' The judge has threatened twice to kick him out of the courtroom. Yelled at me for not controlling my client. Like he'd listen to me."

"Kick him out? Doesn't a defendant have the right to be present?"

"Yeah, but if he's disruptive enough, there's case law allowing it. They'd have to put him in a room where he could hear the testimony. Judge Sinclair won't do it. He's terrified of being reversed."

"I don't understand why they're so gutless. So they get reversed. It's not like they'd lose their job or get a cut in pay."

"I don't get it either," Lourdes says. "I guess that's one of the reasons I've never wanted to be a judge. There are more."

I lie. "I've never given it much thought." I'd like to be a judge but I didn't think I'd have a chance. At least not yet. I'm not even sure what the criteria are other than you had to be in practice five years. I know there's some kind of application process and that the governor ultimately decides. Since the governor and I are in opposite political parties I probably wouldn't have a chance. Lourdes has been talking about her case. I need to act interested.

"My closing argument is a combination of a meaner, higher up gangbanger from Phoenix is the killer and the *victim* deserved to die."

"I won't ask how you think that will go."

Lourdes stands up. "I need to go. Still lots of work to do."

"It's Friday night. You have all weekend."

"I'm in no mood to hang out. I'm really tired. I need sleep."

"Fine," I say. I slide the bill towards me.

She grabs it. "On me." I try to argue, she insists. Like this is our last meal together and she's going to pay. No debts between us. We usually took turns after joking around. No joking today. She doesn't want to invest more time on me. She thinks I'm joining the Phoenix firm. Aren't I?

I'm not ready to go home. Why not a latte or macchiato? I drive two blocks to the nearest Starbucks. In the middle of the store a barista stands behind a table covered with glasses of white wine. Wine at Starbucks?

"Good evening, Would you like a glass of wine? Chablis, or Pino Grigio?" the barista asks. She must have noted my confusion. "It's new. Only in a few Starbucks. We're featuring glasses of wine and we have a dinner menu."

"No, thank you." I walk to the counter and order a latte, classic coffeecake and sit down at a small table. I sip my latte and nibble at the cake. I can't stop looking at the wine. I need to leave. *Drink me. Drink me.* My brain urges me to get the hell out, but my legs aren't moving.

I shouldn't drink. I need to be clear headed. I can't let Sarah down. I can't let Lourdes down. What do I owe Lourdes? She wasn't happy for me. What's the worst that can happen? I'd drink one glass of wine and go home. I have no alcohol there.

It's Friday night. No work tomorrow. Everyone else's out drinking, having fun.

I take a glass of Pino. I don't remember getting up. I go back to my table. I sip it and finish the cake. I feel better. I get another glass. I want a third, but what would the barista think? What do I care?

I feel better than I have in days, maybe weeks. A few stores down from the Starbucks is a Walgreen's. I walk over, pick up a bottle of Pino and drive home.

I throw off my work clothes and slip into my favorite sleep shirt. I check the TV. USA has a twenty-four hour marathon of *Law and Order*. If I stop now, everything will be fine. No one would know I had a couple drinks. I'm not an alcoholic if I buy a bottle and don't open it. Just the opposite. In the kitchen I rummage through the cabinet and find a box of Mrs. Fields chocolate chip cookies. I eat cookies, watch the show and check the time. I've gone five minutes and haven't opened the bottle. The phone chimes. Rose's name appears.

"Hi, Whats' up?"

"Nothing. Just watching TV?"

"Want some company?"

"I'm almost ready for bed. I'm exhausted. I've been, working my ass off to get ready for Sarah's trial."

"I never realized lawyers worked that hard."

"Me either. Anything new with Alfredo, the baby?"

"I'm having my first prenatal check-up next week. I've got this book that tells you how big the baby is almost from the moment of conception . . ."

I zone out. I walk into the kitchen and stare at the wine. Even the label's enticing. Colorful, beckoning you. *Drink me.* Come on, no one will know.

I open the bottle and pour myself a drink, and another . . .

Someone's at the door. What the hell.

"Hold on, I'll be right there." I run into the bathroom and hug the toilet as tonite's dinner tumbles out. I need to answer to the door. Again I hug the toilet, but this time only bile. I'm sweating, my head's pounding.

"Molly, where are you? Are you okay?"

Oh shit Rose. How'd she get in? The spare key? I don't want a lecture. I feel like shit.

I walk out of the bathroom.

Rose puts her arm around me. "Come on Molly. You need to go to bed." I follow her. Of course my bed's not made. She says nothing. Lays me down gently and takes off my slippers. My sleep shirt's covered in vomit. Gently she pulls it off. Goes to my dresser and finds a clean one. Later I learn she washes the pukey one along with my other dirty clothes.

Oh god. Now she knows I'm a drunk.

Forty-Six

"Morning Molly. Breakfast in ten."

Why's Rose here? The thought of food makes me feel sick. I get up and walk into the bathroom, wash my face and brush my teeth without looking in the mirror. My mouth tastes sour. I grab a robe and wander into the kitchen.

"Rose, what are you doing here?"

"Making breakfast."

"I can see that, but why?"

"We were on the phone. The next thing I know you weren't there. Your phone was on, but you wouldn't talk to me. I figured maybe you fell asleep. You said you were so tired. I tried to call back later, but you didn't answer. The line was busy." She hands me a plate with french toast and fruit.

"I'm not hungry."

"Eat what you can." I cut a small piece of French toast, pour on syrup, and take a bite. And another. I don't know what to say. Last night's coming back. The wine at Starbucks. The bottle. We both sit in silence and eat. I wait for Rose to start the lecture. I imagine her calling Dr. Laura. "My sister is a successful lawyer, but she drinks too much. How can I help her stop?"

"I'm sorry. I was exhausted. I should've called you back." Could I bluff it? More bullshit. "It's my first murder case. I want to do a good job."

"I waited awhile but I was worried so I came over. When I got here you were puking your guts out. Almost passed out over the toilet. I'm worried about you."

"I can take care of myself. I drank a little too much, maybe I got some food poisoning from the Mexican food I ate last night." I doubt she'll believe that one.

I get up and pour myself another cup of coffee.

"Are the wedding plans final yet?" I try to distract her.

"Two weeks from Saturday."

"How's the pregnancy going?"

"Talking about my pregnancy seemed to put you to sleep last night."

"I was tired Rose. I'd love to hear about it." I sip my coffee. I'd love to hear anything except that I should stop drinking.

"Nothing much to say except so far so good. Fredo's going to make a wonderful father." She pats her stomach.

"I got a great job offer." Should have told her earlier. Alcoholics aren't offered fabulous jobs. "A big firm in Phoenix. Excellent salary and short track to partnership."

"Congratulations I guess. You'd move?"

"Yeah."

"I'd never tell you not to do something that's best for you, but its been great living close to you, seeing you often. I thought you'd be my baby's special aunt. Like Aunt Margaret was to us."

"I haven't decided whether to take the job. Phoenix isn't that far. I'd still be close to you and the baby."

"What's good besides the salary?"

"It's a prestigious firm. Being a partner is the pinnacle of achievement in the law world." That won't impress Rose.

"Do you want to move to Phoenix?"

"Mom and Dad would be happy."

"You're right. That's one downside." Without a husband Mom might not be so happy.

Rose stands and starts to clear the table.

"Don't do that. I'll get it later. Please sit down." She does. "I'd be closer to Dudley."

"Come on Molly. You don't take a job because of a dog. Will you work less?"

"No, billable hours are how you're measured. It's a different kind of pressure than the PD, but pressure."

"Do you think the job would make you drink less?"

I put down my coffee and look at Rose. I'd heard pregnant women glowed and she did. No way I could stop her from talking about me.

"Okay Rose, spit it out. Tell me how horrible I am, how I drink too much and all the bad things drinking makes me do."

"I love you Molly. I'm worried about you. What would you say to me if you found me puking over the toilet?"

"I'd assume you were nauseous from being pregnant."

"Don't be that way."

"Sorry. Okay, Rose you're right. I drink too much. I stopped a few weeks ago because of the trial. I hadn't had a drink until yesterday. I went to Starbucks for coffee. They had free wine." Even I know that isn't an excuse. "I'm going to stop. I promise."

"I gotta go home. Fredo and I are working on the baby's room. Between that and the wedding I've got lots to do. I'm tired which doesn't help. The doc said it's because of the pregnancy and will pass."

She gets up, gets her things together. Shit. My pregnant sister. My pregnant sister who is exhausted and busy came over and spent the night to make sure I was okay. I'm such a sorry ass.

I walk her to the door and we hug goodbye.

After she leaves the house feels empty. I clean the dishes and sit down at the table. I can't concentrate. I need to make a decision about the job.

I take two sheets of legal paper and wrote Pros on one and Cons on the other. I start with **PRO**: Salary. Prestige. Nice office. Walter? Was he a pro? I liked him, but we had nothing in common anymore. I doubt we'd be friends. Dudley. No stinky clients. Support staff. Civil legal work? Another question mark. Had I enjoyed the work at BARF?

CON: No Rose. No Lourdes. Bad Aunt.

I went back to **PRO** No Jack. No Carl. No bad reputation.

CON: Live in the same town as my parents. No camaraderie. No murder trials. Billable hours. No public defender humor. No one to call when my drinking is out of hand.

I call Walter. It's Saturday. I expect to leave a message. Take the cowards way out. He answers.

"Molly great to hear from you so soon. I assume that means you're in."

For a moment I don't know what to say. Stupid me, of course he works on the weekend. "I can't thanks you enough for thinking of me, but I have to decline. It's hard to explain. . ."

"Stop, you don't have to explain anything. Obviously, you like what you're doing and that's terrific. Maybe we can have lunch again sometime when I'm in Tucson."

It's that easy. I doubt he meant it about lunch.

I call Lourdes. *This is Lourdes. Leave a message and I'll call you back.*

"Lourdes, it's Molly. I turned down the job. I'm staying here."

I call Rose. "I decided not to take the job."

"I'm so glad. I've been praying you'd turned it down."

"I decided I can always get a job, but how many chances do I get to be an aunt."

Forty-Seven

rial is less than seventy-two hours away. We won the critical motion. We can show the jury Sarah's medical records. Smithfield had argued the records were irrelevant, too remote from the date of the shooting, but Quinn didn't buy it. Jurors will find out about Sarah's trips to the ER, her broken ribs, contusions, and concussion.

I convince Lourdes that Sarah should testify. Her story is believable and compelling. She'll have to admit she'd lied to the police, but she'd been terrified. I'd read every cases I could find where the defense was battered women's syndrome. I reviewed law review articles and psychological journals. The jury will want to hear her. They need to hear her. She's less nervous about trial than most clients. She's been through trial even though she didn't testify. Ruth has a great bull-shit meter and agrees with me.

Most defense attorneys will criticize me for putting her on unless we win. How will she stand up to questioning when the prosecutors asks:

"Isn't it true you could have moved out instead of killing him?"
"Couldn't you have gone to a battered women's shelter?"
"Isn't it true he didn't have a weapon on him when you shot him?"
"Why should we believe you say after you lied to the police?"

And those are just a few. But I've been over these questions with Sarah several times and she can answer convincingly.

Lourdes believed she'd be exhausted by the day of our trial. She's doing two murder cases almost back-to-back. Instead she's ecstatic. Her gangbanger client was only convicted of manslaughter. Lourdes expected a verdict of guilty of first degree murder. Everyone in the courtroom was stunned when the verdict was read except her client. The idiot had expected to be acquitted. Jerk. Now he wants a new lawyer. Lourdes hopes he gets his wish. She's running on adrenaline. I just hope it lasts.

The night before trial I can't sleep. I shower, dress and am ready to leave by 6:00 a.m. When we meet that morning, Lourdes tells me Jack offered to help with jury selection. The last thing I need is Jack in the courtroom.

"We don't need him. Anyway I don't want any men at defense table." I say.

"Don't worry, I said no."

It takes more than a day and a half to pick a jury. We are pleased. We have seven women, five men. Four Latina women. If Sarah had been Latina, not Anglo, Smithfield would have tried to dump them. We had discussed what type of jurors we wanted several times. I'd never say it out loud, but I think most Latina women have experienced or heard about men hitting women. Will believe Sarah. I know I sound prejudiced.

Two of the men are retired soldiers who'd been in combat. An article I read said they will make great jurors because they have experienced fear. Will understand our defense. Know how a person can be in fear for their life even when a weapon isn't aimed at them.

At 3:45 p.m. jury selection's finished. Maybe Quinn will send us home. Start the trial tomorrow. I want to practice my opening. Rework it for the hundredth time.

But like most judges she hates wasting jurors' time.

"The State may proceed with their opening statement." Quinn says.

Smithfield rises. I watch him. He doesn't seem nervous. "Sarah Warren murdered her husband in cold blood. She had found and hidden his gun earlier. Not because she was afraid of him. But because she planned to shoot him, kill him. She had other choices. She could have removed the gun from the house. Moved out. Gotten a protective order. But she didn't. She shot him and left him bleeding on the floor. An expert in fingerprints will testify . . ."

I'm cold. Feel like barfing. The jurors listen intently to Smithfield. I think he'll talk for a long time, but before I know it he he's done. His last words sting.

"This woman who vowed to love him in sickness and health, shot him in cold blood, left him on the floor bleeding to death," he turns and points to Sarah, "while she goes shopping." He nods to the jury and sits down.

"The defense may proceed." Quinn says almost immediately after he sits down.

Not even a bathroom break.

Studies have shown 80% of jurors make up their minds during opening statements. I need to do my best. More than my best. Lourdes squeezes my hand under the table. "You don't need notes," she whispers, but I grab them as I stand up.

"Sarah Warren is not guilty of murder. When she shot her husband she was in fear for her life. And for good reason. Sarah will tell you Brian had beaten her not once, not twice, but several times a year, each time becoming more and more violent. Usually she fixed her wounds up as well as she could. She lied for him. Four times he hurt her so badly she went to the emergency room. Twice she was admitted to the hospital. The last time with a broken rib, two broken teeth and a concussion."

I look at the jury and continue. I don't need my notes. I keep talking. Keep eye contact with the jurors. They're paying attention. The words were flowing. Have I made sense, covered everything? It's time to finish. My colleagues told me to memorize an ending. Don't keep going on and on. It's hard to stop, but there comes a point when jurors get restless. You need to stop before that point.

"Sarah acted in self defense. She was in fear for her life, terrified from the moment three weeks earlier when Brian purchased a gun, pointed it at her and said, 'Straighten up bitch or I'll kill you.' "

" 'Straighten up bitch or I'll kill you.' "

I sit down. Sarah and Lourdes smile at me. I'd talked almost thirty-five minutes. I don't remember most of what I said.

We agree the day has gone well. But it can all go to shit tomorrow. Back at the office our colleagues want to hear about the trial. Even Carl.

Lisa and Juan had been in court. "Great job Molly."

Another sleepless night.

Day two. Lourdes and I are in her office discussing strategy when the inter-office line rings. "Nina Cohen, from the CA's office on Line 2." We look at each other. Nina never phones. It's always Smithfield. Lourdes puts her on speaker.

"Hi Nina," Lourdes says.

"Good news for you. We're willing to let Sarah plead to manslaughter, time-served, but the offer's only open till start of trial this morning."

Lourdes takes the phone off speaker and whispers to me, a big grin on her face. "OMG. I can't believe it. Time served?" She turns the speaker back on.

"Come on Nina. We need time to talk to Sarah. They won't bring her up till a few minutes before trial. Sarah feels totally justified in what she did. How about negligent homicide?"

I'd have never thought of asking for a better deal. It's a good thing Lourdes is here.

"I have no authority to change the term of the plea. It's a good deal for her. She can be released today."

"I'm going to ask the judge to delay the start of trial so we can talk to her. I assume you won't object."

"You know how judges hate to leave jurors waiting. But no we won't object." No one speaks. "See you in court." Nina hangs up.

I don't know whether I feel relieved, let down, or both. "Have you ever got-ten a plea in the middle of trial?"

"Haven't you?" Lourdes seems surprised.

"Yeah, but only in minor cases." Not that I've had many major ones.

"It happens. Anne got a dismissal once in a first degree case." Well of course, Anne did. I stopped myself. She probably deserved it.

"Why do you think they're offering this?"

Lourdes begins to pace. "We'll probably never know. Could be a witness refused to testify or went missing. Could be after opening they thought they'd lose. My guess is once Sarah refused to waive time Smithfield never got his shit together."

"You think she should take it?"

"It's a tough call. We've got lots of evidence on our side. But we could lose. Let's see what Sarah thinks."

Lourdes calls courtroom security and asks them to bring Sarah to Quinn's courtroom ASAP. They like her so will do their best even though trial doesn't start for forty-five minutes. I call Nina who meets us outside the courtroom with a copy of the written plea agreement. She knows enough to leave so we can talk privately with Sarah.

Smithfield must make Nina do all the scut work.

We hand Sarah the document and she reads through it. At first she balks. "Why should I plead guilty, when he's been beating and threatening me for years?"

"I think we have a decent shot at winning, but I can't predict what will happen. You lost last time." I put up my hand to let me finish. "I know he was a shitty lawyer, but it was still a loss. It could happen again."

For a few minutes no one says anything. "You're absolutely sure I can get out today?"

I look at Lourdes. "Yes, it is part of the deal."

"Okay I'll take it."

"You'll have a felony on your record."

"But I'll be out of here. I thought you wanted me to plead?"

I don't know what to say. I look down at my notes like they can talk. "You're the one doing the time. If you're found guilty of second degree you're looking at least twenty. If the jury goes for manslaughter, at least seven."

"I want out. My mom's almost sixty. I want to spend time with her while she's healthy."

"Sixty isn't that old. It will be hard to find a job, even get a place to live with a felony record."

"The kind of jobs I'm qualified for no one cares whether I have a record. I can always live with my mom or my sister."

"Okay it's your call."

"I'll take it." Sarah and I sign the plea. Smithfield already has.

I take it to the judge's chambers and advise her bailiff, Henry, we've reached an agreement. He takes it into Quinn's office. Henry comes back in a couple minutes, "As soon as everyone's here, we'll start."

Fifteen minutes later Quinn calls court to order. The jurors remain in the jury room to make sure the Sarah takes the plea. The courtroom gallery is empty of spectators except for a reporter from the local paper.

The judge begins her long litany of questions. "Has anyone forced you or threatened you to plead guilty? Has anyone promised you anything not in the written agreement? Have you had any medication that makes it difficult for you to understand what is happening today?"

Those not-in-the-know think the questions are to make sure the defendant understands what is happening. In reality the Judge wants to make sure the plea will pass appellate court scrutiny. After they plead, no matter how great the deal is, whether they're guilty or innocent, whether they begged for a deal or had to be persuaded to take it, most defendants appeal. Buyers remorse? Free lawyers?

Sarah answers satisfactorily. Sentencing is set for a month away, a technicality since the sentence is time-served. Quinn orders her release. The deputy apologetically handcuffs her for the last trip back to the jail for processing out. Sarah is crying, a first. "Thank you, thank you." As she walks out of the courtroom, a smile replaces the tears. I helped make this happen. She's free because of me.

I never had an experience like this at BARF, and never would at Kavanagh, Cather.

I'm a public defender.

Forty-Eight

No more procrastination. I take my 'Maid of Honor' dress out of the cellophane wrap. No bridesmaids. I got to choose my dress. A turquoise sleeveless sheath. Not some stupid pink flouncy number that ensures the bride will shine and leave the bridesmaids best shot, hoping to catch the bouquet.

Rose shines even though it's clear she's with child. Even though I had picked a sexy dress. I've given up my one-way competition with her.

Mom and Rose argued for days over the wedding. They finally agree the ceremony and dinner will be at the Catholic church the Fajardo's attend. Mom was won over by the lovely grounds which also have a big garden and a pond. The church itself is small. Dad was won over by the minimal price. A woman cellist will play music during dinner, Mexican catered by Alfredo's cousin. No DJ or band. No dancing. Thank god no mariachi's. Both Rose and Alfredo wanted a small wedding, but because of Alfredo's extended family, the guests number almost one hundred.

I've been on a high since Sarah's trial. I don't have a date for the wedding. First time since high school. Even the lack of a man doesn't bring me down. I asked Lourdes to come with me. With her there I'll have to watch how much I drink. I'm not going to abstain, but I want to keep it to one or two. Three at most. Lourdes knows some of Alfredo's family and has met Rose and Alfredo a couple times so it won't be awkward for her.

I had expected to be envious of Rose. Not because I want to get married. And not because I want a baby. Being an aunt is close enough. I want to feel it could have been me in the wedding dress. That I choose to be single. Someday I want to be in a relationship, but first I need to get my act together. My problems have nothing to do with anyone but me. I'm happy for Rose. Glad she came back from Africa. Glad we've grown closer. Alfredo will be a great brother-in-law.

Mom and Dad arrived in Tucson two nights ago. No Dudley. Mom is too frenetic. She worried about every detail of the event. Doesn't like the napkins. Who cares about napkins? Worried they'll be a vegetarian in the crowd. So they'll eat rice and beans. Worried Rose's dress will be too tight. Name it. She worries about it.

She'd been upset with me since I told her I'd turned down the job at Kavanagh, Cather.

"Are you out of your mind? Being a public defender isn't a career."

"I want to live in Tucson. I don't want to be a long distance aunt."

"It's only a ninety minute drive. At that law firm you'd have made a decent salary. You could afford to buy a little condo and come down weekends."

I want to tell her that people live happily on a lot less than they have, but it's hard to make that argument when I live in the house dad paid for.

Mom wouldn't leave it. The three of us were having our hair and nails done. Rose and I were discussing what kind of dog I should get when Mom interrupted, "How are you going to save for retirement?"

Before I can snap back Rose responds. Surprisingly she sounds angry. "Don't give Molly a hard time. She's made a good choice. Money isn't that important. She's going to help people."

Rose's attitude must have had an effect on Mom. She doesn't mention it the rest of the weekend. Goes out of her way to give me hugs and compliments.

Dad alternates between enjoying the festivities and making maudlin comments about losing his baby daughter. You'd have thought she was moving back to Africa instead of living two hours away.

The Priest is surprisingly young and good looking. The ceremony's in English which I didn't expect. Alfredo and Rose have written their own vows. They look at each other, repeat their words of commitment. Lourdes cries more than me.

I have a beer with dinner. Then another. Lourdes gives me the evil eye. She's driving so she abstains. I can hardly wait for the toasts to have another drink. The glass of champagne isn't enough. When Lourdes goes to the bathroom I grab a half-empty glass of champagne on our table. How pathetic? I don't like champagne. Don't know who drank out of this glass.

I want to leave, but I'm expected to wait for the cake to be cut. Lourdes catches the bouquet. My parents had planned to drive me home, but I don't want to wait around till everyone else has gone. I tell Mom I have a headache and need to leave. "Lourdes can drive me," I say.

I hug Rose and Alfredo good bye. Some relative is toasting them so I grab another drink. They're spending the night at one of the fancy resort hotels. No honeymoon. Both go back to work Monday.

I'm finally home. I can have another drink. Oh shit. No alcohol. I check every cupboard. Damn. The store's only a few blocks away, but I'm over the legal limit. I drink a cup of coffee. I'd eaten a big dinner and the two pieces of cake I brought home. I hardly feel buzzed. I'm okay to drive.

I get in the car. Drive carefully I tell myself. I keep to the speed limit. Pay close attention to the stop lights. I park, get out of the car, and walk into Safeway. Pick up a bottle of Pino Grigio. I'm about to pay when I go back and grab another. Just in case. I feel fine.

I get back in the car. Buckle up and pull out of the shopping center when my phone rings. I fumble in my purse, grab the phone and look up. The light ahead is yellow. I slam on my brakes hard as I can. A bicycle has started across the street. Oh shit. I come to a stop past the crosswalk. The bike swerves to avoid me.

The rider screams, "You asshole," and gives me the finger.

Oh my god, I almost hit him. I drive slowly the rest of the way. Could have killed him. I'm still shaking when I get home. Try to open the wine bottle. I need a drink. Now. Finally I get it open. Pour a big one. I check the phone messages. It's Mom making sure I got home. I think about what could have been. Could have hit him, broken a bone or two. Could have paralyzed him. I could have been charged with a DUI, felony DUI if I had an accident. Could have lost my law license. Could have been sentenced to prison.

Oh my god. I'm no different from Terrazas. I could have lost everything even my own life.

I still know Jack's number by heart. He answers. We talk. I ask for directions.

Forty-Nine

My name is Molly and I'm an alcoholic.

Acknowledgments

Once again I thank Meg Park and her writing group below for all their support and critiques: MaryAnn Pressman, Roslyn Schiffman, Terry Tanner, Heather Hatch, Marie Trump, Ann Hammond, Beverly Pollock, Robert Samuels and Starr Sanders.

Special thanks to MaryAnn Pressman, Beth Smith, Kay Kavanagh and Candy Terrell for proofreading and cheerleading.

And a very special thanks to Mary Lawrence for always being a fan, proofreading every draft and cheering me on always.

Any mistakes are mine.

Author Biography

Barbara Sattler spent over three decades in the courtroom as both a lawyer and judge and has tried over a hundred criminal cases.

She began her career as a public defender and later moved to private practice. After seventeen years as a criminal defense attorney, she became a City Court magistrate and later a Superior Court judge.

She is the author of two legally themed novels: *Dog Days* and *Anne Levy's Last Case*. *My Name Is Molly* is her third book. Her blog, *Some Things Considered* can be found at barbarasattler.com She explores criminal justice issues, how one person can make a difference and her love of animals among other issues.

In 2001, Barbara was diagnosed with a rare neurological disease known as transverse myelitis. All profits from her novels go to the Transverse Myelitis Association.

Barbara lives in Tucson, Arizona, with her husband, Kenney Hegland, a retired law professor, author of *Law School Chronicles* and her dogs, Toby and Teddy. Toby and Teddy have yet to publish.

Made in the USA
San Bernardino, CA
22 March 2019